ROYALLY BAD

ALSO BY NORA FLITE

Big City Billionaires

Billion Dollar Bad Boy

Other Books

Never Kiss a Bad Boy

The Bad Boy Arrangement

My Secret Master

Last of the Bad Boys

ROYALLY BAD

NORA FLITE

This is a work of fiction. Names, characters, organizations, places, events, and incidents are either products of the author's imagination or are used fictitiously.

Published by Montlake Romance, Seattle

www.apub.com

ISBN-13: 9781503942790
ISBN-10: 1503942791

Cover design by Mayhem Cover Creations

Printed in the United States of America

To the people at the coffee shop who never got sick of me sitting there all day when my tiny kitchen table wasn't good enough, and who never judged me—openly—for my twelfth double-espresso drink, thank you. You were almost as supportive as my husband, who always knew I needed a shoulder rub, terrible takeout food, and addictive but oh-so-bad reality TV show marathons after every writing session.

Love ya, babe.

- CHAPTER ONE -

Sammy

Fingers crawled up the outside of my thigh. They might as well have been cutting through the layers of my organza dress, because my skin tingled like he was touching me directly.

Who was *he*, you ask?

Dressed in a crisp, midnight-blue suit that didn't fit his bad boy persona—and a cocky smirk that totally did—Kain Badd was the biggest pain in my ass since I'd tried on my first thong. Sure, the guy was cut from marble, and his eyes were the kind of blue that was reserved for Photoshop magazine edits . . . but he was a dick.

He also *had* a pretty nice dick. Please don't ask me how I know.

None of that mattered, because in just a few hours this wedding would be over with, and I wouldn't have to see him ever again. Till then, I was stuck at Kain's side, enduring his constant attempts to work me up until I was hot and bothered. The fucker was winning.

Loud, echoing, bell-filled music sang through the air. Swatting Kain's fingers away again, I shot him a pointed scowl. His smile showed off his teeth, telling me he didn't care that I was getting mad. The bastard was getting to me, and he knew it.

Clearing my throat, I stared down the aisle at the bride coming our way. The gown glowed on her, making me swell with pride. I'd *made* that dress, it was born from my sweat and tears. The clicking cameras let me know that by tomorrow people would be knocking on my door to get my business.

This was all worth it. I had to keep reminding myself of that.

Kain trailed a hand up my spine, whispering in my ear, "She's stealing the show, but honestly, I can't keep my eyes off of you."

Flushing, I hissed, "Shut up and focus!"

"That's tough when I can see your tits rising with every tiny breath."

Kicking him in the ankle, I put on a big smile for the bride. Glossy and golden, she met my stare with glee. The money, the fame, and the fact I'd made this young woman's day. All of it was worth—*what the hell?*

Over the heads of the crowd, I saw dark figures marching through the rosebushes. Their helmets glinted, almost as much as their guns did.

"Get down!" someone shouted.

Everyone came alive in a panic, running or pushing to get away. Kain's fingers threaded with mine—then faceless men in body armor tackled him hard, tearing us apart.

A second later, the full weight of one of the men slammed me to the ground. "Don't move!" That command was fierce; it made my ears ring. *Move?* Was he joking? I couldn't even scream, the air had burst right out of me.

Boots stomped, people roared, and over it all I heard the distinct wail of sirens. An arm crushed across the nape of my neck, metal kissing my wrists.

I was being arrested.

How the hell had this happened?

Two days earlier

I think I might be the worst business owner in the world.

As I packaged up the gorgeous gown crafted from ivory lace and hand-sewn crystal beads, I knew it was true. After all, the gown had cost me several hundred dollars to make, I'd been planning to sell it for a few thousand, and here I was . . .

Giving it away for free.

The young woman rubbed at her cheeks, failing to hide the dewy mist of tears. She'd been welling up with them ever since I'd told her that she was the lucky Platinum Bride of the Month—of which there was no such thing.

It wasn't my best lie, but it would work.

Hazel had been in my store several times with her fiancé. She'd told me over and over how excited she was for this wedding. Marrying the man she'd adored since high school was her dream.

She'd promised to pay off the dress by the end of last month. That hadn't happened. Then she'd said she'd pay by last week, but again, nothing. I didn't need to be a psychic to know something terrible had gone wrong. Hazel wasn't the type to screw anyone over.

Yesterday, driving down the highway, I'd seen her fiancé on the corner holding a sign: out of work, will do anything for money.

Like many, he'd lost his job when the local soap factory closed last month.

Call me weak, or frail, or just . . . stupid, but there was no way I was going to let this poor woman walk away without her dream dress.

"I can't thank you enough," she sniffled, laughing nervously at her own reaction.

I shoved the package her way with my biggest grin. "Like I said, you're the winner this month! You don't need to thank me at all. It's out of my hands."

Scrubbing at her nose, she hugged the box tight to her chest. She was red from throat to eyelid, a total mess from how happy she was. "I'll send you some photos from the wedding," she promised.

"You better!" I laughed.

Hazel didn't take her eyes off of me until she got to the door. I was afraid she might start bowing. "Seriously," she said, pushing at the exit and making the bell jingle. "If you hadn't given me this, I don't know what I would have done. Canceled the wedding, lost the deposit, I just—"

"Shh shh shh!" I flapped my hands. "Send me those photos. I'll hang them on our monthly winners' board." I didn't have one of those, either.

Her smile went so wide it almost touched her ears. "Thank you. You've got a good heart."

I swelled at her compliment. It was hard not to.

But good hearts don't pay the bills.

The instant she was out of sight, I slumped behind my front desk and put my face in my hands. *I am such an idiot.* Giving away what I needed to keep my bridal shop afloat was pure insanity. *That's what's going on*, I thought to myself. *Somewhere along the way, my brain has cracked.*

I'd opened my business just three months ago. It had been a quick, messy process. Moving back to my hometown had been even messier. It wasn't like I had a choice in the matter; what daughter wouldn't rush back to take care of her sick mother?

Regardless, I was here. I meant to make the best of it.

Too bad I was also my worst enemy.

Sighing, I slapped my cheeks to shake myself from my funk. *Focus. Put on some music and make yourself useful.* Cranking up my small radio, I shuffled through the songs until I found "Hide Away" by Daya. The piano began, pumping me up, guiding me out from behind my desk.

This was what I needed. Music had a way of sinking into your bones and erasing your worries. It was magical, forcing me to swing to the fast-paced beat, demanding I forget all about my problems.

My mistakes.

Bouncing on my heels, I grabbed a wedding gown from the rack. It was glittery, miles of tulle. I meant to just move it to a mannequin so I could tweak the ribbons on the corset that I hadn't finished yet. When the chorus of the song began, I swung the dress in a circle.

My hips rocked, my hair flipped, and I jammed it out on my shop floor with that white gown in my arms. Laughing, I twirled around with the dress like it was my private lover . . .

And found myself staring into the crisp, blue eyes of the most gorgeous man alive.

Gasping, I curled the dress up like it was a wet washcloth I was wringing out. The stranger's dark eyebrows crinkled, his smile hooking into my heart. I was torn between being charmed and humiliated.

"I—um—hi!" Coughing, I hurried over to turn my radio down. "Can I help you?"

He didn't speak, the woman behind him did. "Oh. My. Stars." Wheeling my way, she grabbed at my wrists with unwieldy gold nails. Her sapphire eyes were stuck on the dress I was holding. "That is the *cutest* fucking dress I have *ever* seen!"

The guy glanced her way—had he been watching me this whole time? "Good," he said. "If you can find a dress you like that fast, we can get this over with."

A flicker of disappointment made my mood settle. *Of course he's engaged to her.* How could a guy as hot as him be single? In my head, I stopped living my brief, imaginary wedding to Mister Stranger, and instead I focused on the young woman. "So you're looking for a wedding dress?"

"More like looking for my fifth," she laughed. Winking, she offered her hand. "Francesca Badd—with a double *d*." She wiggled her chest to drive home the joke. "It's a pleasure, doll."

Had I heard her right? Her last name was *Badd*? Smiling, I shook her hand and watched the giant gold hoops in her ears shake. I could smell a difficult bride from a mile away. *Five dresses? Jeez.* "I'm Sammy. I'd be happy to show you a few things, do you know what you like?"

Francesca pointed at the gown in my arms. "That. I like that. I *want* that."

Over her head, the guy cleared his throat. "The brat is used to getting what she wants."

She twisted around, her piled-high hair flopping. "Please ignore my brother, he's a little bit of a dick."

"Don't use the words 'little' and 'dick' in the same sentence with me."

"Watch your damn mouth, Kain!" She pointed at me. "You're being rude in front of this nice lady!"

I was blushing, but not because of the swearing. I'd grown up here, bluntness and foul mouths had numbed my ears years ago. What I was freaking out about was one thing:

He's her brother? Not her fiancé?

For the second time, I ate the man up with a casual glance. The dark-gray shirt he had on was hugging his broad chest. It vanished into his belt, highlighting his slim hips while his tight jeans showed off his muscular legs.

His perfect skin was enhanced by the twisting tattoos that coiled along his arms. I could even see one peeking near his collarbone. I didn't normally go for inked men, but for him, I'd make an exception.

Feeling incredibly silly . . . and incredibly relieved, I moved toward the changing stall. "I'm glad you like this dress! Here, come try it on. It's not finished, but it shouldn't take me more than a week. When is your wedding?"

Francesca slid the curtain open, taking the gown. Before she ducked inside, she gave me her sweetest smile ever and said, "It's the day after tomorrow."

The curtain shut, and my stomach fell into my knees.

The guy—Kain?—stood next to me, his hands in his pockets. "That's how our family does things. 'Spontaneous and messy' should be our motto." His chuckle warmed me, but not enough to shake off the reality of the situation.

"Francesca," I said carefully. "Maybe you should look at some of my finished work."

Spinning out of the curtain, she held the corset closed behind her with one arm. The gown sparkled in the light through my large windows. I'd designed the tulle to hang and flow like snow from a mountain, the top half extra-creamy white against her tan skin.

Admiring herself in the mirror, she laughed. "Why bother? This is my dress! This is it right here! Kain, how does it look?" He opened his mouth, but she cut him off. "*Isn't it beautiful?* Ah! I love it!"

Breathing faster, I struggled to keep smiling. I hated letting people down. "Francesca . . . listen. It's gorgeous on you—"

"I know, right?!"

"But two days is just not enough time to finish this."

Picking at her teeth in the mirror, she made a low humming sound. "I don't understand."

Kain put out his hand, resting it on the small of my back. His touch was scalding; I was too aware of it. "Make sure you check out the ribbons, Francesca."

She spun, eyeballing the corset with glee.

Confused, I let Kain push me toward the front of the store. When he let me go, I still felt his phantom fingerprints. "Listen," he said. "How much money do you need to make sure that dress is ready in time?"

I shook my head. "It's not money that's the problem. I'd need to stay up all night and some of tomorrow to finish it. And even then I'm not sure I could do it."

Digging out his phone, he started tapping it. "Just tell me the magic number."

"There *is* no magic number. Are you listening to me? I'd have to kill myself to get it done!"

His steely eyes scraped upward from my toes to my raised brows, the force of them as strong as being gripped by his thick fingers. "I haven't stopped listening since you opened your pretty mouth, sweet thing. If you don't want to give me a price, I'll give *you* one."

Clenching my hands, I braced myself. I was ready to snap at him—who had the balls to talk down to me like that?

Kain spun his phone, showing me the screen. He read the number out loud, which was good, because my vision went blurry at the sight of it. "Will twenty grand be enough?"

My tongue was too heavy, I was slurring. "Twenty . . . grand?"

His silent smile said he wasn't kidding around.

Twenty grand. With that, my money worries would be gone. I could pay off my mother's growing medical debt and still keep my business afloat. *Who are these people?* I'd never heard of the Badds, but were they so rich that throwing twenty grand at their daughter's dress was nothing?

In the back of the store, Francesca called out, "Sammy! Do you have any veils that match this gown?"

I leveled my eyes on Kain. He looked and smelled like a predator, all crisp pine and silky musk. This was a man who always got what he wanted. If I'd been wondering why Francesca would bring her brother along to shop for dresses, now I knew. Who could say no to her with Kain around?

Spinning away from him, I shouted, "I have just the one!"

I wasn't watching Kain anymore, but his expression was imprinted in my mind. It was the strangest thing, that look he'd given me. He'd acted like we'd been facing off. More than that, he'd acted like he'd *won*.

In that moment, I understood him. It didn't matter how handsome Kain was, or how fit . . . or how he moved like water through a river; this guy was arrogant as hell, right down to his core.

Kain was bad news.

And believe me, I know bad news.

My life has been full of it.

- CHAPTER TWO -

SAMMY

I stayed up all night, just like I'd said I would have to.

First I used coffee.

Then I used energy drinks.

Finally, when the early hours between night and day arrived, I looked at the red-lettered debt collector bills piled on my desk. It was the last push I needed to get me through my task.

Yawning for the millionth time, I rubbed furiously at my eyes. In the sharp orange-sherbet light of sunrise, the gown shone like a bronze sea. It was some of my best work, and picturing it draped on Francesca was almost enough to shake off my weariness.

Almost.

Yawning, I stumbled into my shower. If there was any hope of meeting her today for her fitting, I needed to get my act together. Hanging my head under the stream of furious water, I closed my eyes and hummed.

The last time I'd pulled an all-nighter was back in college. I'd been determined to show off a series of full-length couture gowns for my finals. It was an insane task to take on. It left me with bleeding fingers and a hatred for chicken wire.

But that collection had gotten me my dream job in New York.

It was a pretty good job, too, while it lasted. Laughing to myself, I flipped wet hair from my face. *Stop thinking about that. It doesn't matter now.* Besides, who needed the high-paid, fast-paced lifestyle of New York City?

I didn't let myself answer that question.

Wrapping a towel around my body, I stepped across the cold tile toward my bedroom. The blinds were open, pointing right at the building rubbing shoulders with mine. Not keen on giving anyone a show, I tiptoed over, tugging at the cord.

In a masterful display of craftsmanship, the blinds snapped right off the window.

Gasping, I jumped back before they smacked my feet. I was left standing there in the early sun, in nothing but a towel, with a broken string in my fist.

In the apartment across the way, a baffled older man stared at me.

Inhaling through my nose, I looked around my room for a solution. In the corner, next to some of my still-not-unpacked boxes, there were some sheets of cardboard. Grabbing one, I snatched up some of the packing tape and faced the window.

Then my towel started to slip.

With nothing but some cardboard between me and the stranger, I groaned loudly. Was this really how my day was going to go? Gritting my teeth, I quickly taped the most haphazard excuse for a curtain into place.

Stepping back, I scooted the towel higher on my boobs and observed my work. *About as good as the blinds were.* I really needed to get out of this shitty apartment, but it was all I could find in my budget on such short notice.

It wasn't like I'd grown up having it easy, but we'd been middle class—comfortable. It was only when my dad died last year that things went to hell. There was no insurance policy, and what little money that had been squirreled away went straight to my mother's doctors the sicker she grew.

But that's going to change. Twenty grand was enough to set things straight again.

Scratching at my wet hair, I didn't stop my towel when it fell to the floor that time. It was dark in my room now; that was fine, I didn't need much light to find some clean clothes.

By the time I managed to tug on some jeans and a black button-up blouse, it was crawling close to ten a.m.

Stumbling into the tiny kitchen, I made up a quick pot of coffee. I hovered over it while it percolated, drumming my nails anxiously. It was still dripping when I yanked the pot out, pouring the black nirvana into my stallion-head-shaped mug.

Sitting down, I took the biggest gulp ever. *Fuck,* that was good. That was what I needed.

I was only twenty-three, but I was way too old to pull all-nighters. Weren't people constantly talking about how important sleep was? Something about how every hour you lost took a day off your life?

I was pretty sure I'd heard a doctor say that. A television doctor, but still.

Tapping on my phone, I checked for directions to the address where Francesca wanted to meet. When my Google Maps told me the drive would take over an hour, I choked on my coffee.

She lived in *Newport?* Damn, I hadn't accounted for that in my timing. Scooping up the plastic-wrapped wedding dress, I set my mug gently in the sink. I was in a rush, but I was still careful not to chip the cup. It was my favorite one—a gift from my father.

Throwing everything into the backseat of my weathered but treasured Dodge Avenger, I grimaced at the bright sun. It was just turning the corner into summer, the sky managing to be the sort of primary blue you found only in children's toys.

Fumbling in my glove box, I found a pair of oversize sunglasses. The bronze Guccis were an artifact from my time in New York, I'd bought them for myself as a gift for landing the job at Filbert's Bridal.

It was a heavy reminder of the comfortable future I'd thrown away. *I did it for the right reason*, I reminded myself. *And besides . . . I just landed a twenty-k gig. That's more than I made in four months at Filbert's! Things are looking up for me.*

With determination, I slid the sunglasses onto my face and ground down on the gas pedal.

When this job was over with, I'd buy myself something even nicer than my Guccis as a reward.

◆ ◆ ◆

This couldn't be right.

Flicking my eyes up, then back down to the map on my phone, I wondered what was going on. How had my GPS gotten so fucked up? Because it *was* fucked up. It had to be. That was the only explanation for why it had taken me here.

The long, wrought iron gate spread like two linked arms in front of me. It was both intimidating and oddly pretty, the way an attacking hawk could be pretty. The mansion beyond was dazzling.

I just couldn't believe this was the right place. *Then again, they DID pay a premium for that dress.* Was it possible the Badds lived here? No, I couldn't quite believe it. I'd watched people blow tons of money on weddings, it didn't mean they were rich—just desperate.

And this went beyond *rich.* This was the kind of estate the president would live in!

Bouncing my skull into my headrest, I made a long, low noise. Why could nothing be easy for me? Now I was going to have to call up Francesca, tell her I'd be late, and ask her for better directions because I was freaking lost.

Gritty, mechanical snarls filled the air. Black and gold, the motorcycle slammed to a stop next to my driver's-side window. Throwing myself sideways in surprise, I gawked at the reflective helmet of the rider. I could see my own shock in the mirrored surface.

Hard hands with oddly clean nails yanked the helmet away. "Sammy?" Kain asked, looking me over with amusement. "That you? I almost didn't recognize you under those clamshells on your face."

Shoving the sunglasses up onto my scalp, I regained my composure. "Why are you here? Were you following me?"

Kain stared—then he bent over, cracking up.

Still laughing, he smoothed some of his hair. In spite of the helmet, the rich, mahogany strands were still styled. His bike rolled forward, his hand clicking something he slid from his pocket. In a grand gesture that was free of rusty squeaks, the gates spread open in front of us.

"This," Kain said, gesturing, "is where I live, darlin'."

Gazing at the tiled stretch of driveway in front of me, the green gardens, and the sprawling estate in all its glory . . . I had a single thought:

Look on the bright side, you aren't late for the meeting.

Kain rode ahead of me, his bike purring with his low speed. I followed, marveling at the gorgeous landscape that could have been cut from an oil painting. The rose garden was a galaxy of pinks and reds, made brighter by the white of the mansion.

Beyond the grassy field, I spotted a few structures. Squinting at them, my heart started to race. Were those stables? Did they have horses here?

Pushing my sunglasses back onto my nose, so I wouldn't look like a tourist, I set my mouth in a serious line. Francesca was rich, this whole family was rich. That was why they could throw twenty grand at me to rush a wedding dress.

Understanding the situation I was in, I started to twitch. This wasn't just intimidating, this was exciting. Maybe I could get a tour of the estate before this was over with.

Kain parked his motorcycle in the corner of the driveway, where the giant spiral of stones reached its biggest curve. I stopped near him, unsure where else to go. In the long silence of the death of my engine, I filled my chest with air. *It's go time.*

Grabbing the dress, I pushed my door open and stepped out.

Right into Kain's chest.

"Ah!" I gasped, bouncing back into the hard blockade of my car. He didn't move an inch, not in body or his ever-present smirk. The air around us was crafted from the heavy scent of his leather jacket and the musky pine that was just naturally him.

Kain leveled his wild eyes on me. I'd never felt so judged. Did I pass, did I fail? Did I *care*? Chuckling, he leaned sideways as if he had all the time in the world to loiter here. "You didn't expect this, did you?"

"This?" Waving around at the estate, I shrugged. "How could I?"

His full lips slid closer to mine. "Then you really had no clue who I was when we met. I should have guessed you weren't from around here." His attention bounced to my sunglasses.

I'd thought of them as protection; now they felt like an anchor. Bristling, I took them off, dropping them through the crack in my window. "For the record, I *am* from here. Born and raised, thank you very much."

He revealed the whites of his eyes. That was the first thing I'd said that had surprised him. Shocking a man like Kain felt *good*. It didn't last long, he stole my confidence with a casual trace of his finger down my shoulder.

"Then you should've known what you were walking into, sweetheart."

It was a threat . . . it was a warning. Not appreciating either, I smacked his hand away and sidestepped him. "Back off, I've got business to get to."

Fingers coiled around my wrist, twirling me like a dancer. Thick pieces of my ponytail blinded me, my heart swinging up and out. Vertigo replaced every other sense.

When I came back down to earth, Kain was holding me in his arms.

It was a low back bend, my weight supported by him, my hair tickling the grass. His face was made from shadow, his smile no longer teasing me. This was the mouth of a hungry man, and I felt like the morsel he wanted to devour.

We stayed like that for far too long. Long enough that I realized it was my fault we were still tangled together. Deep in the black-and-blue depths of his eyes, I watched Kain's humor shift ever further.

Before, he'd wanted to play with me. It had been a game with no stakes.

But now . . . everything in his body, his breath, screamed, *I want to have you.*

And I wasn't ready for that.

Pulling away, I tumbled to the ground. I grunted, but the brief pain was good; it jostled my senses back into place. Grabbing the wedding dress tighter, I stood, dusting grass from my jeans.

I was about to whirl on him and tell him off. The way he straightened, seeming genuinely unsure of himself, stopped me. Kain blinked, then he scratched the back of his neck and turned away. "I better put my bike in the garage before someone else tries and fucks it up. Go inside, my sister is waiting for you."

He strutted away from me, moving with a swimmer's grace in the body of a warrior. It was easy to forget how tall he was. Whenever he got close, he always made sure to bend down so we were nearly touching noses.

My heart hadn't calmed down; I clutched at my shirt, lost in a tornado of emotion. What the hell had just happened? What *was* that?

There was a noise behind me. Glancing back, I saw the large doors of the mansion opening. Francesca ran my way, her arms wide. She was going to knock me over, my muscles were already weak from Kain's assault.

Throwing up my hands, I waved the dress like a flag. "Careful!" I cautioned. "I spent all night on this!"

Pulling up short, she looked appalled. Then she started bouncing, hands clasped to her full and animated chest. "Aah! It's here! You're here! I can't wait to put it on!"

Francesca's energy helped dissolve the last of the lingering unease brought on by Kain's body pressing against mine. Swallowing around my dry tongue, I cleared my throat. I had to be on, this was *my* show—and the bride's, of course. "You're going to love it. Just ask my hands."

I meant to make her laugh, except instead, she darted her attention to the Band-Aids still wrapped on my fingertips. "Oh, shit! Hon, did you bust yourself up just for me?" Catching my wrists just as easily as her brother had, Francesca frowned.

"It's fine!" I made my voice lighter. "Really, focus on what matters—how great you're going to look."

Half a second later, she was beaming. "Gawd, I can't wait. Let's go inside so I can see."

I'd never been inside of a mansion before. It was like seeing the ocean for the first time. It made you feel small, and scared, and itchy with curiosity.

The ceiling stretched so high they surely could have ridden a giraffe inside. Maybe several. My heels tapped on smooth-as-glass tiles, black with smoky gray weaving through it all. Two staircases curled upward, the white walls decorated with modern art and paintings of—probably—members of the family.

As we passed a large portrait of several faces, I realized it had to be of the Badd family. I could spot Kain's glittering grin from a mile away. There was Francesca standing beside him, and nearby, a large, hulking man I assumed was their father. And unless I was seeing things . . . was that two other brothers?

It must have been a recent portrait; Kain looked similar to how he did now. I didn't have time to study the painting closer because Fran was yanking me over the steps with increasing excitement. At the top of the stairs, she pulled me down a hall and threw a door open. "Here we are!" The bedroom inside was some horrific dream of golden glitter and pink crystal. A unicorn wouldn't have been comfortable in there. "Isn't it to die for? Now, let's see that dress!"

I unfurled it from the plastic dramatically. Clasping her cheeks, she squealed appropriately. Before I could ask her to undress, she was stripping down to her underwear. Francesca wasn't the shy sort.

On her ribs, just under her right arm, there was a small tattoo of a black-and-red crown. It was the only ink on her body. Resisting my urge to ask her about it, I guided the dress up her hips. "Once I have you in," I said, "I'll have to fix any spots that seem loose. I did my best to use the measurements I took from you at the store, but . . ."

To my sincere amazement and delight, the dress clasped around her, snug.

She stepped back, posing in front of her giant floor-length mirror. "Oh. Em. Gee. Sammy, it fits perfectly!"

I couldn't control my smile. "I mean, I'd have liked to adjust the length a bit more, and the hem isn't as even as I prefer . . ."

Her pursed lips shut me up. She lifted her hair off of her neck and admired the low-cut back. "I love it. I can't wait till Midas sees me in it."

"Midas?"

Francesca was oblivious to my reaction. "Midas Tengelico, the sexiest man in the world."

A funny thought wriggled through my brain. I couldn't catch the tail of it before it got too far. *I bet Kain is sexier.* Sitting up straighter, I fidgeted. *Where the hell did that come from?*

I knew the source; barely fifteen minutes ago, he'd spun himself around me like silk. His smell, his heat, his firm muscles . . . everything about him had sunk into my memory. *Think about something else!* But what could possibly take my focus away from Kain? *Actually . . . I do have one nagging thought.*

Taking a look at Fran in her dress with a pair of new eyes, I asked the question that had been chewing at me. "Hey, sorry if this is too forward, but how do you earn your money?"

"Why?" she asked, looking awfully offended. "What have you heard? Did some stupid girl say something about what I'll do for the right amount, because I *swear*, it was just a rumor and—"

"No, no." Laughing, I pointed around her bedroom. "This place is a mansion. How does your family afford it?"

Understanding flashed through her eyes, replaced by sharp suspicion. "Oh, that." Gathering herself, she spoke with flat, indifferent ease—like she'd had to say this a million times. "My family runs a super successful maid service company, Badd Maids. It's where all of our money comes from. All of it."

"Badd Maids," I said.

She stared me down. "Yup."

There was no way I believed her. But on some level, I wanted to. I liked Francesca; I didn't want to slow down enough to consider that she might be involved in something less savory than the obvious lie she'd spit at me. But really, a cleaning service? That's what had paid for all of this?

As if talking would erase my nervous thoughts, I focused on Francesca. "All right, I get it. If you don't want any tweaks to the dress, I guess I'm done here."

"What, you're leaving?" Pouting, she grabbed her hips. "Stay for the dinner party! The food will be great, the music . . . the drinks! You can't go yet, Sammy!"

"I didn't get much sleep." *An understatement.* "And I don't know your family well. I should go."

Could she pout *more*? How was she doing that? "Fine," she sighed. Eyeing her reflection, she twisted, rubbing the corset. "Can you get me out of this?"

With agile precision, I unstrung the ribbons and set her free. Then, with some pointless chit-chat and good-byes, I hurried out into the hallway. The soft rugs chewed at my flats as I power walked. Francesca was sweet to invite me to the party, but I had other priorities.

Things like . . . getting as far away from Kain Badd as possible.

I couldn't pin down why he made me so nervous. Something about his energy threw me off; it made my mouth tingle and my tongue buttery. *The sooner I get to my car, the sooner I don't have to worry about him.*

That was all well and good.

Except . . . I couldn't *find* my car. I couldn't even find the way I'd come inside! In my haste, I'd gotten turned around in the cavernous mansion. Perspiration pooled inside the dip in my throat, growing by the minute.

Every corner looked like the last. Each hall was a mirror of another. Had I seen that painting before? Was that gray swirl in the floor new?

Rounding into a passage with large windows, I spotted rich green grass, tall hedges outside.

And a door.

Yanking at it in relief, I threw myself out into the air. The midday sun was beating down, the sky empty of clouds. Shielding my eyes and wishing for my sunglasses, I studied where I was.

The back of the house?

All around me was a large field, the ground beaten by traffic in some spots. The scent of hay hit me before I saw the stables. With adrenaline flooding my veins, I looked on as a young woman guided a chestnut mare into a stall.

The Badds really did have horses. I hadn't imagined the stables when I'd driven up.

Eyeing the large backyard, I noticed the curling tendrils of rosebushes to my right. That had to lead back to where my car was, I was sure I'd seen the garden from there.

But I don't want to get lost again.

Debating with myself, I gave in to my secret desire. I loved horses, I'd ridden them when I was a child. I'd had to stop riding once I hit fourth grade; my father blamed it on money being tight.

Approaching the stable, I slid my palm over the smooth grain of the support beams. The rich scent of animals and nature made me dizzy. "Excuse me?" I called.

Instead of a face, big, bouncy curls of black hair poked around the corner. I saw the person they were attached to a second later. She peered at me from around the mare, and though her eyes were confused, her smile was friendly; it showed off her freckles. Was she my age? She felt . . . younger. "Hey there!" she chirped. "What can I do for you?"

My stare was fixated on the horse. Its giant eyes, so wet and honest, studied me. Every fiber in me wanted to pet its velvet nose. I held back. "My name's Sammy. I'm . . . well, how do I explain. I was here—"

"Oh! The wedding dress maker!" Laughing, she rubbed the horse's flank. "Frannie would not shut up about you and that gown."

"Right. I finished up with her, and now I'm kind of turned around."

"The estate can be intimidating to first-timers." Dusting her palms off, she came my way, then she kept going. "Come on, I'll show you out. Name's Matilda, by the by."

I lingered, watching the horse as long as I could. Finally, I chased after Matilda. She was shorter than me, though not by much. Her hair made up a lot of her height. Even among the rosebushes she took us near, she still smelled like hay. I loved it.

We wove through a short maze of hedges. "Here you go," she said, gesturing as we broke out onto the hard tiles of the driveway.

I was about to thank her. I didn't get that far, the two of us stopping in our tracks as we saw what was going on. A red car was parked near mine, an older woman shouting furiously at a man in a gray shirt and purple tie. Throwing her arms up, she said, "You're done! Get out of here!"

"Mama, you tell him!" I hadn't noticed Francesca. She bounced nearby, her arms wrapped around a fluffy white thing—some kind of dog? "Get the fuck outta here, you scam artist!"

The man scowled, but there was fear in his narrowed eyes. "I'm not a scam artist, Miss Badd. I told you weeks ago, you can't keep changing the plans. I said I'd arrange things for noon, you were the one who changed the rehearsal lunch to a rehearsal dinner *last night*."

Francesca opened her mouth, but the larger woman—who had to be her mom—stomped forward. The man ducked, nearly feeling the wrath of her ring-encrusted fist.

Holy shit! Was this about to get ugly? Mama Badd screamed, "Go! Get your scammy ass off my property! We'll do the party without you!"

He didn't need more convincing. Ducking into his car, he started to reverse. Francesca ran forward, kicking her sparkling gold heel into the side of his front bumper. Squealing tires broke through the clean air—he drove away in a flurry of dust.

Breathing heavily, Francesca spun on her mom. "What do we do now, Ma? Who's going to organize the party tonight?"

"Oh, honey, we'll figure it out. I can call another planner. Anyone would feel honored to help throw a party for us!"

Next to me, Matilda made a small snort. There was no way Francesca heard her, but still, her dark eyes flew my way. I stood taller, unsure if I should smile or run into the rosebushes.

"Sammy!" she shouted, drawing her mom's attention to me. She waved, nearly dropping the fluffy dog thing. "You're still here! Thank fucking gawd!"

My face scrunched. "I was actually about to go." Could I make it to my car if I moved quickly enough?

Hugging her dog, she moaned. "You can't! I need you to save the day, please! I don't have time to find another planner."

Chewing my lip, I glanced at Matilda. She was hovering, picking at her nails and looking at her feet. She acted like she wanted to turn invisible.

I said, "Party planning isn't my expertise." Mama Badd swished my way. Literally swished, because her long dress was dangling with threads of crystal that brushed her calves loudly. "Hon, you're the one who made Fran's dress, right? You've seen your share of wedding parties. We just need someone to help us set up, keep it all together."

"Ah . . . well . . ."

My hesitation was obvious. She sniffed, eyeing my dented car and smiling knowingly. "We'll pay you, of course."

Jeez, this family and their money. They threw it around like it was candy on Halloween.

Matilda whispered, "You should do it. It's better to help them than to run."

Run? It wasn't running.

What else do you call escaping because you're scared of bumping into Kain again? That sounds like running to me. I cursed my blunt inner thoughts.

With everyone watching me expectantly—even the dog—I smiled weakly. "All right. Just tell me what you need me to do."

- CHAPTER THREE -

SAMMY

Have you ever planned a party in just three hours?

Me either.

Until now.

Luckily, I wasn't alone. I had a range of helpers, from cooks to servants to bussers. I'd never had to lead so many people. In my drained state, the hours melted into a weird swirl of white noise and murky colors.

I was surprised they needed me, honestly. I was sure that anyone else could have directed the waiters to bring out drinks and appetizers, and certainly any old person could have told them to choose cloths for the garden tables that complemented the bride-to-be's bright orange dress.

White and green, thank you.

Exhausted, I wiped my forehead and leaned against the kitchen wall. I did have a better idea of the estate's layout now, that was a plus. *You won't be spending time here, why does it matter if you know where things are?*

Again, my sharp inner voice was right.

Sipping a big glass of water, I rubbed my hands on my dress. Francesca had insisted I change into something more presentable. Finding an outfit in her closet that wasn't covered in faux fur, animal spots, or giant rhinestones was a challenge.

I'd settled on a green satin dress, the bottom pleats glinting with gold. It was still flashy, but it would work.

"Ma'am?" a young waiter asked. He was wearing the same starched, black suit as all the others, though the way he shifted around, he seemed uncomfortable in it. "Miss Badd says you can go if you like. They're done eating and are enjoying after-dinner drinks now."

I flashed an appreciative smile. "Thanks—ah, what's your name?"

"Jameson."

"Thanks, Jameson. I'll head out in a minute."

He nodded, his slicked-back hair moving as much as a helmet would. I had the distinct sensation that he was lingering, watching me with interest. Before I could ask him if something was wrong, he hurried off.

Pushing my hair behind my ears, I closed my eyes and pointed my nose to the ceiling.

What a day.

"Did you move in or something?"

Blinking, I stared at Kain. He'd snuck up on me, his arms folded over his gray jacket. He looked oddly clean and crisp in such fancy clothes. In one hand, he held two champagne flutes.

We were alone in the kitchen. That fact sat heavy in my belly.

Gripping the counter behind me, I said, "Your sister needed the help."

"Careful." He stepped closer, his eyes never straying from my face. "Once you start with her, she'll never stop asking you to do things."

Helplessly, I measured the distance between us. I was trapped in my corner; he'd corralled me so easily. "I like helping people."

"I have something you could help with. Something pretty *big*."

Flushing, I bounced my attention down to his zipper. I didn't mean to, it was as if his gritty voice had taken hold of my neck and guided me down.

And his smile said he'd seen me do it.

I cleared my throat. "You're a big boy, you can help yourself."

"Oh, I do. And I will." His foot came down, the shiny shoe transfixing me the closer he got. "I'll jerk this cock off to thoughts of you, sweetheart. Especially to the memory of how you felt in my arms earlier."

My muscles were useless. All I could do was squeeze the counter harder. "Fine. Go do that."

"Tch." His chuckle caressed between my legs. "You can pretend all you want, but I know I got to you, too. That's why you've been avoiding me all day."

"I was busy with your sister," I argued.

"And after that?"

"I was planning to go home."

"But you didn't."

His lips were only a foot away. How had he gotten into my personal space so smoothly? When I spoke, it was a whisper. "I was just about to, you interrupted me."

"Let's get some honesty going." His arm came forward. I flinched, expecting him to touch me—he put one of the glasses next to me on the counter. "You want me. I can *tell* how badly you want me. And you also want nothing to do with me."

"That last part is definitely true."

Grinning, he bent against the counter. "You're not looking for some long-term baby-making plans with me, right?" Fuck, I was so red. "You want to never see me again? Fine." His low tone flooded my ears, making me dizzy. "Get me out of your system. *Fuck me,* sweet thing. Fuck me and forget me."

Could he hear my heart? "That . . . that's not . . ."

Cupping my chin, he leaned his weight into me. I bent, I crumbled, and I let my facade crack. Kain was too tempting. I wanted to know how his smirk would feel on me, how his quick tongue would taste.

He was right. I wanted him.

I didn't know I'd closed my eyes until he breathed out. Blinking, I watched him study my eyes. Thumbing my chin, then my bottom lip, he said, "You're too curious to walk away."

Kain stared me down. I kept wondering when he was going to kiss me.

Stepping back, he nudged the champagne into my hand. On impulse, I took it. "Drink. Then come find me in the garden."

"What?" It came out louder than I wanted it to.

"You're not from here." Such a flat accusation. It was almost an insult. Kain watched me over his shoulder, his body angled so I could admire the slimness of his waist, how the black pants hugged his ass. "You were lying earlier, I don't know why. But it's clear you don't know who I am . . . or who my family are." He hesitated. "Drink that, take some time, and if you still want to mess around, come find me in the garden."

There was nothing else to be said, apparently, because he walked out of sight.

Sliding down to the floor, I hugged the glass. Holy shit, that walking stack of sex and passion . . . he'd left me a total mess.

And we hadn't even kissed.

Staring into the golden drink, I watched the bubbles pop. Some floated to the top, others clung to the glass as if trying to hold off their fate.

Which was I? A fighter . . . or a bubble that wanted to be popped?

Putting the glass to my lips, I sipped.

Champagne had never tasted so much like sin.

I hadn't slept . . . I wasn't thinking straight. Alcohol was part of the blame, too—after the one glass, I'd refilled mine twice. I kept looking for every excuse in my arsenal so that I could justify what my body was eager to do.

The sky was a deep shade of ocean tide. Under it, my world felt suddenly smaller.

"Oh, Sammy!"

I'd hoped to sneak past the family as they sat under the tiny, star-shaped lights, but Francesca was too vigilant. She waved at me, getting the attention of everyone else so that it was impossible to just walk away.

My lungs flared. *Kain can wait.* Hell, if I took enough time to clear my head, maybe I could get out of here without giving in to my stupid urges. Smiling, I approached the long tables that were set nearly end-to-end.

Francesca stood when I got close, pulling me against her with a big grin. "Everyone!" The people were talking among themselves; she shouted louder. "Hey! Shut the hell up!" That worked, every set of eyes fixing on my furiously hot face. "This is Sammy, and she's the best damn person I've met in a long time. If it wasn't for her, the wedding tomorrow couldn't even happen."

"Oh, no," I said, flapping my hands.

"Don't be modest," Mama Badd said, tipping her drink at me. From her half-shut eyelids, I suspected she was feeling the alcohol. "Frannie is right. You got her dress ready overnight, and you saved this dinner party."

There was a large man across from Mama B. His jaw was thick as a melon, but the hard angles of his cheeks and nose revealed a familiar handsomeness. Neurons fired in the base of my brain. I knew he was Kain's father before he spoke. "Thank you, Sammy," he said, all silk and brass. "You've made my little girl very happy, and so you've made me happy."

"Hear hear," cheered a guy beside the big man's elbow. He couldn't have been much older than Kain, his eyes a black so pure I wondered where his pupils were. He was wearing a pearl-gray suit, but it didn't hide his muscles one bit.

Francesca let me go, throwing her arms around her father. "I love ya, Daddy!"

Chuckling, he patted her back, then reached past her to offer me his hand. "Maverick," he murmured. Linking my fingers with his, I had the unsettling thought that, if he wanted to, he could have crushed my bones without a struggle.

Maverick hooked a thumb over his shoulder. "That's Hawthorne, my second oldest."

The guy winked at me. He took after his mother, the telltale blue eyes of his father replaced by wicked black holes. "Seconds can be better than firsts." He chuckled.

I didn't doubt that he was trying to flirt, but I was busy wondering . . . if he wasn't the oldest, who was?

"Hm," Maverick mumbled. "Where's Kain? You've met him, right?"

Fuck, I was blushing all over again. "Uh, yeah. I have."

Mama Badd turned in her chair, frowning at the darkened garden. "Maybe I should go look for him."

"No!" Lifting my hands, I smiled appealingly. "Let me do it. I was going to wander around and get some air, anyway. It was nice to meet you all." I'd hardly met half of them by the looks of all the unfamiliar faces, but that was fine with me.

I had too many sinful, sticky things in my head to wonder about Kain's family tree.

That impossible man . . . he'd told me to drink, then find him. He'd probably expected me to back out. When I found him in the gardens, just outside the rows of tables everyone was gathered at, his face didn't give his thoughts away. Had he heard us all talking or his father asking for him?

He had to, I can hear them just chatting from here. That meant he'd decided to ignore them all . . . and wait for me.

"Guess you made your choice," he whispered.

On unsteady feet, I approached him. He was standing against a tall hedge, surrounded by roses that looked black instead of pink in the shade. It was cool enough to see my breath, the ghostly smoke rolling between us. June in New England loved to shift weather patterns by the damn hour.

I was a magnet to his iron touch. He snatched me up, his hands prowling over my stomach and hips. I was grateful for the chill; he'd turned me into a furnace.

Shivering under the slow rolling of his thumbs, I leaned upward. "You really think I'm not a local girl, huh?"

Light from the stars morphed his blue eyes into diamonds. "You're not eager enough to get in my pants to be from around here, hon."

We came together; I didn't know who moved first. Running my lips across his, I tasted the last tangy drops of champagne. I'd wanted to be soft, but Kain gripped me tighter, his teeth battling with my tongue. Pulling back, I fought to catch my breath. "How about now? Still not convinced I'm eager?"

"No," he growled. "Convince me more."

The garden was fresh, it smelled green. Around us, his family and friends chatted and laughed into the cool night air. They didn't see me take Kain's hand. They didn't see me drag him toward his house.

They definitely didn't see me reach out to grab his ass.

We made it inside, up those treacherous stairs. It's amazing we managed, everything felt like a fuzzy dream I'd barely remember later. *Good*, I told myself, following him into his bedroom. *Once this is out of my system, I won't want to remember.*

He shoved me through the doorway; I stumbled, giving up any chance of taking control of our interaction. My vision spun, I could see dark walls, a darker bed, and a single window that hinted at the world outside.

It was a setting that deprived me of all senses . . . all distractions . . . but one.

Him.

Kain hooked my dress hem and lifted it, digging his hands into my ass. He didn't ask. He wasn't the sort to waste time asking. A trickle of fear crawled along my spine. *Will he go too far?* Had I forgotten what kind of man he was so easily?

We'd only met yesterday—it felt ages ago. I'd known then that he was trouble. A man who demanded, a man who consumed until he was sated. How had I let myself forget why I'd been avoiding him?

Then his fingers cupped my pussy, and I stopped caring.

"You're already wet," he murmured. That raw sound shivered through my cells.

Taking his hand, I pushed him against me. "Don't get a big ego. I just haven't had sex in forever."

I could feel his grin when it rubbed over my lips. He didn't believe me. Riding his own arrogance, Kain threaded his fingers through the side of my panties. He outlined my lips, tracing outside, then along my slit.

Heat rippled through my core. I crushed my thighs around his wrist; he kept petting me, never bothering to remove my panties. "Fuck, you're so ready."

I wasn't about to let him act like I was the only horny one in the room; I felt for his cock, expecting him to be hard . . . but I didn't think he'd be so damn huge. "You're ready, too." I meant it to sound confident, except I was too overwhelmed.

"Of course I fucking am." He yanked me down, dropping us both to the floor. Under my spine, his rug was thick and plush. "I've wanted to stretch you out with my cock since I saw you dancing around that shop of yours."

That was news to me. Baffled, I thought of what to say. He saved me the effort, his erection pressing roughly into my middle. He rocked back and forth, his belt jingling. His zipper cut through the silence.

Ripping his pants down to his thighs, then his shirt over his head, he showed off his naked torso. The edges of his muscles were illuminated by the garden lights peeking through the window. Kain was more of a statue than a man; how else could he be so flawless?

Then my eyes tracked down, and I spotted two things. The first was almost lost among the parade of tattoos on his skin. If I hadn't seen it on Francesca, it wouldn't have stood out to me. The red-and-black crown sat on his ribs, the same spot hers had been.

I was intrigued, but then there was the second thing:

His scar.

It curved along the lower right side of his stomach. Immediately I pictured a butcher's knife, or . . .

A bullet wound.

It was a crazy thought. Kain seemed wild, but that didn't mean he got into gunfights.

"Oh, baby girl," he said, reaching for my dress. "I want to see those tits of yours in all their glory."

His flattery caused my heart to stutter. I grabbed for the fabric, helping him pull the dress up and over. It messed up my hair; I was quick to smooth it. Kain wasn't paying attention, he was fixated hungrily on my chest.

Taking the hint, I reached back, popping my bra off. The air swept over my nipples; it would have firmed them, but Kain had already pushed them to their peak. He breathed in sharply, flicking his stare up to mine. "You might be the most beautiful girl I've ever seen."

Kain leaned in, fingers wrapping in my hair, ensuring I couldn't break away when he kissed me. Each swirl of his tongue on the roof of my mouth brushed my nerves away.

My worries.

I was melting into the floor, the heat between us boiling. His cock flexed, I could feel the thick veins through his briefs and my panties. The fear that he might be wide enough to cause me pain was turning me into mush. Riding him would be like riding a roller coaster.

Reaching between us, he tugged his underwear aside. The warm, naked flesh of his prick ground along my slit. I cooed as he bumped my clit, but my hands came down, gripping his shoulders. *Fuck*, his muscles were solid. "Wait. Use a condom."

He laughed darkly. "Don't worry. I wouldn't do you wrong like that, you don't want to carry one of my kids, trust me."

It was a weird thing to say. It made me pause, my lusty haze breaking under his sobering warning. Kain slid a foil packet from the pants around his thighs. The condom peeled cleanly down his full length—watching was erotic.

"Lean back," he said flatly, "and brace yourself. I'm about to find out if this pussy is as homebred as you keep trying to say, or if you're about to fall apart from how hard I fuck you."

His eyes roiled like an animal's in heat. Did mine look the same? "Shut up and show me what you can do. You told me to fuck you and forget you, right?" Gripping his ass, I pulled him against me. "Do it. Rock me until I forget who you are, Kain."

Shivering, he angled himself. "I love hearing you say my name. Try to do it while you're screaming, baby girl." Then he plunged forward, his cock head stretching me so abruptly I saw flashes of color behind my eyeballs.

Kain drove into me like he wanted to make a point. Maybe he did—maybe he wanted to show me I couldn't handle him.

That I couldn't forget him.

No, I told myself, wrapping my legs around his waist. *This is a one-time hookup. One and done. I'll never see him after this.*

And that was just fine.

Just . . . fine.

Closing my eyes, I moaned at the sensation of his hard hips cutting into my skin. Each thrust caused his ridges of muscles to bump my breasts or graze over my swollen clit. He bent me in two, the rug tickling my cheek as I sank in.

Somehow, Kain found a way to dig in further.

In my skull, the echo of his force thumped over and over. Anyone below us in the house could hear. He bit my earlobe, thrumming my clit with a free hand—and they *definitely* would hear my screams from that.

"Kain," I breathed, lashes fluttering like a hummingbird. "Fuck, Kain! That's so damn *good*!"

"I know." His arrogance had always pissed me off. In this setting, it made my pussy squeeze around his shaft even tighter. The crest of orgasm teased me, my muscles clenching in delicious pressure.

"When you come," he hissed, wrenching my hair so that I had to look into the furious pits of his stormy eyes, "count for me."

Confused, I opened my mouth. "What?"

Licking my lower lip, then my teeth, he inhaled. "Count out each time you come. Do it, or I'll stop fucking you right before you finish. I mean it."

Kain was too serious, too . . . unstable. I believed him, his harsh words sending static down into my pussy. My thighs shook, and his knowing smirk knocked me over the edge. "Count," he reminded me when I started to whimper.

Shaking violently, my hips twitched as the orgasm took hold. It was in my veins, my bones, my everything. I was a single hot point of pleasure. Making words was hard . . . but I did it for him. "One!" I shouted it like it was my last breath.

His groan was lower than the center of the earth; lava and pure, unfiltered rock. He found speed where surely there should be none, his fingers circling my sensitive clit faster and faster. "Again," he demanded. "Come for me again, beautiful."

Buzzing with energy, I arched into his strokes eagerly. I'd never had multiple orgasms before, but in this little black bubble with a man who was secretly a beast . . . I knew it was going to happen.

"Two!" I cried, sweat sliding down my throat. He licked me there, tasting my salt as I panted with the strain of climax. My inner walls milked him, the condom too thin to hide each swell of his nearing release.

"More, I'm not done with you. *More*, Sammy."

Hearing my name broke down another mental wall. My nails cut into his back, I lavished attention over each of his rippling muscles. I imagined his ink would rub off on me from our friction.

I didn't need to imagine the third orgasm.

"Three," I whispered, the word sticking in my throat. Kain filled me to capacity, his teeth bared. He looked at my face as he came, but he never slowed down. The monster kept fucking me, his seed shooting into the condom.

I didn't stop counting; I just *couldn't* count anymore.

Blackness crept into my vision. Kain had made me come until I passed out.

The last thing I saw as I faded away were his tender, unguarded eyes.

Even if I wanted to forget what we'd done . . .

I could never forget how he looked at me.

- CHAPTER FOUR -

Sammy

Slipping out of the room, I concentrated to make sure every step I took was as quiet as a church mouse's. I wasn't about to wake Kain up and let him see me fleeing, and worse, what if anyone else in the house saw?

Closing the door, I faced the hallway and took my first real breath of air.

Francesca slammed into me, her arms choking away that single breath.

"Sammy!" she screamed, the noise raking over my nerves. "How could this happen?"

"It—it's not what you think!" I blurted, staring wildly at Kain's door. Was she going to kill me for sleeping with her brother?

Hugging me harder, she rubbed her cheek on my shoulder. That was when I realized she was crying. Was this that big of a deal?! "Sammy." She sniffled. "I don't know what to do. I can't believe that bitch! I hate her. I *hate* her!"

My brain ticked like a clock, striking twelve. *This isn't about me.*

Carefully, I untangled her and held her at arm's length. It was early in the morning, but mascara and makeup ran down her cheeks. Francesca was a mess. "What happened? Who's a bitch?"

Pushing out her lower lip, she stepped backward. "That fucking Monica, that's who. She was supposed to be my maid of honor, Sammy! Then she goes and texts Midas pics of her vajayjay! How the hell am I supposed to let her be my bestie now, huh?"

Lifting my hands cautiously, I kept my voice calm. "It'll be okay. I'm sure you'll think of something."

Wiping at her face, she focused on me. I took the opportunity to put on a reassuring smile. Slowly, she copied me—going from depressed to thoughtful. Digging her nails into my forearms, she leaned closer to me. "You're a genius, Sammy!"

"Ha-ha, thanks, but I'm not."

Bobbing her head, she gripped me until I winced. "Yeah," she whispered, almost to herself. "This will be perfect."

"Um," I said blankly.

"You'll be perfect."

My mouth crinkled up like a flatlining balloon. "Hold on."

She threw her arms around me in a hug that was much more cheerful than earlier—but just as painful. "You're going to be such a good maid of honor!"

Inch by inch, my stomach crept into my feet. "Francesca . . . I can't do that, we barely know each other."

"I feel like I've known you forever!" Staring me in the eye, she put on her saddest tone. "Plus, if you don't, I'm screwed. Sammy, I'll have no one! My whole family and friends will laugh, they'll say, 'Oooh that Frannie, she's too much of a bitch to have a bestie! See?'" Her eyebrows knitted together. "I'd fall apart in front of everyone."

She was being ridiculous . . . and even still, I felt a twinge of sympathy. I wasn't close to being married, but if it was my big day and my best friend had destroyed our friendship, and I now had no maid of honor . . . wouldn't that be awful?

Kain warned you about this. I snapped a peek at his door. *He said if you helped her, she'd keep asking for more.*

Like always, I couldn't turn down someone in need.

Sighing, I pulled her in for a hug. "I just hope I can fit into her dress."

Francesca squealed, jumping in a circle and taking me with her. When we made a full rotation, I spotted Kain watching me through the crack in his door.

My heart floated up and away. He was still mostly naked, a tight pair of black briefs wrapping against the morning wood he sported. I'd seen that cock in its full magnificence last night. It didn't take much to imagine it all over again.

He saw me watching, his hand reaching down to graze himself. One firm, quick squeeze of his shaft and my clit twitched in response. Dammit.

I didn't like how satisfied he was by my open-mouthed reaction. Gripping Francesca, I faced her. "We don't have much time until the wedding. Tell me everything I need to know."

Wrapping my arm around her shoulders, I let her guide us down the hall. She gabbed and giggled and flipped her hair. All the while, the hungry stare of a certain Kain Badd burned slowly through the back of my skull.

He was watching me. He didn't stop until I was out of sight.

The next few hours were a blur of arms, busy hands, and ear-splitting shouts. There was an entire team on foot, all dedicated to making the daughter of the Badd family into a star.

Two women coiled her hair, another worked on her toes. She had three makeup artists—even her little fluffy white Yorkie had someone working on him.

I'd planned to just put on a dress and shoes. Francesca would have none of it.

Forced into a chair, I was set up like a piece of meat for some hyenas. The women chattered and yanked at me, forcing my hair into such a tight twist that my eyes watered. I finally put my foot down when they tried to do my makeup like the bride's.

There was *no way* I was letting them pancake it on.

My stomach rumbled as I sat there. I was grateful when I was offered a mimosa. Someone else handed me a tray of pastries, so I took a raspberry Danish—okay, two.

Eventually the room quieted down, the staff clearing out. Francesca stood by as the remaining assistant strapped her into the dress I'd created. I sat in front of the vanity, observing with genuine pride.

She really was beautiful.

"I have to show my dad." She giggled. Swishing her veil, she beamed. "I'll be right back! Get your shoes on!"

When she charged out the door, the last of the attendants went with her. Left alone in the fluffy white sitting room, I leaned down to straighten out the low-cut top of my dress. No matter how I pulled at the material, nothing could make it less . . . what was the word? Streetwalker?

It was a style I'd have never worn. The rose-cream color didn't fit a wedding, if you asked me, though they'd clearly paid someone a lot of money for the outfit; I was positive that was real gold on the zipper.

At least they match the heels. They were meant for Francesca's former friend, and she must have been a fan of height. Scowling, I wiggled my toes into the pink and glittery torture devices. I tested them, wobbling after a couple of steps. The door opened behind me. "Francesca, do you have any other heels besides these?"

Kain slid inside the room, and just as fast, he slid into my blood. I went hot all over, scanning the way his rich navy suit fit across his muscles. It brought out the flecks of silver in his eyes . . . eyes that were busy roaming my nearly naked chest.

"What the hell are you doing in here?" I hissed.

He came my way, not stopping. Kain walked his fingers up my ribs, brushing dangerously close to my breast. "I'm getting ready for the wedding."

Glowing pink, I summoned enough strength to push him away. He smiled, leaning on the wall to watch me. "Get ready elsewhere, I have to practice walking in these heels."

"Don't worry. I'll hold you up in case you trip when we're walking together."

Tiny hairs stood up on my arms. The confident slant to his stare had my blood pumping ever faster. "You're not serious. You're the best man? *You?*"

Plucking at his suit jacket, he looked down at his knuckles. "Am I not best man material?"

I was too stunned to banter. Slumping into a padded chair, I dug my nails into the back of it. When I'd agreed to help Francesca, I hadn't considered that it would throw me closer to the one man I wanted to be miles away from.

"It's actually perfect, when you think about it," he said. "Now I get to dance with someone I actually like. It helps even more that I know how *good* you can move those hips of yours."

The memory of grinding my pussy deliriously on his pelvis rocked my brain. Grabbing the mimosa, I used it to wash the dryness from my mouth. "I might have to walk down the aisle with you, Kain, but I don't have to spend another moment with you before or after."

"'Walk down the aisle,'" he teased. "Like we're husband and wife. I know I fucked you into a blackout last night, but I don't know if I'm ready to marry you."

"Marry you?!" Standing quickly, I threw my hands down. The glass was empty, or I would have gotten mimosa all over my dress. "I don't want to be *near* you!"

Laughing, Kain pushed off of the wall. "Please. You really think you're done with me?"

He was getting closer; I tightened my jaw and stood tall. I wasn't going to let him intimidate me. I *definitely* wasn't going to let him get under my skin . . . or on my skin . . . and fuck, now I was thinking about his naked body all over again.

Kain was on me, his breath caressing my cheek. "You're all red," he whispered. "That because of me?"

Pressure pounded in my ears. Every air particle was affected by him, the distance between us pointless. He wasn't touching me yet, but my lower belly flipped and went wiggly like he was.

I ran my tongue over my lower lip—he followed it with his eyes. "Kain, what happened last night was a mistake."

"This mistake made you scream so hard I think the whole house heard you."

My eyes shot wide. "That—don't act like you were that good!"

His arm passed my ear, his palm touching the vanity behind me, blocking me in. Every wave of heat that came off of his body sank into me. Were my knees *shaking*? "Listen to me, beautiful. I know I was good. And you know I was good. So stop playing, and if you ask nicely, maybe I'll take you for another round. I'd love to eat that sweet pussy of yours, didn't get to last night, ya know? I'd hate for you to think I wasn't a gentleman."

Words failed me. Even my muscles were failing me. Gripping the top of the chair, I sank back onto it. Kain didn't let me go, he followed me down, his sharp nose brushing the tip of mine.

When he licked his teeth, my clit swelled, imagining his tongue on me.

Rubbing my legs together, I swallowed loudly. "You're definitely not a gentleman."

"Then what am I?"

A jerk, an asshole, a dickhead . . .

The best fuck I've ever had.

Francesca busted into the room. "Okay! Let's finish up and—Kain!"

Her brother spun away from me, all evidence that he'd been soaking my panties vanishing. "Sis," he said, grabbing her shoulders. "You look amazing."

She blushed, doing a twirl for him. "Think Midas will run from the altar?"

"If he does, he's a damn idiot."

It occurred to me as they laughed together . . . just how similar they looked. She had the same angular jaw as her brother, and he had her thick lashes and sparkling eyes. They were comfortable together. It made me a little envious that I had no siblings.

Studying how Kain treated his sister, my mood shifted. He was protective, kind, even sweet. None of the sides he'd shown to me.

No. I saw something like that in his eyes . . . right before I passed out.

I had to forget that moment. Guys who were full of themselves just hurt the women who fell for them. I was not about to fall for Kain Badd. Not a fucking chance.

Francesca fanned her face. "Oh, gawd, it's just a few minutes away. Sammy, get up and make sure this dress is on me right."

"It's fine, really." Standing, I weaved around Kain, leaving a wide berth. There was never enough room between us. Tucking the ribbons on her corset, I pulled—then nodded. "You're perfect. Trust me."

Pulling at the top of her dress, she puffed out her cheeks. "Whoo. My tits are sweating, I'm so nervous."

"Let's get you out there," I said, eyeing the clock. "It's almost showtime."

Francesca marched in front of us as we left the room. The plan was to head out a back kitchen door and into the rose garden. The groom wasn't allowed to leave the pavilion near the front of the house until she was stashed away in her own personal tent.

It was a quick trip, most of the grass was flat and even. When we turned into the garden, I tried to lift my dress and step over a few rocks.

My weight shifted too fast—I started to fall, my ankle going out under me. "Aah!"

Firm, strong arms circled my waist and under one arm. Kain cradled me against him, his chest on my mostly naked back. "Careful," he said in my ear. "Don't want you getting hurt. Then how will you tempt all the boys with your fancy hip moves?"

One heartbeat. Two. That was how long it took for me to decide I shouldn't be settling in this man's comfortable embrace. "Hah," I mumbled, standing quickly. "That's ironic, coming from a guy who probably keeps notches on his headboard."

"Excuse me," he said, adjusting his crimson tie. "I'm classier than you realize. I keep a list on my laptop, thank you."

Was it worse if he was joking? Did I *want* him to be the cocky playboy I'd pegged him for, or was it possible he wasn't . . . and that scared me more?

Shaking myself, I hurried—carefully—after Francesca. Inside the white tent, her mother and the priest were waiting. "Oh, there you are!" Mama Badd gasped. Ignoring me, she pulled Kain closer. Dusting off his shoulders, she pressed an orange boutonniere into his pocket. "Now remember, you go when the music starts, but not *before* your cousins."

"I got it, Mom," he said, kissing her cheek.

Crouching, Francesca petted her little dog. Someone had set him up with a tiny silver vest, a box tied to his collar. "Mic! You're so cute!" The dog wiggled, licking her cheek.

The priest smiled kindly. "I'd better get up to the altar. See you in a few minutes."

"Me too," Mama Badd sighed. With a final pinch of her daughter's cheek, she beamed. "I'm so happy. I've already ruined two packs of tissues. Make me proud, honey." Fluffing her dress layers, she slipped out of the tent, followed by the priest.

Francesca stood up, flapping her hands at her hips. "This is it. It's happening. Ah, oh no, I'm sweating. Can you tell?" Her skin had turned an amazing cranberry color.

"You're fine," I consoled her, handing her a tissue from the box someone—probably her mother—had thoughtfully left behind on the table. "Besides, nothing happens until the music begins."

As if I'd summoned it, the sweet bells careened into our ears.

Kain said, "*Now* it's happening. See you, Sis." He peered out of the tent, then motioned at me. "Let's go, cousins are already walking."

Grabbing Francesca in a hug, I laughed. "You're going to make your husband very happy."

Squeezing me, she sniffled. "Damn straight."

"Don't cry!" I cautioned. "Your makeup!"

Dabbing her eyes, she shooed me. "Go, go! Get out there. See you soon."

I balanced on my painful heels and followed Kain. The sun blinded me for a moment when we stepped into the open. I lifted my hand to shield myself; in that instant, he linked his fingers with mine.

Such a simple touch shouldn't have electrified me. It defied all logic, but logic doesn't care a whit about emotions. *It's just lust*, I promised myself.

Fuck, let it just be that.

Together we walked, and true to his word, Kain kept me from tumbling the several times my ankles wobbled. The number of people sitting in foldout chairs was amazing. Was this all family, or friends, or what?

The more I gleaned about the Badds, the more curious I became.

When we reached the end of the aisle, we were supposed to part ways. Kain wasn't much for tradition, I guess, because he held my hand and followed me to stand on the left of the altar.

Every set of eyes fixed on us. Sweat pooled along my collarbone. "What are you doing?" I hissed at him under my breath.

He didn't answer, he just let his fingers drag from my palm to my hip. He went further, outlining the shape of my ass . . . the edge of my thigh. Kain didn't give a shit who saw him or what he was doing.

This was a man on a mission.

I was his mission.

What happened next . . . well, we've caught up to the start. Kain tried to finger fuck me in public, Francesca glowed in the sun, and everything looked awesome and grand, and how could it ever go wrong?

That was when the police showed up.

And then my world was changed forever.

- CHAPTER FIVE -

SAMMY

Whatever the floors in jail cells are made of, they had to be pretty hardy stuff. I'd paced back and forth over the same four-foot stretch for about an hour, and amazingly, the ground didn't show a sign of it.

I was still wearing the ridiculously floofy and too-tight maid of honor dress, though I'd removed my heels the second I'd been freed of my cuffs. Hugging myself, I marched back and forth behind the bars, my teeth chattering. It was cold, but in spite of everything . . . I did have one thing going for me.

I was *pissed as fuck*.

Fury is good for keeping you warm.

I'd never been arrested in my life. Initially, I'd been terrified for myself—for everyone. The mayhem had been deafening, making me sure that it had to end in violence somehow. When I'd been set on the grass away from the still-gathered-but-dispersing wedding attendees, I'd gotten to finally look around.

Black cars and more obvious police wagons hovered on the fringe of the estate. I could see them around the edges of the house and rosebushes. Slowly a parade of cuffed people began marching up toward the vehicles.

Francesca in her wedding dress . . . lord, that cut hard. But she wasn't crying; her makeup was clean and crisp. When I followed her glare, how she kept wrenching around to glare at one of the others behind her, I began to get a bad feeling.

"Daddy!" she screamed, shaking her wrists and yanking at the officer who was struggling to hold her back. "What the hell did you do *this* time?!"

"Francesca!" Mama Badd snapped, dragging the officer on her forward from the pack. "Keep your mouth shut! Mister Finch will straighten this all out."

"This is supposed to be my wedding day!"

"Francesca, shut it!"

"Up," someone said, ripping me onto my feet.

Stumbling, I eyeballed the cop and said, "Please, this is wrong! I didn't do anything, why am I being arrested?"

Mama Badd looked my way as she passed. "You, too," she growled. "You keep your mouth shut. Don't say anything to the cops."

"Anything about *what*?" I shouted.

That was the last I saw of the Badds before the police cars carted them off.

Dropping my forehead on the cool bars, I took a moment to consider all the mistakes I'd made in my life. What had led me to *this*, of all things? Jeez, I'd never been more embarrassed in my whole life than this morning.

Even waking up, remembering that I'd hooked up with Kain when I'd explicitly instructed myself not to, hadn't been as bad as this.

Keys jingled, and I glanced up anxiously at the sight of another nameless police officer. "Come on," he said, wriggling the cell door open. "They're ready for you."

"Who's ready for me? What does that even mean?" I didn't like how my voice broke; I was just too exhausted to hold it together. "Why am I being held here at all?"

The cop was older than me, and I guess he'd seen all sorts of people pleading in the cell I was standing in, because not a flicker of sympathy lightened his gaze. "Are you coming out of there or not?"

Scooping up my high heels, I walked past him with the last of the quiet dignity I could muster.

He led me down the hall, past other cells where people either curled up in drunken sleep or watched me with curious eyes. While I wondered what they had done, it was obvious they were thinking the same about me.

Except I hadn't *done* anything! I had no clue why the wedding had been raided, or why I'd been swept up in the mess and carted off to the police station. All I knew was that I was tired, hungry, and beyond frustrated with the world.

This is all a mistake, I told myself, forcing my heart to calm. *Once I talk to someone in charge, they'll release me.* They had to. Didn't they?

Mom.

The thought of her sitting alone in her apartment filled my guts with razors. She wasn't going to know what had happened to me, why I hadn't come by yet to help her with her meals or to keep her company. If anything happened to her because I wasn't there . . . I'd never forgive myself.

And I'd *never* forgive the Badds.

"Here we are," the cop said, pausing beside an unremarkable white door. Through the tiny window in it, I saw there was a new man waiting at a table inside. His head came up, like he'd sensed us before the officer even opened the door. "Detective Stapler will take it from here."

"Stapler?" I blurted before I could stop myself. "And who are you, Officer Paper Clip?"

Officer Paper Clip stared at me flatly. "Have fun."

I regretted my idiotic question; I blamed it entirely on my unstable mood. Turning, I watched as the detective at the table rose with a friendly smile. "Miss Sage, please, have a seat."

Glancing around the blank room, I moved to the metal folding chair and settled on it across from him. "Detective Stapler, right? Listen, I don't know why I'm here, but it's all a mistake."

"Oh, I'm sure it is," he said, nodding seriously. "We'll get it straightened out right away."

I sank into my seat, breathing out. "Thank you. I need to get out of here fast; my mother, she's not well, and she's probably wondering where I am."

"Your sick mother, is it?" he mused.

My nodding head stopped mid-motion. "I know that sounds like a cheap excuse, but I'm serious."

"I'm serious, too, Miss Sage." He slid his hands apart, and I finally noticed the pale folder he'd been resting his arms on. I didn't know what was in it, but my nerves started to spark. "This situation is no joke."

"*What* situation?"

Stapler had fine lines over his bushy brows. Those lines crunched together, growing deeper as he spoke. "Tell me what you know about the Badds."

"Almost nothing. I only met them yesterday."

His chuckle scraped through my ears like old pottery over glass shards. "Funny, how could the maid of honor of their youngest daughter know almost nothing about her family?"

Pushing a hand against my forehead, I laughed weakly. "I get it. No, see, you're confused."

"*I'm* confused? Enlighten me."

"Francesca was just a client. I made her wedding dress. Yeah, I also ended up as her maid of honor . . ." Plucking at my orange frills, I smiled at him as hard as I could, hoping he'd give in and smile back. No such luck. The tension remained. "It just kind of happened."

"You're telling me you became the maid of honor for a woman you only met yesterday?"

"It's a funny story. You'll laugh, I swear." My chuckle came out as stiff as cardboard. "Her best friend sent some rude photos to her fiancé the night before the wedding. She was in a pickle, I stepped up. How could I not?"

Opening the folder with a flourish, Stapler slid a photo my way. Then another and another. Lifting them, I stared at the vibrant images of me waiting at the end of the aisle. There was even one of me from behind, and you could clearly see Kain's hand on my ass cheek.

I was going to kill Kain. Seriously kill him. Tear-his-balls-off-and-dance-on-top-of-them kill him. Flushing, I pushed the photos back across the table. "I just admitted that I was her maid of honor, there's no need to show me these."

"There's a story in those pictures, Miss Sage." His grin cocked sideways, a fat finger jabbing at the photo of Kain and me. "You're acting pretty familiar with someone you don't *know* so well. Or is this just how you are with strangers?"

"Fuck you," I snapped. Swearing at a detective wasn't my proudest moment, but being accused of being some kind of whore wasn't winning him any points. "You've got everything all mixed up, and I *still* have no idea what you're trying to prove."

Stapler watched me closely. "You're really telling me your only connection to these people was a wedding."

"That's all. Can I go?"

With careful pacing, he pushed two new pieces of paper at me. They were photocopies of checks; the payments from Kain for the dress and from his mother for the help with the party. "My math isn't great," he said slowly. "But this looks to be about thirty grand right here. Tell me, who gets paid thirty grand to make a wedding dress?"

Licking my lower lip, I met his serious eyes. They were kind of pretty for such a weathered man. "Is it a crime to get paid to help people out? Is that what I'm being charged with?"

"You aren't charged with anything. Yet." He shrugged. "Help me out. This looks suspicious to me. Here you are, walking closely with the children of Maverick Badd on the day of his daughter's wedding. And then, after we raid their estate to find the illegal weapons they're holding, you walk in here with thirty grand in your pockets from the family itself."

"I didn't walk in, you guys dragged me in, and—wait." I stiffened. "Hold on. You're saying you raided their estate because they were hiding weapons?" Reality tap-danced across my guts.

Stapler said, "The Badds have always been lawbreakers. Blackmail, greasing the palms of dirty politicians to keep things the way they like in this city. You name it, and they're involved. I've even got a few homicides I suspect they're responsible for."

Homicides. The wobbling, too-tangible memory of Kain's naked flesh crept through my memory. How his torso had rolled like the waves in a dark storm. How he'd been so perfect . . . except for that single, puckered scar on his stomach.

Weapons. Bullets. The leap was easy to make. How dangerous was a man like Kain? I'd been worried that he'd be wild, maybe kind of crazy—and definitely too alpha for me.

Being a murderer had never crossed my mind.

"Holy hell," I whispered. "You think I had something to do with all of *that*?"

Stapler—honestly, who had a name like that?—reclined in his seat. The photocopied checks sat between us like nuclear weapons. "You're carrying funds from an illicit source, paid by a family known for bribery and selling black-market goods. How else do I look at it?"

Lifting my hands, I flailed them side to side. "Slow down. I had no clue about any of this." *Is he serious? Are the Badds that kind of family?* "Francesca walked into my store the other day. I've only been back in the state for a few months, I'd never met her *or* her brother before." Chasing my thoughts in a circle, I wondered how to prove I was innocent.

Wait. Narrowing my eyes on the detective, I hesitated. *Maybe I don't have to.*

Tilting his head, he smiled curiously. "What are you thinking, Miss Sage?"

"I'm thinking . . . that you already said I'm not under arrest. You don't actually have anything to charge me with, do you?"

He went so very still. "Not yet."

Breathing faster, I pushed myself unsteadily to my feet. "Then I guess I'll be going."

"Miss Sage?" he asked. Peering at him, I grabbed the doorknob. "I'll say this once. I'm not the bad guy here."

Sucking in my lower lip, I weighed my words. "You might be right about them. I don't have a clue if anything you've said is a lie. It could easily be all true. But between the both of you?" I opened the door. "You're the only one who's tried to frighten me. Good guys don't do that."

He said nothing as I made my exit.

It would have been much more dramatic if I wasn't carrying a glittery pair of stripper heels.

- CHAPTER SIX -

Kain

My shoe kept tapping on the busted tile floor. Every few minutes the cop behind the front desk would glare at me with distaste. When he did, I made sure to smile and wink. Every time the same smile, the same cocky wink.

I hated cops. Had since I was a kid. Plus, it was easy to dislike the guys who'd dragged me in here and left me in a cell for two hours. To be fair, it wasn't very long—but our family lawyer was usually much faster.

It probably didn't help that he represented both sides of my family, and in the span of one morning, needed to assist all of us.

Simon Finch was one of those men who just appeared out of thin air, often with his hair wobbling in the breeze like he'd sprinted straight from wherever he'd been waiting. He'd pointed out how the arrest had been made without cause, that they had no proof to keep anyone here, and then he'd e-mailed my father his invoice and traipsed away to help other would-be convicts out of prison.

I admired him. It's not that I thought I deserved to be in jail, but Finch definitely got me out fast enough each time that if I *was* doing something wrong, I could go right back to it before the cops could even get another warrant.

After things were straightened out, my brother Hawthorne had brought me my motorcycle and a change of clothes. It had felt good to get out of the suit, even if I knew I looked amazing in it.

Recrossing my legs, I leaned forward, trying to peek around the corner. Sammy was back there; I didn't need to see her to know. Fuck, in a way, I even felt it. That made no damn sense, but the tugging in my stomach acted like there was a bit of bait hooked inside of me, and Sammy had the fishing pole.

I didn't need to be here. I definitely didn't need to try and explain things to her nonexistent lawyer about how to help get her out of trouble—I still couldn't believe she didn't have one. Who didn't? Either way, once I was confident that they had no plans to actually arrest her, I'd parked my ass to wait.

I just . . . felt sort of responsible for Sammy getting caught up in the raid. But I'd warned her from the start; she didn't know who I was, *who my family* was. If she had, she wouldn't have gotten so involved with my sister.

And then we wouldn't have kissed.

A kiss. Fucking hell. Was I really mooning over one of a thousand pairs of lips? Yeah, it had happened under a perfect starry night in a rose-filled garden, but harping over those little details was something a wannabe pretty princess did. Not me, and probably not Sammy, either.

She was a no-nonsense kind of woman, even if she did reek of high-end prissy New York City life. Spending time with her as her guard slipped, more and more of her genuine, hard-edge, ball-busting, heart-of-Rhode-Island attitude slipped out.

No, she wasn't the fairies and glitter type.

Not at all.

Sammy walked around the corner, sparkling high heels swinging in her hand. My heart pulled side to side; I wanted to laugh. I could have rolled on the floor and made the whole room stare at me.

She spotted me. Her rich green eyes flipped from uncertainty to molten lava. It was the sort of look reserved for roadkill stuck to the tires of your brand-new Corvette. Pulling her dress layers over her full hips, she spun to face the thick man behind the front desk.

"Hey," she said. It took him a minute to look up from his newspaper. "I need my things."

Yawning, the cop raked his bored eyes over her. "Name?"

"Sammy Sage."

The plastic box he dropped on the counter contained a purse, some earrings, and a cell phone. He pushed some yellow papers at her as well. "Your car was taken to an impound lot, info is on there."

Sammy dug through everything, shoving the items into her purse. "Excuse me." Tapping the counter, she waited until the large man was staring at her again. He looked as uninterested as ever. "There's some stuff missing."

"What stuff?"

"Two checks, both made out to me."

His face remained frozen. "Confiscated."

When I saw her pretty features twisting, I felt a stab of guilt. "Why would they be confiscated?"

"They're part of an ongoing investigation." Shrugging made his jowls shake. "Sorry, ma'am. Until someone decides they're clean, you can't have them back."

Bristling, she took a deep breath . . . and then she just rubbed between her eyes. "Fine."

She took that well. I changed my opinion the second she faced me. Every bit of rage she'd muted for the clerk, she was pointedly stabbing at me with it. "Jail was kind to you," I said with a half smile. "You didn't even get any pen-cap tattoos. Or are they just hidden somewhere sweet?"

Sammy adjusted her dress as she turned pink. "I didn't want to see your face again. But now that you're here . . . I've got some things to say."

Pushing off the bench, I stuck my hands in my pockets and wandered closer. We stood in a way that seemed casual, but I was intentionally blocking the one exit out of the station. She had things to say? So did I. "Sammy, listen. I'm sorry as hell about what happened this morning. It was all a misunderstanding."

She looked me up and down. "Everything the detective said to me, was it a lie?"

My smile cracked just a hair. "I don't know what he said. I wasn't in there."

"But you do know." Her head tilted, sending a cascade of disheveled hair down her elegant neck. "It's in your face. You're too comfortable in here. This isn't your first time getting arrested."

Ah, shit. "Sammy, whatever Detective Office Space said back there, it doesn't matter. That's why you're walking out, and why *I'm* walking out." Leaning closer, I took a quick, short breath. Even with sticky sweat on her, Sammy smelled intoxicating. "Give me a chance."

"I've got something else I'd love to give you," she grumbled. "You're lucky my father raised me so well." Her hand fisted at her side, clenching and releasing over and over.

"Are you thinking about punching me? Careful, I *love* tough women." I couldn't stop my grin. "So your dad taught you manners, huh? Is he also the one to thank for your good looks, or is that your mom? Either way, I'd definitely like to shake his hand."

Sammy's eyebrow twitched. "Get out of my way."

Turning sideways, I motioned with my arms. "Sweetheart, you've got all the right in the world to walk out of here. But I think you'll want to listen to what I—hey!"

She'd lowered her chin and passed me by so fast that the air stirred the fringes of my hair. Weren't people supposed to let you finish a sentence? "Just hold up!" I followed her out into the early afternoon. "Sammy, hear me out! I'm trying to explain what went wrong back there!"

Pulling up short, she whirled on me. "What went wrong was me letting myself get mixed up with you."

I *knew* not to do it, but . . . sometimes, I don't know why I do the things I do. I was a secret to even myself. "Think about what a story it'll make for our kids."

The edges of her eyes filled with fine lines: steel swords aiming right at me. "You're such a jackass." *Shit!* Why couldn't I resist making stupid jokes? "Sammy, wait!" Laughing to ease the mood, I followed her as she walked along the chain-link fence with her phone in hand. The front of the police station was quiet, cars shining in their parked spots. "Seriously, I'm sorry. Let me explain myself. I'm not a bad guy, honestly."

"You really want to explain what happened?" Without facing away from her darkened phone, she glanced at me. "Why did Francesca's wedding get raided?"

"Because some asswipe or *asswipes*, plural, are jealous of my family. You saw my estate, is that so far-fetched?"

She gave me a blank look. "I got dragged into a jail cell and humiliated, and you want me to believe it's because some random person or *persons*," she pulled the word out, "are jealous? Nope. Wrong answer."

"Come on," I said, tracking after her toward the road. "Where are you going now?"

Waving her phone, she tapped at it. "I'm getting a taxi back to my car. They said they towed it nearby."

I was getting ready to think of another way to keep this startling woman from exiting my life completely. As I watched her expression fall, her fingers poking frantically at her phone, I found one. "It's dead, isn't it?"

"I didn't get to charge it last night because . . ." Blushing, she eyed me, then her phone again.

Because you were fucking me until you passed out. I didn't say it, she was pissed enough at me. "Let me give you a ride."

"How? Didn't they tow your motorcycle, too?"

"My brother brought it here, so I could leave when I was ready." Jerking my thumb, I indicated the stretch of sidewalk up the street. My bike was shining under the orange sun.

Sammy looked from me to her phone, then back again. Finally, she cupped her cheeks and gave a dramatic groan so loud that the police officer sitting by the front doors sat up like she'd pointed a gun at him. She bent over, head between her knees.

"Are you okay?" I asked, reaching for her.

Before I made contact, Sammy unfurled so quick that her back cracked, her hair finally flying free of the last of the woven wedding design. "Fuck me!" She laughed at the sky. "Can things really never go my way?"

"They can at least go to the impound lot," I said. Sammy studied me, looking me over like I was some demonic creature she'd unearthed. I did my best to smile reassuringly.

Eyeing my bike, she next looked down at her purse. Carefully, she wove the strap through the loops of the high heels, giving them a place to hang. "Okay. I'll let you give me a ride."

A surprisingly airy flutter swam from my toes to my throat. It forced my voice to come out lighter than usual. "Then let's get out of here."

She held me like I was the only thing keeping her on the planet. It was a grip reserved for lovers or, in her case, people who had never been on a motorcycle before.

I didn't have a spare helmet, so I'd forced her to wear mine while I went without. My father would have praised me while my mother would have cracked me upside my temple for choosing someone's safety over my own.

But she wasn't here.

And Sammy was.

I mean that. Sammy was *here*, right here in the moment. Fear is the perfect divider for separating you from your fucked-up thoughts. When you think you might die, clarity shows through better than black clouds on a red sky.

Riding my bike didn't scare me, though, so unlike her . . . I wasn't free. My skull rampaged with the hoofbeats of my thoughts. *Is helping her all right? Does this make any sense? Will Hawthorne care that I'm not at the club yet? Will my father? And Francesca . . . how is she holding up? Shouldn't I be spending time with her instead?*

Twins have connections deeper than blood.

My engine crackled, gravel flying away from my front tire as I pulled up outside the impound lot. The metal beast purred between my thighs, then it went silent. "Here we are," I said, twisting to look at Sammy.

Inch by inch, she eased her hands off my middle. They were bent like claws, clearly cramped. I missed them instantly. When she pulled the helmet off, her hair fell from it in tangled strands.

The sight of her stunned face—wide lips, sparkling eyes, and tomato cheeks—made my cock jump as quickly as my heart. It was a confusing sensation that left me dizzy; did I have enough blood in my body to endure two demanding parts of me at once?

"Are you okay?" I asked.

She focused on me, blinking. "I know how it feels to be a cannonball."

Laughter exploded from me. "That's one way to describe it." My hand came up, stroking hair from her forehead before I could stop myself. We touched through our skin . . . but it was more than that.

Heat plucked at the base of my neck. I couldn't stop how my brushing fingertips became a firm palm cupping her cheek. My mouth tingled; I knew how she'd taste, I wanted to experience her soft lips as they buzzed with the last of her adrenaline.

Sammy started to lean in. In the blackness of her dilating pupils, I saw my half-open mouth. She must have seen her own expression in my eyes, too. My thumb grazed the corner of her lips; her hand closed on mine, pushing me away.

"Come on," she said, leaving the helmet on the seat. "Let's go."

Recovering from the rejection, I followed her down. Her bare feet touched the hot gravel, but it was her bones—still vibrating with the violence of my bike—that gave up. Sammy buckled sideways, her dress flipping upward as her face crashed straight toward the ground.

Faster than I had any right to be . . . but I just *needed* to be . . . I caught her by her elbow. It was like the other day in my driveway all over again. We were tangled dancers, and while no one had seen us yesterday, a confused impound worker gawked at us now.

Gentle as a breeze, I scooped her up in my arms. Sammy gasped, which was good, because it muted my subtle groan. Holding her against me was pure pleasure. Her weight was perfect, just enough to keep me grounded so I wouldn't float into the heavens.

"Kain, put me down."

"Nope. Have you seen this place?" Stepping over rocks and broken glass, I headed for the gate. "You don't want to put those heels back on, that's fine. But if you try to step on this shit with your silky feet, you'll be seeing blood."

"My *silky feet*? Jeez, don't tell me you have a foot fetish."

Chuckling, I spoke into her ear. "Was I rubbing your feet last night or your pussy?"

Her mouth went white and tight.

The man waiting by the gate stood up like we were royalty coming his way. He had no clue that one of us actually was. "Hey there," I said, squinting at his name tag. ". . . Larry. My lady friend here has a car she needs to grab. Show him the paperwork, Sammy."

Pulling her purse into her lap, she fumbled the yellow papers out, handing them over. The young man took them hesitantly, saying, "Uh, all right. Give me your key, I'll go grab it."

Sammy gave them up, then we both watched as Larry trucked off across the giant lot of vehicles. It was like a graveyard for cars, their bodies in various degrees of decay.

The wind kicked dust up, and on instinct, I shielded Sammy from it. Doing so pushed my face close to the top of her head. Hair strands tickled my cheeks, a sensation as nice as her fingers would have been on the small of my back.

"Kain," she whispered.

My veins quickened. "Yeah?"

"After this . . . I don't want to see you again."

I wasn't ready for the torrent of brackish ice that slammed through my ribs. I couldn't see her face; was she serious? And what was I supposed to say to that? When I'd hooked up with Sammy, I'd expected to have to turn *her* away later.

When was the last time someone had turned me down?

Larry drove her car up to the gate. The second he stepped out, she jumped free of my arms. It looked like some twisted apocalyptic scene: Sammy in her dirty but clearly fancy dress, her hair flying in the hot wind.

She ducked into the driver's seat, giving Larry just enough time to move before she peeled out through the gate. Sand billowed as she passed me—and then she pulled up short, the brakes squeaking.

Her window slid down; I approached, still unsure what to do. "Here," she said, holding something out to me.

Grabbing the glittery heels, I stared from them to her. "Sammy—"

She jerked forward, driving off onto the road and taking the corner in a sharp swing. Just like that, Sammy was gone. There was no fanfare, no long good-byes. I didn't get to argue my case or explain my family. None of it.

Larry stepped beside me, watching with me in the moment of silence. "Why did she give you her shoes?" he asked. "Was she Cinderella or some shit?"

His words made me laugh, and that felt good—that release was what I needed.

"Yeah. I think she was."

Have you ever smelled stripper ass?

It's not a bad smell. It's just a memorable one. It's the kind of thing no girl can recreate outside of the club, you only wear it if you're the sort who's busy taking off her panties and shaking it for her rent.

My eyes took a second adjusting to the dimness. Reno, by the door, nodded at me. I didn't have to pay a cover; my family owned the Dirty Dolls, among other strip clubs. The place was huge, the second-floor balcony situated above so that you could see straight down to the stages below.

If you stood at the top rail you could watch the few girls capable of climbing to the top of the poles doing their tricks right in front of you. You could wonder why they'd risk their damn lives doing upside-down contortions when most of the money was made by hustling for lap dances—and it was a whole lot safer.

Strippers don't get health insurance.

Walking past the bar, I brushed off the onslaught of each and every dancer. They all knew me, so you'd think by now they'd realize I didn't buy dances. Maybe they just wanted to stroke my ego in the hope I'd reward them with the kind of favor only powerful people are capable of.

The man sitting sprawled out on a wide couch by the stage wasn't easy to miss. There were three strippers sitting beside him. They swooned and giggled and tried to rub against him, but I knew my brother. Hawthorne was much like me.

Maybe we'd sleep with a girl if she was our type . . .

But we'd never waste our time with a lap dance.

He'd left various stacks of bills beside him and scattered on the floor; the girls were stuffing them all over their bodies as I approached.

"Hey, man," I said, leaning against the edge of the couch.

His black eyes jumped to me. "What the fuck took you so long?"

"Chill. I just had some stuff to take care of."

Hawthorne sat up, eyeing me in the subtle way he was good at. "Shit. Were you with that girl?"

Rubbing the side of my head, I didn't deny it. "Just gave her a ride to her car."

"We have too much going on to mix in unknowns."

"She's not dangerous."

"No?" Hawthorne cut a hand out in front of him so sharply and suddenly it made the dancers lean away nervously. "We don't know who the hell the mole was. Someone at that wedding told the cops where to look for our goods, and it's a fucking miracle that Dad was in the middle of shipping things out so we didn't get caught."

It did feel like we lucked out, but . . . "Someone stirred stuff up, but come on. Sammy makes dresses."

Shaking his head, my brother straightened out the tight, dark red shirt he had on. It showed off his muscles the same way mine did, though his tattoos were less obvious. He was a fan of the yakuza, and his tats remained just beyond of the edges of his cuffs and collar. Beneath, he was a sprawling mass of ink.

I wanted to explain myself further—who was he to judge me—but the DJ's voice boomed over the music. "All right, gentlemen! Top of the hour, time for our new set! Here's Gina, Rosey, and Melina!"

The new girls took their spots on the stage. I looked on as the glimmering bodies gyrated, asses bouncing and tits swinging. If I'd had any doubt, I knew it now. Sammy Sage was more interesting to me than any other woman. Nothing was better than a strip club to prove it, though I was sure no one else would think that was romantic.

But Sammy wanted nothing to do with me. She'd decided I was bad news, and honestly, she wasn't wrong.

I didn't blame her . . . I was just determined to change her mind.

A waitress swung our way. She was a cute thing, her blonde hair long and smooth down her back. The corner of her nose had one of those tiny piercings. "Drinks?" she asked, peering between me and my brother. "Anything for you, Thorne?"

"Nah," he said, smiling so his teeth showed. "I'm good, Scotch."

I had to look twice to make sure I'd heard right. But there, stitched into the right side of her figure-hugging top, was the name Scotch. It had to be a fake name, which, among the array of strippers called Swanky and Sensual, wasn't so strange. She gave me a quick smile before she strolled off to manage the crowd.

"Listen," Hawthorne said, motioning for everyone else to go. Once we were alone, I sat beside him on the couch. "Felt and Robert are digging around to find out who ratted on us. They knew where our guns were stored, that means they spent time at our home. Dad thinks it was one of the Deep Shots."

"Deep Shots." I snorted. "More like the Deep Shits. How could they even slip inside?" The Deep Shots were an old gang, but they hadn't been on our radar until they'd changed leadership about a year ago. After that, they'd been starting trouble all over our city. It had always been small stuff before; having the guts to call a cop raid on us was new.

Thorne lifted one of his eyebrows. It was as dark as the rest of his thick hair. When I was younger, I used to think Hawthorne was full of shadows, that they peeked out of him wherever they could. "Frannie invited so many people. We were too cocky, Brother. Anyone could have gotten inside and dug around, told the cops where to look."

"But *why*?" That was bothering me the most. We didn't have a great history with the Deep Shots, but why try and fuck us over, was it just for kicks?

Hawthorne sank deeper into the couch, his knees spreading. He looked for all the world like a king on a throne. It was a heavy reminder of who we were . . . what ran in our blood. "Dad has some ideas."

"He told you but not me?" I bristled, fingers digging into the couch.

"If you had been here an hour ago," he said bluntly, "he would have told you himself. Talk to him tonight. I'm not going to cross him by spilling his thoughts."

My mood was already sour, this just tipped me over. Pushing myself to my feet, I hooked my thumbs into my belt loops. "Anything else, *Brother*?"

Those inky eyes fixed on me. He had a deadly stare, and even after years of seeing it, I still felt a twinge of unease. "Watch that girl."

"I—what?"

"You're into her anyway. If you really think she's not the mole, not connected to the Deep Shots or anyone after us, then keep an eye on her. Find out for sure."

My tongue stuck to the roof of my mouth. I wished I'd asked for a drink from Scotch. "All right. If you think it's best."

He gave me a knowing smirk. "As if you wouldn't have done it anyway. You act like you aren't incredibly obvious, Kain."

"Isn't that what makes me so likable?" Reaching down, I gripped his hand and gave a firm shake. "Be safe, Thorne."

"Look around," he said, grinning. "I'm surrounded by soft things. What's safer?"

Weaving back through the growing crowd—it always got busier as night came on—I nodded at the bouncers as I exited. The cool air ate away the stripper-ass smell, but it would take a few minutes for the music to leave my ears.

She told me to leave her alone. I couldn't. I didn't want to anyway, but . . .

Now I had no choice.

Will she understand? There was a good chance this would push a bigger wall between Sammy and me. I'd have to take that chance, because the other option meant I'd never talk to her again. Never hold her . . . and never kiss her.

My bike was waiting for me.

On one side of the handlebars, her shoes sparkled.

- CHAPTER SEVEN -

Sammy

Though I knocked first, my key was already clicking in the lock. "Mom?" Pushing into the tiny apartment, I looked around. "It's me!"

I would have lived with her if she'd allowed me. Her place was too small for the both of us, but I'd have done it. As weak as my mom was, though, she was eternally proud.

"Samantha!" she said, leaning her head around the corner of the bathroom. "You're finally here!" Her attention went to my bare feet and my frazzled hair and dress. "What happened? Are you okay?"

"Me? Are *you* okay?" Dropping my purse, I hurried toward her. I'd come as fast as I could, not even bothering to change clothes. Opening the door, I saw that she was sitting naked in the tub. "Did you fall?"

"Oh, it's nothing." Chuckling in her throat, she covered herself. "Just a little slip during my shower. I turned the water off."

"How long have you been stuck in here?" Her eyes met mine, then moved away. "Oh, Mom. I'm so sorry." Yanking down a towel, I wrapped her in it, then helped her stand, guiding her over the lip of the tub.

She put her weight on me just as long as she had to. Then she let go, hugging the towel tight. "Did you go to a wedding or something?"

"I . . . did, actually. It's a long story. Did you eat?" I didn't let her answer, I just headed into the kitchen while she walked into her room to get clothed. Shouting, I said, "You must have missed your medicine this afternoon, too. I'll get it all set for you."

She came out in a long white shirt and loose tan pants. "Honey, I can do all that."

I'd learned every smidge of pride I had from her. It was hard for her to stand by as I served her up a ham sandwich, her pills rolling in a tiny cup. "It's nothing. Sit, eat, relax. I'm really sorry I didn't come by this morning."

Settling onto her tiny excuse for a couch, she took a bite of food. Her mouthful—her silence—told me more about how hungry she was than she'd wanted to say. Guilt burned through my veins.

Swallowing the pills, she chased it all with water. "Your long story. Go on."

"Uh . . . oh." *I can't tell her I got arrested. She'd be mortified, and her poor heart . . .* "An old friend called me up last minute. She needed me to stand in at her wedding, it just took longer than I expected. Again, sorry."

"Stop apologizing." Waving her skinny fingers, she smiled in a way that made her look younger. "Weddings are fun. And a good way to meet boys," she said, winking.

Laughing, I shook my head furiously. "Last thing I need is a 'boy' in my life." *Kain is no boy. He's almost more than a man.* Shifting where I stood, I looked at the floor.

"Oh-ho," she said slyly. "You met someone. Was he hot?"

"Mom!"

Grinning, she nibbled her sandwich. "That's a yes."

"Give me a break."

"Give me details."

Covering my burning face, I said, "I can't. I won't. It doesn't matter anyway, he wasn't right for me."

"No?"

"No." I meant it to come out firm, but the edge of the word wavered.

My mother heard, but bless her, she changed the subject. "How's work been?"

I started to smile—I almost said good and meant it, too. *The checks.* Right. I'd never gotten to cash all that money. I was out a wedding dress and worse off than ever.

Lifting my chin, I leaned closer. "It's wonderful. Everything is good."

My mom studied me for a long minute. "I'm glad. I'd hate for you to regret moving back here and—"

"Mom, no. Stop." I was hugging her before I could think it over. In my arms she felt like a set of sticks in a cloth bag. Sickness had ravaged her, a fact I didn't like to dwell on. I couldn't tell how much was her depression over losing my dad or what was from her weak body. "I love being back. I get to see you all the time. Plus I don't miss the noise and pollution of New York at all."

Patting my back, she squeezed, then pulled back. There was warmth in her eyes. "I'm glad to hear that. My mother used to say that coming home brought good luck."

"Luck," I said, tracing the word with my tongue. Cleaning up the mess as my mom chatted at my wandering mind, I had a funny little oddly comforting thought.

This has to be rock bottom.

From here, I could only go up.

Right?

I ached all over when I crossed the threshold into my own home. The floor creaked, only slightly louder than my overworked joints. Clicking on the light above my stove, I used the flickering illumination to pour myself a cup of water.

What a fucking day.

Leaning over the sink, I stared at my warped reflection in the metal faucet. It was all stretched out; it was exactly how I felt. Every bit of me had that too-tall, too-strained sensation. In the sink, my stallion mug sat collecting water. It was hard to accept that it had only been waiting there for a day and a half.

Heading up the stairs, I kept expecting my bones to disconnect on every step.

I debated taking a shower—I definitely needed one—but sleep clawed at me until I couldn't fight back. In my bedroom, I reached back to strip the dress off. I struggled with the zipper, tugging at it side to side. "Come on, you piece of—urgh."

Breathing in desperately, I fought a wave of cresting anger. I was beyond drained, I just wanted to drop into my bed and forget this whole day, and now this torture of a dress was resisting me.

"Get the fuck . . . off!" Grunting, I felt the threading give way. The zipper tore, it was enough to wriggle the dress down to my ankles. I'd been wrong earlier when I'd thought the zipper was real gold. *Poor craftsmanship*, I noted, kicking the garment aside. My dresses never ripped like that.

I enjoyed my nakedness briefly. Rocking side to side, my arms overhead, I groaned. There were marks along the undersides of my breasts from the support wire. Rubbing at them tenderly, I pawed through my dresser for pajamas.

Man, it's seriously cold in here. Wasn't it summertime? This state was plain unpredictable. Shivering, I pulled a long shirt over my head, then tugged on some thick black sweatpants. *The wind cuts right through the walls of these old houses that landlords love turning into cheap apartments.*

I shouldn't complain; cheap meant *I* got to live here.

Turning, I jumped at the sight of my own shadow on the bedroom wall. "Jeez," I laughed nervously. "Calm down." The outside streetlights made every corner appear darker, richer, and bleaker than ever.

Streetlights?

For a while, I stared at my window. The glass stared back at me. Something about that was wrong—but what?

The blinds. They broke yesterday morning and . . .

I'd covered the whole window with a big piece of cardboard. Now it was sitting on the floor against the wall, propped up exactly like someone had taken it down and set it aside carefully. But I hadn't done that, so who—

In the hall, I heard my stairs squeak.

Someone is inside my home!

Whoever it was, they'd broken in through my bedroom window. Good people didn't do that shit. Panic gripped me, smothering any chance I had to scream. Shooting my eyes all around the room, I made myself focus. Fear swirled up, my mouth tasting like the inside of an aluminum can.

I need my phone. Shit, my purse was downstairs. *A weapon. I need a weapon!* Twisting, my eyes bulged and throbbed—everything in my skull was pressurizing. I'd never imagined I'd be in a situation like this. Was it a robber, a *murderer*?

I caught motion in the hall just outside my open door. I froze, and whoever was standing there froze, too. I couldn't see their face—it was too dark—so to me, this intruder could have been the devil himself.

We stood so still that I began to hope maybe he'd just go away.

Maybe . . . maybe everything would be okay.

He stepped forward, moving into the light. He was big—and I could have sworn I knew that face somehow.

His hands came up, as threatening as any weapon. In that second everything shattered. Filling my lungs, I *screamed.* My ears rattled, and the man rushed forward to silence me. He never got that far; the pile of dress on the floor caught around his ankles.

He slammed onto his chest, giving me the chance I needed to run past. I hadn't stopped screaming, my voice echoing through the stairwell. A thousand bees stung my throat, and still I just pulled in more air and began again.

Get your phone—no, get to the door!

The stairs behind me stormed with the thudding of heavy boots. He was following me, and the only advantage I had was that I knew my home in the dark better than he did. Or did I? Had he been waiting in here for me? Had he wandered my home for hours?

Had he seen me getting naked minutes ago?

The idea made me want to throw up. I felt violated, and that made me bristle with rage. Who the hell was this person to break into *my* home?

Don't do anything stupid! I cautioned, taking the corner of the stairs so hard I bounced off the kitchen wall. *Get to the door, just—*

Fingers dug into my hair, yanking at me. Somehow I slid away, creating a distance between us that I wished was a mile wide. Vertigo conquered my world as I spun; I stumbled against something cold. *My sink.*

The attacker hadn't said a word, but his heavy, rasping breath filled the nearby blackness. He didn't know my home as well as I did. He didn't need to.

He just had to be faster.

Lifting my eyes, I saw the shiny faucet. My face looked back, the figure moving over my shoulder. He was coming for me, and whatever he had planned, it was going to happen. If I did nothing else . . . this would be it.

The only item in the sink looked back at me with the familiarity of a prized possession.

In the metal, I saw him waver closer. He was on top of me. This was it.

When had I stopped screaming?

Whirling around, I lifted the horse-shaped coffee mug high. It connected with a satisfying crunch against my attacker's skull. He flew back, cradling his face and yelling louder than I even had. "You bitch!" he shouted. I didn't stay to listen to what he would say next. The mug fell, shattering; the noise was soft in my blood-throbbing ears. Every noise had become a faint buzz, my focus on running for my front door. My other senses were shutting down.

Fumbling with the knob, I exploded out into the night. "Help!" I choked, falling onto my elbows in the street. "Please, help me! Call the police!" I had the awful premonition that no one would step up. I lived in a bad area, people heard gunshots the way other neighborhoods heard the laughter of children.

Tires screeched, headlights blinding me. "Sammy!" a familiar voice yelled, his firm hands lifting me to my feet.

In disbelief, I gazed on the man I'd never wanted to see again. "Kain?"

Impossible. Why was he here?

His warm eyes fixed on me, imploring—concerned. "Are you okay?"

Realization hit me in the stomach. Shoving forward, I climbed onto the back of his motorcycle. "Go, drive! I need to get out of here!"

Kain didn't ask me to explain. I liked him so much more for that.

He kicked the bike forward, my fingers digging into his perfect stomach. We tore down the street, my head twisting so I could stare through my wind-whipped hair at my apartment.

No one was looking back.

My savior—fuck, he was, wasn't he?—drove until I gave him a hard tap on the shoulder. We were miles from my house. That, plus the well-lit and busy city streets, made me feel better.

He pulled up beside a convenience store, parking the bike but not shutting it off. "What happened back there? Are you okay?"

"Give me your phone. I need to call the cops."

"The cops?" His gorgeous face turned ugly. "Sammy, what *happened*?"

Throwing my arms up, I became aware of my situation. I was in my pajamas, no phone, no wallet, sitting astride the growling metal bike belonging to an apparently dangerous man. *Who was I?* This stuff had never happened to me before!

Taking my face, he spoke with a precise calmness that soothed the terror in my heart. "Sammy. Tell me what happened."

I swallowed loudly. "Someone broke into my house and attacked me."

Releasing me, he bent over his bike and revved it. "We're going back there."

"What? No!" I grabbed at him, shaking his arm. "Kain! The last thing I want is to go back there, it's dangerous!"

"Not with me it isn't."

"I want to call the cops!"

"Someone *attacked you*!" Fury unlike anything I'd faced burned in front of me. Kain could be a jerk, but he'd never actually scared me. Sitting inches from him, our legs brushing, I warred between being flattered . . . and being afraid.

He must have seen it, because his eyes melted. "Sammy, if someone hurt you, I'd never forgive myself."

The thudding in my chest became unbearable. "Come on. It's not like it's your fault." His silence stirred the embers of terror that had hardly started to die in my gut. "Kain. Tell me that this had nothing to do with you."

"I can't say." Wincing, he faced away from me. "But just in case, we can't call the cops. And if you don't want me to go back there—"

"I don't."

“Then we have one other option.” He turned enough for me to see how serious he was. “I need to take you back to my estate. It’s the only place you’ll be safe for sure until we can figure this out.”

“*We?* I’m not a detective!”

“‘We’ as in my family. If someone went after you because of us, we need to know. Sammy, my family can keep you safer than any cop ever could.” He faced me fully, his leather jacket the only source of any sound. It whispered like a boat on the sea, daring me to break the tranquility . . . the confidence . . . that emanated from him.

If it had just been some act of dominance, I could have rolled my eyes and told him to take a hike. If he wouldn’t call the police, I’d walk barefoot into the gas station and ask them to do it instead.

But Kain wasn’t acting tough. He didn’t posture. The low boil of his stare was helping me forget that I was sitting, unsheltered, on top of a motorcycle in my pajamas. I’d even stopped shaking with fear over the realization that I’d been attacked just minutes ago.

My home wasn’t safe.

Being with Kain felt like it was.

What other conclusion could I come to than to stay with him?

“All right,” I said. “I’ll go with you.”

Kain tilted his head up so imperceptibly higher I would have missed it if I wasn’t already close enough to count his eyelashes. “Thank fucking goodness.”

“But,” I added quickly, “if things feel fishy, I *am* going to talk to the police.”

Peeling his jacket off, he draped it on me, not giving me a chance to turn his kind offer down. Gripping the collar of it, he tugged it into place, staring straight into my face. “Let me do it my way, *then* you can call the cops.”

Does he always need to get his way? If I spent any more time with this guy, I’d have to teach him that every interaction didn’t have to be about someone "winning." Snuggling into the warm jacket that smelled exactly like him, I breathed deep—then choked.

Wait.

Did I really just consider spending MORE time with Kain?

The guy who treated police stations like hotel lobbies? The son of a family that Detective Stapler had warned me about?

I really, *really* needed a break away from all of this insanity.

But as Kain slammed his heel into his bike, propelling us off into the night toward the estate I'd vowed to never return to . . .

I had an idea things were just getting started.

- CHAPTER EIGHT -

KAIN

Someone tried to hurt her.

It felt like someone had shoved a pine branch down my gullet. Every taste bud was bitter, the flavor of my fear and disgust cloying. How *dare* someone pull Sammy into this? Whoever had more balls than sense was going to get a set of knuckles in his teeth.

I'd personally make sure of that.

The entire time we flew down the highway, my mind was ensnared by tendrils that kept pulling me back into a pit of hate. No one messed with my family; that was a given. This new attack had crossed into a whole other realm of bullshit.

Someone tried to hurt her.

That phrase tattooed onto the wet mass of my brain. It remained there the whole drive, I knew it would remain till the morning, and there was a good chance it would remain long after I was dead and buried.

Crushing the handlebars, I felt the high heels clattering against my wrist. Sammy hadn't commented on the shoes, but why would she? She'd thrown them at me to give back to my sister. To her, the shoes being with me made sense.

She couldn't know how illogical it was. She just couldn't.

I'd been thinking of her as my Cinderella. I was already a prince—in a sense—so why couldn't it work? We'd dance, I'd put the shoes on her perfect feet, and we'd kiss and laugh, and all would be fucking sparkles and hearts.

Someone. Tried. To hurt her.

Did fairy tales ever end with the prince murdering someone?

The iron gates split as I approached, welcoming me back home. The estate was a huge, sprawling mass of gardens and fields and forest. I'd lived here since I'd been born, I'd never felt unsafe.

The police raid hadn't even registered as a blip to me. I didn't like being cuffed, and Frannie was still fuming about the whole mess. But was it dangerous? Nah.

What had happened to Sammy was.

Bright lights illuminated the large front doors. A shadow moved behind the decorated glass. *Probably Mom.* She'd called me a few times today, telling me to come home and rest. I couldn't tell her that I was busy spying on Sammy.

Hawthorne thought she was an enemy.

Tonight, I'd learned she was a target.

If I hadn't been watching her . . . Fuck. I hoped she never asked what I'd been doing so close to her house. Surveying her place from the street wasn't going to sound normal, even I knew that.

Parking the bike, I helped her off of it. Her toes touched the flat rocks of the driveway, then she looked up at me through her messy bangs. "I think I've gone without shoes for a full day, almost."

I pulled her by her elbow. "Let's get you inside."

Together we climbed the steps. The overhanging roof darkened us, and the lamps glowing through the warped windows created gold highlights all around. Sammy tightened her fingers on my forearm. I luxuriated in that touch; so basic, so *real.*

For a second, I felt like this badass of a woman needed me.

That she trusted me.

I'd have traded a year of my life for more of that feeling.

"Kain!" My mother threw the door open, shocking us both. Sammy pulled her hand away, the gap between us as good as a mile. "There you are! I was getting worried!"

Scratching my neck, I shrugged. "Ma, come on. I texted you an hour ago."

"An hour is a long time." Her serious eyes focused on my guest. "Wait. Sammy? Why are you here?"

Motioning with my chin, I walked around my mom, trusting Sammy would follow me; she did. "Where's Dad?"

"Kain, what happened?" Closing the door behind us, my mother wrapped her long, silken blue robe tighter. The suspicion in her elegant face melted into fear. "Never mind. I'll hear it from you when you tell your father. Come on." Her slippers scuffed along the polished floors. Even in her before-bed state, my mother was graceful.

Like a true patriarch, he was waiting for us in his sitting room. He was dressed like he had plans to go out on the town: fine trousers, an ironed button-down of deep black. Maverick Badd had never been cruel to me, but even as a grown-ass man, I was still unnerved by my father.

But I didn't have time for that.

"Mav?" my mother asked, stepping to the side. She followed the thick man's gaze as it rolled over me, then Sammy.

He looked at me with a patience so heavy it could crush my lungs. Seeking out the still-crisp anger in me, I stepped forward. "Dad, someone broke into Sammy's house and attacked her. This has to be related to the raid, there's no way it's a coincidence."

His eyes traced over to Sammy. "The Deep Shots caused the raid. Felt talked to our inside man and called me an hour ago to confirm it.

Why would they go after her, of all people, afterwards? She's a nobody to them—no offense, sweetheart."

Sammy's face went all pinched. "Calling me sweetheart offends me more. I don't care who you think attacked me or who I am to anyone. I'm only here because Kain convinced me that it was better to talk to you than to the cops." Her glare cut my way. "I don't know why I listened to him. Give me a phone."

Disbelief darkened my dad's expression. I had to cover my mouth; I was too close to cracking up. I didn't want him getting all pissed off, but fuck, seeing him lose his cool because of Sammy was just too delicious.

My mother broke the silence first. "You've got a pair of balls on you, girl." Unlike me, she didn't hide her amusement. "Mav, hear what she has to say."

He'd gone from slumping to leaning forward. More than ever, he looked like some beastly gargoyle, ready to pounce. A heartbeat passed, two of them—then he sat back and smiled at my mother. "Only because you asked, Carmina."

"Go on," I said to her.

Sammy gave me a quick look. Facing my father, she stood as tall as possible. "This evening, a man broke into my upstairs bedroom. He tried to attack me, but I got away."

"How?" Maverick asked.

She took a second, then said, "I cracked him in the head with a coffee mug."

That made me look at her all over again. "A coffee cup?" I whispered.

She just shrugged sheepishly.

My father leaned sideways in his chair, he didn't seem certain what to think. "I'm still not sure what that has to do with us. Kain, let her talk to the police if she wants. It sounds like a robber just tried to sack her place and got a concussion instead. Why don't—"

"Wait," Sammy blurted.

Each of us stopped, gazing at her curiously. "What is it?" I asked gently.

Her eyes widened, then they kept going. It was the sort of look you had when you suddenly remembered not just the dream you'd had, but how awful the details had been. "It wasn't a random robber. I've *seen* him before."

"Where?" I asked.

In wonderment, she looked my way. "Here. He was one of the guys serving drinks at the dinner party."

All muscle and fury, my father pushed out of his chair. "Call your brothers," he snapped, pulling out his cell phone. "Tell them to get their asses here."

He didn't say who he was going to call instead, and I didn't ask. I had other things to worry about. "What should I tell them?"

"That we need to find out the name and face of every single person that was here yesterday." Leveling his fierce blues on me—eyes so unlike my mother's—he loomed closer. His voice came out softer than it had any right to be. "A rat in our kitchen can be handled, but it sounds like this one has brass balls and rabies both."

I'd started to dial, but the sight of Sammy stopped me. In my oversize jacket and no shoes, she was the epitome of vulnerable. Yet there she was, standing right in front of my hulking father, her face daring him to knock her aside.

What the hell was she doing?

Her hands fisted by her hips. "Listen," she said, like she wouldn't consider letting anyone interrupt her. "I know the face of the man who attacked me. Maybe he's even the one who got me arrested. But the more I think it over, the more I want to call the police so they can handle it."

"Sammy," I started.

Maverick held up a hand, not looking away from her. "My gut says the reason someone went after you tonight had to do with us. I owe it to you to keep you safe."

She was already shaking her head. "The police can keep me safe."

His laugh was a bellow, it made his shoulders shake. "That's what you think? Do you have any *idea* what the police care about? Here's a hint: it isn't bystanders like you." Leaning down so they were eye-to-eye, he said, "Money. It all comes back to money."

Sammy thought we were all scum, but the cops were more corrupt than my family could ever hope to be. They also sucked at doing their jobs. If she went back with them, they'd do nothing to keep this mystery man from getting his hands on her again.

The cops around here were dirty.

I knew too well that promises from dirty cops meant shit.

Sammy didn't break their staring contest. She didn't even twitch. "You want to act like my bodyguard until, what, you find the guy who's after me?" she asked.

Lowering his brows, he considered her as if seeing her for the first time. I had to smile; I knew he was recognizing what I had. He said, "I'm not going to be guarding you." His attention jumped to me. "Kain is."

Her mouth quivered: the first sign of her uncertainty. Sammy watched me with such wide, emotive eyes that I thought I could stare hard enough—long enough—and eventually peek right into her soul.

She spoke to me, but she was addressing Maverick. "I'm flattered. But I seriously don't need anyone to watch over me."

He was halfway to the door, his phone to his ear and my mother at his side. "You don't have a choice. No one leaves these grounds until I know what's going on."

"I—what?" She looked so small; had she always been like that? Turning, she took two steps after him. "I can't stay here! I've got a business to run, and my mother . . ."

Her mother?

Maverick slowed in the doorway. "Tell Kain about anything you need. My family will take care of you, Sammy." His hand braced on the frame. "We're not your enemies," he said firmly. "We can keep you safer than anyone."

She watched him go, his broad back tight as he vanished. I could hear him murmuring into the phone, my mother whispering as she hung on his arm. Then we were alone, just me and the girl I'd whisked away from danger like a hero from a fireside story.

Except the way she was glaring at me . . .

I didn't feel like I was her hero at all.

"Sammy," I said.

Slipping my jacket off, she dropped it on the floor. I winced at the sound it made, a gentle rustle that rang as loud as funeral bells in my heart.

"Sammy, listen. This is only temporary, my father just wants—"

"Did you know he'd do this?" Sammy had barely moved. Every fraction of the air that she touched, I felt it resonate with me. I was hyperaware of her, and I had no idea how to turn it off.

My arms came up; her eyes went down. "No. I did plan to guard you until this was figured out, but I didn't think he'd forbid you from leaving."

"I never thought I'd be a prisoner twice in one day," she whispered.

"You're not a prisoner."

Smiles should never be so hurtful. "Don't joke around. We both know I am."

She's right. Sammy was trapped here, and I was trapped by her very existence. I was impossibly connected to a woman who looked at me like I'd just run over her pet dog. How could I survive this kind of torture?

As I watched her leave the room, I had one simple, morbid thought.

Maybe I won't.

- CHAPTER NINE -

Sammy

He followed me down the hall. I didn't have a clue where I was going to go, I just needed to move.

I needed to be away from him.

From all of them.

These damn people! I couldn't have predicted this situation. I was without any of my things, stuck in a mansion belonging to a corrupt family. They didn't want me to leave . . . and I didn't know what I could do about it.

And he had the gall to say I wasn't a prisoner. Shooting a look over my shoulder, I froze him where he was lingering on the other side of the room. "Quit following me. Aren't you supposed to be summoning your brothers or whatever?"

Waving his phone, he gave a half smile. "I can walk and text at the same time."

"Well, aren't you talented."

"I like to think so."

"Don't try to be cute," I snapped.

Kain crinkled his nose. "I can't exactly control it."

I was done with his jokes. Pulling a 180, I stomped his way. I'd told him before that my father had raised me right. I didn't believe in violence, but I was at the end of my already-frayed rope. It was so easy to blame Kain for all the bad things in my life.

His back thudded on the wall; I'd pushed him so roughly that the impact made a framed photo clatter to the floor. Glass spread, tinkling like sweet music. "How dare you?" I growled, fingers curling in the front of his shirt. "After everything, you think you can pretend we're fine? That we can *joke* like we're friends?"

My voice was rising; I couldn't stop it, I didn't try. Upstairs, I heard movement. The ringing in my ears blocked the world out, my eyes aching as I glared at the man I wished I'd never, *ever* met.

Kain put his hands on mine, gripping so I couldn't escape. Even now, his touch was warm. "Sammy," he hissed. "Look at me."

"I am!"

He held me tighter, his nose coming close to mine. "Do you see your enemy? Do you see someone who wants to hurt you? *You, of all people?*"

His words were a fuse that started to light a firecracker. It sank into me, more acid than fire, burrowing low into my belly. Kain talked to me like he knew me, but he didn't. He couldn't.

So why was I suddenly listening?

Black clouds swam through the blue sky of his eyes. "You ran out of your house screaming for help. What the fuck was I supposed to do?"

My wrists were numb where he was squeezing. "Take me to the cops."

The dark storm grew deeper. "No," he growled. "That's what we keep telling you. If I turn you over to them, they won't do a thing to keep you safe! If someone wants you dead, then . . . anywhere but here, anywhere I'm not . . . you'd be—"

"No," I blurted.

"Yes." I'd never heard such certainty from anyone. "I couldn't live with myself if that happened."

The skin around my eyes tightened. "We're strangers, don't care so much." I was trying to distance myself, but his honest admission was wrapping around my ribs. I couldn't breathe without tasting him, and my ears were full of his promises.

His fears.

Kain's mouth made a shape it never should have. *Is he going to kiss me? Now, here, after everything?*

His voice slid over my lips, stirring my heart. "I don't know how to not care about you."

Gravity pressed on the top of my head until every grim thought began to compact and crumble. Down they went, past my eyes, which were trapped by his, through my lungs, which were full of the same air he breathed.

Each bit of hate collapsed until there was nothing left in me but a thread of disbelief. How did Kain do this to me? I'd wanted to hurt him . . . to make him see he was wrong.

I didn't know what I believed anymore.

But I did know that I wanted to kiss him.

Behind us, a feminine voice squeaked, "What the hell? Kain, don't make out with your side chicks right out here where everyone can—Sammy?" Francesca was gawking at me, her skin covered in some kind of mint-smelling cream, her long hair piled on her scalp.

Hot shame kicked me in the teeth. Ripping away from Kain, I choked on some sort of explanation for why I was here. Why she'd witnessed me about to kiss her brother.

Francesca rushed at me, her hands tangling in mine. I wasn't ready for her hug, she was deceptively strong. "Sammy! What are you *doing* here?"

Holding her at arm's length, I glanced at Kain. "It's a long story."

"I love long stories!"

Scrunching my tongue against the back of my teeth, I thought over what to say. Kain pushed forward, acting like he hadn't just been pulling back the veil to the vibrant emotion in his soul. "She's going to be staying with us for a while."

His sister froze. I watched the gloss in her eyes turn into suspicion. "Something happened. Tell me."

"Fran—"

"Kain," she seethed. "Fucking tell me."

Footsteps marched down the hall, three men rounding the corner. I recognized two of them: Maverick and his intimidating son, Hawthorne. The third was a lean man only a hair taller than all of them, his smooth skin marred by a scar that stretched from right eyebrow to the bridge of his nose.

If anything, the old wound added to his sharp looks. I couldn't have said if he was more gorgeous now than when he'd gotten the scar. I just knew that few people could have made such a blemish look so bold—so complementary.

He locked his eyes on mine: blue like Maverick's, lighter than even Kain's.

Hawthorne pulled up short, studying all of us. "You guys having a party?"

"Daddy!" Francesca shouted, whirling on him. "What's going on? Why is everyone here?"

"Good to see you, too, Sis," the stranger said.

She ignored him, her stare was forever frozen on Maverick's face. I paid attention, though, because I felt like I needed to learn who everyone in this family was if I was going to get out of here.

Another brother, I thought curiously. Was he older or younger than Kain? I needed to start taking notes.

Maverick looked down his nose at his daughter. Whatever kindness was in his voice was rivaled by the severity of his words. "Our family is being threatened. Your brothers are here to help me take precautions."

"Threatened?" She pushed a hand to her mouth. I caught her wary look in my direction. "Sammy's in danger, too, isn't she?"

I tried to smile, but everyone's somber faces made it a struggle. "Someone attacked me tonight, but I'm fine."

"Who?" she demanded.

Her question felt like an accusation, but I didn't know why. "He said his name was Jameson. He was this tall, reedy kind of guy. He spoke to me for barely a minute in the kitchen." I realized they were all hanging on my words. "Reddish hair, kind of pale."

I almost added that he'd had a crooked, sweet smile, but the memory of his sneer when he'd stalked me through my home made it impossible to associate anything sweet with him.

Kain put his hand on my shoulder. That was when I noticed I was shaking. Francesca looked me over, from my bare feet to my long, white nightshirt.

I didn't have a bra on; I hugged myself, suddenly uncomfortable under their stares.

"I'll need you to look over photos from the wedding," Maverick said to me.

"Not tonight." It was Frannie who spoke, her arm circling my shoulders and brushing away her brother's. His eyes darkened, but she didn't care. "Sammy needs to rest. Can't you all see how freaked out the poor girl is?"

I didn't feel like a poor girl, but Francesca was getting me away from this weird interrogation. I appreciated that, because I *was* burnt out. I itched for a hot shower and a warm bed.

Blue Eyes spoke, his voice quiet but hard. It was the kind you couldn't ignore. "Francesca is right."

She scoffed. "Of course I am, Costello."

Costello? So that was his name. The longer I looked at him, the more he reminded me of a feral wolf. He watched me from under the heavy fringe of his eyelashes, light skin contrasting against the rich, mahogany, ruffled hair on his head.

A warm, welcoming scent prickled my nose. It was electric: distilled alpha male. Kain had drawn close to me again, his body subtly separating me from the rest of his brothers—especially Costello.

Kain brushed my fingers beside my hip. "Fran is right, everyone back off. We're not getting anything done tonight. She can look at photos tomorrow when she's fresh."

I was so thankful I came close to hugging him.

Maverick shook his head, grunting low in his throat. "Fine. Get her settled in, make sure she has anything she asks for." His chin swung through the air, aimed at the other two brothers. "Come with me to the den. Kain, join us as quick as you can."

He nodded, standing like a sentinel beside me long after the other men had tracked from the room. Kain's shadow fell over me; I was kissing distance from his Adam's apple. His heat was all-encompassing, his nearness sapping the last of my strength away.

I was supposed to be angry with him . . . not comfortable.

Not eager.

I saw the corner of his mouth rise. The tempo of my heart was infectious. It demanded I move, so I did. I backed up, my bare heel crunching on something that bit into my sensitive skin. "Shit!" I screamed, stumbling sideways.

Kain caught me, supporting me as Francesca bent down. "Oh, no!" she gasped, noticing the shattered photo. Lifting it, I saw that it contained the smiling faces of five kids of various ages, as well as two older people—Maverick and Carmina.

Fran shook the last of the glass shards off of the family portrait. They tumbled like diamonds over the laminated floor of the hallway. "Are you okay, Sammy?" she asked.

"It's just a small cut." Balancing on Kain, I eyed my heel. A tiny fleck of blood shone there. "Show me to your bathroom, I'll clean it out."

Francesca shook her head. "Gawd, why aren't you wearing any shoes?"

"I was getting ready for bed when that guy attacked me."

Her face fell. "Oh. Sorry." Too quickly, she glared at her brother. "Well? Carry her upstairs."

"Oh, no!" I laughed nervously. "That's not—"

"You heard the lady," he said, scooping me up. "I didn't think I'd get to hold you like this twice in one day."

"Whaaaat?" Frannie gasped, flapping her hands like a bird.

Blushing to my ears, I bit my tongue. "Please don't ask."

Kain took a path I remembered. I recognized the stairs that led to the landing and past his bedroom. Just passing by it made me feel scandalous.

The bathroom we entered was gigantic. The tub on one side was big enough for a horse, and the shower could have held multiple people. He set me on the edge of the double sink, grabbing a few tissues and wetting them.

"I can do it," I said firmly.

Ignoring me, he knelt down and grabbed my ankle. With a tenderness not meant for men like him, Kain dabbed at the glass, working it out with hardly any pain. "Relax," he said quietly. "I'll be gentle."

Gentle is exactly what I'm afraid of. The nicer he was, the more I couldn't hold on to that slippery monster called resentment. Kain washed my cut, placing a bandage over it when he was finished. "There," he said, looking up at me. "All set."

I'd never looked down on him before. Somehow, it made me feel smaller. It was like being a flimsy piece of ribbon caught on a tree branch before it vanished into the world, never to be seen again.

"What are you thinking about?" he asked.

Gripping the edge of the counter, I locked up so hard that my joints popped. "Nothing."

The cockiness that fit him best rolled through his almond-shaped eyes. "Must be about me, then."

"I—what? No!"

"You're not the best liar."

Flushing, I stepped gingerly to the floor. Testing my heel, I said with some surprise, "It doesn't even hurt."

"I'll take that as a thank you." His smirk split his hard jaw. "Or a kiss will do."

"Like hell." But my lips buzzed at the very mention of kissing him. Rolling my ankle experimentally, I said, "Your dad said if I needed anything, to make sure I got it."

"Of course. Just ask."

"I need to make a phone call."

He arched an eyebrow. "You know you can't call the cops."

"I'm not. It's someone else."

"And you won't tell me who?"

Chewing my bottom lip, I thought it over. *If I tell him about my mother, can it be used against me?* I didn't know if I could trust this family. I'd been told they were dangerous, but Kain had also rescued me from harm.

But I *was* trapped, so . . .

Who was really a threat to me?

"No," I finally sighed. "I can't."

Shaking his head, he ruffled his thick hair. "In that case . . ." One step and he was looming over me, the sink at my back. "It'll *definitely* cost more than a thank you."

The thumping of my heart vibrated into my teeth. "You think you can blackmail me into kissing you?"

"I don't think I need to blackmail you at all." Chuckling warmly, he showed me the edge of his teeth. That grin shredded my defenses, and the thickness in his voice did the rest. Kain had me pinned, his hips pushing into mine. "I think you've been wanting to kiss me all day, Sammy."

Swallowing, I whispered, "You're wrong."

"Am I?"

Darting my eyes to the side, I breathed faster. His scent was in my brain. "For most of the day . . . I wanted to punch you."

He started to laugh. His body rippled, muscles rubbing over my chest. His joy was contagious. Everything he *did* was contagious.

The last of his laughter went down my throat, tickling into my heart. He kissed without limits. His strength pressed me into the porcelain, but it was his lust that held me still. Kain Badd was a man who consumed whatever he desired.

I was ready to let him eat me whole.

- CHAPTER TEN -

Kain

I could see myself in the mirror behind her. Arousal colored my skin and coated my tongue. Her taste was like a deep breath after years below the ocean. I'd never kissed—or wanted to kiss—like this.

My cock reached for her through my jeans. Her moan when she felt me grinding against her sweatpants sent a new throb through my shaft. Each brush of my tongue on hers sent pulses of excitement through my pores.

Our heat met, her hips pushing back on mine. Sammy had stopped pretending she didn't want me. Whatever wrongs I'd done, they wilted when compared to her desire. I knew the feeling.

"Fuck." I bit the word off, my teeth chasing her lower lip. "I've been wanting to do this since I saw you outside my room this morning." It could have been years ago, it felt like forever; another time, another world.

Sammy buried her hands in my hair, trailing her nails down my neck. Her touch called forth goose bumps. "I'm still mad at you," she whispered. Her eyes dared me to challenge that fact.

Grinning, I set my thumbs on her cheeks and kissed her again. "That just makes it more fun."

Her whimper made my cock swell uncomfortably.

Scooping her ass into my palms, I lifted her so she was sitting on the counter all over again. Before, I'd tended to her foot, but it was the rest of her I was interested in now. Sliding my hands down her thighs, I squeezed her knees, vising me between them.

Sitting as she was, her eyes were level with mine. Fisting her hair, I forced her chin back, exposing her long neck. My grip was rough, but my mouth was soft as butter. I tasted the hollow of her throat, the corner of her ear.

Sammy tried to look at me. That half-lidded stare revealed the wet edges of her green eyes. She was aching as much as I was, and fuck if that wasn't a rush. Her excitement pushed mine over the edge. I was free-falling into helpless lust. It was a ride I'd take again and again, if she let me.

Her nipples were hard through her shirt. Without a bra, it was easy to see them and the shadows they cast down her front. Leaning forward, I let her hair go so I could dig my fingertips into her spine. I forced her to arch into me, her body shaping like a bow about to fire an arrow.

My phone buzzed in my back pocket; I jumped forward, startled.

Sammy laughed softly, her forehead pushing into mine. "For a second, I thought your dick was vibrating."

"Yeah? Would you like me more or less if my cock could do that?"

"I don't think I'd complain."

Reaching back for my phone, I chuckled through my teeth. "I'll remember that." Eyeing the text, I frowned sharply. Between my heavy need to get laid and Hawthorne calling me, I knew which I'd rather focus on.

She leaned away, sensing our moment was fading. "I'm guessing that's your dad."

"Brother, actually." My phone buzzed again. "Oh. No. That time it was Dad." They were blowing up my phone, telling me to get my ass downstairs. Frustrated, I ran my fingers through my hair.

Sammy gripped the counter, her legs spreading farther. It was the pose of someone relaxing—taking it easy—but it just made her look more tempting than ever. Groaning loudly, I pushed my shaft back against her. "Why can't they leave us alone a little longer?"

Her smile lit up her eyes. It was so *good* to see her happy. "It's fine. Go see them, but first . . ."

"I bend you over and rail you until you can't stand?"

Blushing hard, she shoved a hand into my chest. "Let me make that phone call."

Right. I forgot about that. For a second, I endured a twinge of self-doubt. Had she been making out with me just to get her way? Was it all a show? *No. She couldn't fake it like that.* I'd spent the night with her once already, her touch . . . her moans . . . they were the same as then.

Handing her my phone, I backed up. Sammy stayed as she was, her eyes tracking down to my palm as I adjusted my painful erection. When she saw I'd caught her, I winked. Her perfect teeth crushed her bottom lip, making my core swim.

"Can I do this alone?" she asked.

Shrugging, I headed out the door. My father would have told me I was an idiot for not listening in. But truthfully, I trusted Sammy. I couldn't find a reason not to. She'd gone out of her way to help my sister three different times, and while money had been involved twice . . . no one had paid her to be the maid of honor.

Lifting my hand, I brushed my mouth. Everything was still tingling with the feel of her. It was the way a lightning bolt must feel if it slid beneath your skin.

As awful as it was, I comforted myself with the knowledge that she wasn't going anywhere tonight. If I couldn't have her to myself yet, there'd be a chance soon enough.

The door opened behind me. "Here," Sammy said, offering the phone back.

I didn't take it. "You're done already?" That seemed too fast to talk to anyone.

Her chin dipped, like she didn't want me to see her expression. "They didn't answer. It's probably fine, but . . ."

"But what?"

Hugging herself, Sammy rocked side to side. "It's a lot to ask, but if I gave you an address, would you go check something out for me?"

I scooped her hands up. The touch made her jump, her wide eyes flying upward to mine. If I'd doubted it before, I was sure now: Sammy was terrified. "Tell me what you need me to do. I'm here for you, Sammy."

I could swear that I saw her heart as it filled her mouth. It took her a full minute to find her voice again. "It's my mother. She isn't well, and if someone came after me tonight, there's a chance . . ." She stopped herself, or maybe the words just wouldn't leave her tongue.

Her mother? So I had heard her say that earlier.

Rubbing the backs of her palms, I smiled solidly. "Tell me where she is. I'll go over there and check things out. I won't even let her see me unless I have to. Okay?"

Relief pulled her shoulders down. I expected her to be happy, but I didn't expect her to embrace me. It's strange how much more intimate a touch like that can feel after you've caressed someone's naked body in the dark.

Holding her close, I shut my eyes so I could lose myself in her arms. We breathed together, our lungs matching speed—growing faster by the second. Sammy untangled herself, typing into my phone quickly. "That's where she lives. It's kind of far from here."

Nodding, I pushed the phone into my back pocket. "It's fine. I'll go see everyone downstairs, then I'll head out." I motioned down the hall. "Frannie will set you up for the night."

"I'll take a shower first, if that's all right." Her fingers crinkled in her hair. "I'm a serious mess. You can probably smell me from there."

"Definitely." I lowered my face, inhaling the side of her throat. "And it's wonderful, babe." Kissing her once—okay, twice—I stepped away. Her fingers touched her skin where I'd just been.

With a smirk, I started down the stairs. "Kain," Sammy said, stopping me. When I looked back, she was still cupping her neck. "Thank you. Just . . . thanks."

"You already thanked me, remember?" Brushing my lips, I flicked my fingers like I was throwing her a kiss.

I thought she'd just blush some more. Her hand came up, clasping the air to catch my imaginary lips. Though she grinned, I realized she was just as surprised by her reaction as I was.

What's going on between us? It was a question that had been tickling in my skull for some time. The weight of all my missteps with this woman had been ruining my mood the longer time went on.

She'd told me with conviction that she was still mad at me.

But did angry people catch air kisses?

I wanted to leave with an aura of indifference. I was known for being the cocky bad boy, that was who I'd always been. I didn't keep souvenirs like sparkling heels, and I didn't tend to tiny cuts with genuine tenderness.

When I exited down the staircase, I took the steps two at a time.

- CHAPTER ELEVEN -

Sammy

"Mic," I hissed, pushing the fluffy dog away from my face. "Leave me *alone*."

It was the eighth time the animal had come over to snuffle at me. It wasn't entirely his fault, I *was* sleeping on Francesca's bedroom floor. I was easy access to his little, wet nose.

After I'd showered, I'd entered the darkened room to find the girl had already gone to bed. Not wanting to wake her, I'd curled up in the bathrobe I'd found and just tucked myself into a corner of the room.

Shivering, I rolled away from the panting dog again. *Okay. This is too much.* In a mansion this big, there had to be a place I could go to find some privacy. Standing, I stepped around Mic and slid quietly into the hallway.

The big clock on the wall said it was after three in the morning. My eyes were puffy, my skull heavy on my neck. Creeping along the soft rugs, I tested the doorknobs of several rooms. Most were locked, and I didn't have it in me to sneak into Kain's bed tonight.

Especially not after our bathroom heavy petting session.

Burning from the memory, I headed downstairs. As I passed the hallway, I slowed down. I hadn't seen it happen, but at some point, someone had hung the photo I'd broken back up.

There were a few low lights along the ceiling. They allowed me to squint at the photo, studying the people in it. Maverick was easy to recognize—he was younger, but just as big as ever. Carmina still held the same elegance she did now, though her hair was shorter.

The children were clearly theirs; I bent closer, intrigued by what Kain looked like as a child. It didn't take me long to spot him; he and Francesca were nearly mirror images of each other with their blue eyes and dark hair.

He couldn't have been more than six in the photo, his grin just hinting at the cocky guy he'd grow up to be.

Next to him, his eyes black as pitch, had to be Hawthorne. That left two others; Costello had to be the tallest of them, a young boy who lacked the ragged scar he now sported.

And that leaves . . . Blinking, I leaned back an inch. *Another girl?* I didn't know that the Badds had a second daughter. Why hadn't I met her yet?

With more questions in my head, I went back to exploring. I didn't go far before I found another row of doors. The second one I tested opened, so I peeked through the crack. It was a bedroom for sure, and the blue night colors showed an empty mattress.

Shutting myself in, I rubbed at my face. *Should I turn the lights on?* No, what was the point? No one was here, I had it to myself. No dog, no snoring Francesca, no handsy Kain.

Crawling under the blankets, I snuggled into the warmth with an appreciative groan. Now *this* was a nice bed! I'd have to find out what it was made of. Not that I could afford it, I was sure, but still.

Lying there in the dark with the blanket to my chin, I tried to turn my mind off. It was a struggle, especially because I kept thinking about my mother. I wanted her to be fine—and she probably was—but . . . *After losing Dad, I can't imagine her being gone, too.*

It had only been a year since my father had died. The pain was still fresh. *Oh, no!* A heavy rock rolled around in my stomach. I'd just remembered that it had been the horse-shaped mug he'd given me when I'd gone away to college that had ended up saving my life tonight.

The cup had been precious to me.

Now it was just pieces on my kitchen floor.

Hot tears pushed against the insides of my eyes. *No, don't cry.* This wasn't the time or place for it. If anything, I should be grateful; the mug had let me escape whatever harm my attacker had planned for me.

Right. Think of the positive side of this. My father had taught me to be strong, to smile at your fears. Wouldn't grieving hurt his memory? I didn't know, but avoidance was so easy.

Ugh, just pick a new topic to dwell on if you're going to lie here awake.

Except the only other thing on my mind was the fit-as-hell and ever-smug Kain Badd. That guy, he'd put me through the ringer in such a short time. I'd wanted distance from him, but now I was trapped in his home.

And then I let him kiss me again. At least I hadn't initiated it. I also hadn't stopped it. Was that really better?

I didn't know I'd fallen asleep until something heavy slammed into my face. Gasping, I shot up straight, the pillow falling into my lap. "Bwah—hwa—huh?!" I stuttered.

Francesca stood beside the bed, her hands on her hips. She was wearing a bronze, silky nightgown—but her eyes were liquid fire. "What are you doing in here?" she asked, her tone biting.

Scrubbing at my eyes, I stared at her. "I . . . was sleeping." My mind was sluggish. I took a second to stare around the room. In the early sunlight through the window, I saw that the walls were a robin's-egg blue. Everything else was white or red, a large bookcase on one wall stuffed so full that books were piled beside it. There were a few photos on the wall, but I couldn't see them well enough to study the faces in them.

Turning back to Francesca, I asked, "Should I not be in here?"

"There are guest rooms in the other hall." Mic rustled around the door, bouncing at her heels. Francesca lifted the dog up, snuggling him. "Sorry, I'm not trying to be a bitch. It's just that . . . this is my sister's room."

"Oh!" Sitting up so that the blanket fell free, I rolled over the side of the bed. I meant to land gracefully, but in my haste, I stumbled onto my hip. Fran reached for me; I bounced up quickly, laughing to calm her. "I'm fine! It's all fine."

Her shiny lips—was she already wearing lipstick? What time was it?—made a smile. "Aw, Sammy. It's okay. You don't gotta rush."

Fixing the blankets, I said, "Where's your sister at? I was wondering why I hadn't met her, I'd actually started thinking you only had a bunch of older brothers! Was she not at the dinner or the wedding? No one introduced me to her."

I hadn't known her for long, but even so, Fran's sudden silence was strange. Looking down at Mic, she spoke with casual disinterest. "She's just really busy. She would have come to the wedding if she coulda, but . . . it doesn't matter. She could be back any minute, and she'd want her bed free, that's all."

My hands drifted to my sides. "I . . . see." I didn't see at all. I had no idea what was going on here.

Sensing the tension, Fran put on a giant grin. "You're wrong, you know."

"I—wrong about what?"

"My brothers." Scratching Mic's ears, she set him down. "I'm not the youngest, I'm technically a few minutes older than Kain."

Click-click-click went my brain. "Holy hell. You're *twins*?"

Giggling, she flipped her hair and winked. Every bit of similarity the two shared shone back at me like a full moon. I'd thought it was just their blood, but after meeting the others, it should have been obvious. "I'm much better looking than him," she said coyly.

In my opinion, Kain was grade-A dyno-mite delicious. Francesca was very beautiful as well, though. She had his long features, and he had her delicate eyelashes and fuller lips.

Lips that were perfect for kissing and touching and . . .

Coughing softly, I marched toward the door before she could see my red neck. "Is there any chance I could borrow some clothes? I kind of don't have anything with me."

"Of course!" she gushed, chasing after me until she beat me up the stairs. Opening her bedroom, she grabbed my arm and yanked me in. "I *love* dressing people up! Gawd, you'll look so hot when I'm done."

"Oh, no, hot isn't . . . I just want to not be modeling a bathrobe or my pajamas."

Shutting us into the room, she waggled her eyebrow at me. "Girl. Just you wait." Heading to her giant closet, Francesca began throwing clothes onto the bed. Occasionally she'd mumble about how "this isn't your color" or "nope, this is too slutty."

My worries only grew when she threw a lacy pair of blue panties and a bra my way. They looked extremely expensive, and extremely sexy. But . . . it was better than nothing, so I struggled into them.

As I tried on the tight black pants she'd handed me, I faced away from her. Clipping the button, I spun back and said, "These might be a bit tight—jeez!"

Francesca was as naked as a babe on its birthday. Blinking at me like *I* was acting crazy, she held up a white crop top next to her full-on bare breasts. "Do you think I need a bra with this?"

Covering my eyes, I peeked through my fingers. "Yes, yes, double yes."

Sighing in a way that showed me exactly how her boobs could shake and shudder, Francesca dropped the shirt. Even if I hadn't wanted to, I again saw the small tattoo of a crown across her upper ribs.

Now that I knew that she and Kain were twins, I was extra curious about the meaning behind their duplicate ink.

Turning away to hide my hot blush, I wriggled the pants to loosen them. "Hey, uh, can I ask something?"

"Sure thing." I heard clothing rustle. "Hm. Maybe I can rock some cutoff jean shorts instead. It's supposed to be warm out."

Sliding the too-low-cut green tank top on, I adjusted the front. "That tattoo of yours." *Just say it!* "Kain has one just like it."

"Of course he does." A zipper crunched. "We all do. Well . . . everyone but my sister, I mean."

I glanced at her—saw her bare ass—and looked away again. "Why do you all get them?"

"Daddy says it's tradition. We do it when we turn eighteen to remind us of who we are."

"What, rich as kings?" I asked, laughing.

"Almost." She clicked something shut loudly. "We're royalty."

I spun around so fast that I knew I'd feel it in my neck for days. "Ex-fucking-scuse me?"

Dressed in jean shorts that showed off her excellent legs and a tight black top that hid her chest—thank goodness—she stared at me. "Did Kain not tell you?"

"Of course not! I—are you serious?"

Tugging her shirt lower, she eyeballed her floor-length mirror. "He usually tells it to every girl he likes. I figured that was how he got you into his bed."

"That—I—bwah." Stumbling over my words, I fought for what to say. "It's not . . . what you think."

Her mouth shrank into a little pucker shape. "Gawd, I don't care if you did anything with him. If anything, I have him to thank. If you weren't still here the next morning, that dumb bitch Monica would have walked down the aisle with him instead."

This was all too much. Sitting on the bed, I stared blankly at my feet. *Kain is royalty? How is that possible?*

"Here," she said, offering me a pair of white flats. "No hurting your feet today."

I took the shoes, but I was still dazed. "Fran, it's hard for me to believe all of this."

"Why?" She pulled her hair up, watching me in the mirror as she tied it back. "It doesn't change anything. We're not ruling the world, it's all just a technicality. Dad's brother is king in his homeland. I'm not sure why he left, but hey, he met Mom and they had babies and now I'm here to give you awesome clothes and make the world a better place." Laughing, she winked at me. "Too bad, though, I would have kicked ass as a princess in a royal court."

Kain's a prince.

I'd slept with a prince.

If I'd kept a sex bucket list, I might have made a check mark next to that.

"Instead of running a country or getting married, I just get dragged off to jail thanks to my asshole family," she mumbled.

That's right. The ceremony was interrupted. Studying her, I noticed how tight her jaw was. "I'm really sorry about that. When are you and Midas going to finish tying the knot?"

"Never, at this rate." Slamming her palms onto her vanity, she huffed. "Daddy isn't going to let anyone onto the estate until things settle down. He trusts no one right now, not even a priest, of all people."

An idea crossed my mind, but I didn't get to voice it. Knuckles banged on the door, startling us both.

"Hey," a rough, oddly quiet male voice said. "Is she in there with you?"

"It's Costello," Fran said, scowling at the door. "Give us a fucking minute!"

I flinched at her swinging mood. *She really doesn't like him.* I wondered what the scarred brother had done to earn her ire.

Opening the door, I stared up at the tallest brother. He didn't wear a comfortable smile like Kain. He also lacked that casual, predatory curiosity that I'd seen on Hawthorne. With a face as still as a pond in spring, the pale-eyed brother looked down on me.

I'd meant to tell him to relax, here I was. Somehow, faced with his steady, somber eyes that dug through mine and kept on searching, I lost some of my backbone. Maverick didn't scare me, but Costello . . .

Dressed in a loose, burlap-textured shirt with a laced-up neck, his lean body was like a master swimmer's. Everyone in this family was graced with stupidly good genes.

Has he even blinked yet? I wondered.

Costello turned away, and I had the oddest sense that I'd failed some test. "This way," he said boredly.

Collecting myself, I followed him down the stairs. "Where are we going?"

"Maverick wants you."

"Did you guys find photos from the wedding?"

"We did."

Making conversation with him isn't easy, ugh. I was saved from having to bother. Pushing the den open, he motioned for me to enter. I slid under his arm, not having to duck to do so.

The men were all standing around a table inside. They looked up, the air full of expectancy. How long had they been waiting for me?

Kain's eyes were hollow, the lower edges purple and shiny. He looked flat-out tired. When he spotted me, his exhaustion lifted away so that he could grace me with that half smirk of his that I found so thrilling.

"There she is," Maverick grunted.

I waved, but the soft rumble of my stomach said hello before I could. I didn't blush, though; how could they not expect me to be starving?

"Good," Hawthorne said. "Let's get this going."

A wave of lightheadedness shook me. "Before I do anything, I need something," I said.

The guys all shared a look. Maverick eyed me warily. "Whatever it is, just ask."

With all seriousness, I said, "Food. I need to eat something before I collapse."

Kain covered his mouth, but it didn't muffle his snort. His father shook his head, lips pushing together into a tight line. He seemed irritated, except that I sensed that—like Kain—he was trying not to laugh. "Fine. Hawthorne, go get something from the kitchen."

"What? Why the hell do I have to do it? Send Kain, he's the one banging her."

My cheeks were glowing bright enough to help a ship sail safely in heavy fog. I had a counter on my tongue for Hawthorne; no way was I going to let him say something like that without a response.

Kain leaned close to his brother. "You're right," he said carefully. "I *am* fucking her. And it's great. But the only one who gets to talk about that is me. Is that clear?"

He didn't ask it like it was a question.

Hawthorne lifted his chin higher, posturing so that his chest nearly bumped Kain's. "Little brother, you should know better than to try and tell me what to do."

Before the intensity could get worse, I stepped forward. "Hey, yoo-hoo." My arm cut between them, waving rapidly to get their attention. "I can feed myself, no need to break bones over who has to get me a stupid muffin." I paused, my eyebrows scrunching. "Tell me that there *are* muffins."

Maverick's laugh shattered the tension. Slapping his thigh once, he swung his chin side to side. "I like her." I didn't have a chance to be confused *or* flattered; the large man narrowed his joy into flat expectation, all fixed on Hawthorne. "Go get her some damn food. You heard me."

Through all of this, Costello had managed to blend into the wall he was leaning on. "I'll do it," he said. Pushing forward, he moved past all of us in two steps of his long legs. "Not like I'm going to be much help here."

Kain shoved Hawthorne once, his attention following Costello out the door.

Pinching the bridge of his nose, Maverick huffed. "Fine. Sammy, come over here while we wait." The round table in the den had been covered with photos. He stood next to it eagerly.

He didn't need to explain anything to me. I knew what they wanted. *But will he be here?* Could I identify the man who'd spoken to me in this very house, then lurched at me from the shadows of my own home?

The memory lifted prickles on the backs of my arms. Looking over the piles of photos, I ran my fingertips across them. One by one, I pushed together a pile of useless pictures. The ones of Kain and me made me shift side to side; Detective Stapler had shown me copies.

I guess these came from the same photographer. Rapidly, though, it became clear to me that Jameson wasn't in any of the photos. There were plenty of other servers, just not him.

Hunching over the blurring images, I slid them back and forth frantically.

Why isn't he here? "I don't get it," I whispered to myself.

A shadow darkened the table. Looking up, I saw it was Kain. His eyes were glistening with concern. "Are you okay?" he asked.

"No." My hair flipped side to side. "Something's wrong. Why isn't he in any of these?"

"Maybe you missed him," Kain said, looking over my head. "You should eat. I can barely think when I get hungry."

I saw he was looking at Costello, who'd returned with a tray of food. My stomach rumbled, but I wasn't hungry anymore. Hovering back over the photos, I closed my eyes and racked my brain. *Why why why why why?* What was I missing?

Cold touched my elbow; I jumped two feet.

"Sorry," Kain said, offering the glass of orange juice again. "Just drink something and relax a minute."

Drink something. In a daze, I took the glass, but I didn't taste it. "Holy shit. That's what's wrong." I whirled, facing all of them. Their eyes were various degrees of doubtful and curious. "Are there photos from the dinner party the night before the wedding?"

Hawthorne glanced at Kain. "Frannie must have taken a bunch with her phone. Mom yelled at her over it a few times."

Their father jerked his head at the door. "Go get her."

Hawthorne didn't argue with that order at all.

"What is it?" Francesca asked, swaying into the room. "Why is Thorne saying you need my phone?"

"Did you take pictures at the party the other night?" I asked, hurrying her way.

Lifting her eyebrows, Fran's face morphed into delight. "Of course I did. I got some great selfies. Did you want to see them?" Digging into her purse, she yanked out a thick phone that was stuffed inside a glittering white-and-black case. I was pretty sure it had real diamonds on it.

One by one, I slid through the photos as she chatted next to me. Francesca was explaining what she did or didn't like about her selfies—and there were hundreds—or why she'd taken a photo of every food course. I wasn't listening; I was on the hunt.

Where . . . where . . . come on—yes! Shaking with excitement, I literally ran toward Kain. Behind me, Frannie shouted, "Hey! Be careful with that!"

"There!" Shoving the screen in his face, I tapped it repeatedly. "That's him!"

Kain squinted at the photo. It was a long shot of the table, just before everyone had gotten settled into their chairs. Men in black suits were poking into the image on the fringe, their faces blurry or turned away.

Except for him.

Jameson was bent over the table, his hand half-touching a champagne glass as he filled it. The sight of his hard features and reedy torso made my blood race. And not in a good way.

He looked so normal here. When I compared him to the man who'd stalked through my hallway, hovering outside my door as I'd gotten naked . . . it was too surreal.

"Sammy!" Kain grabbed me with one hand, stopping me from crumbling.

Sweat dotted my forehead; I locked my knees, gripping his firm arm with a grateful smile. "I'm fine. Maybe I should eat that muffin now."

"You need to sit." Guiding me to a chair, Kain helped me into it.

I noticed I was trembling, but I didn't want everyone else to see. I nodded at the phone he still held. "Show them." *Give me some privacy over here*, I thought, willing him with my eyes.

Kain understood. Turning, he brought the phone over to the others. "She says this is the guy."

Hawthorne folded his arms. "One of the servers?"

"I doubt he was really a server," Costello whispered.

Puffing air through his lips, Maverick said, "I don't recognize him, could be a disguise or just a hired goon. Go meet with the Deep Shots, find out who he is."

I wasn't watching them, I was hanging my head between my knees and holding my forehead. Footsteps came my way, a hand tucking against my temple, then scooping my hair up and away. Kain looked down on me, his face tight with worry.

"Here," he said, offering me the orange juice. "Drink."

I didn't argue, I tilted the glass and let the tart liquid wake me up. "I'm fine," I assured him. "It was just a blood sugar crash."

"Sure." Kain was polite enough not to push it, but he knew I'd been freaking out. Seeing that man again, remembering everything, it had been too overwhelming.

I'd been burying the situation under a wave of denial. I couldn't keep the act up once I saw that damn face. Jameson had seemed nice. *Normal.* If *he* could attack me in the middle of the night, then . . .

"My intuition sucks," I mumbled. "I had no clue he was dangerous."

"I don't know," Kain said. "You knew *I* was no good right from the start."

Grinning, I finished off the drink. "A broken clock is accidentally right some of the time."

The charming dimples he had went deeper. "You feel better now?"

"Good enough for a muffin." Pushing myself up, I headed for the tray of food. There were a few options; I was surprised Costello had bothered to put in the effort. Lifting a pastry, I nibbled the top. "Now that you know who you're looking for, I'll need a ride home."

No one said anything. I endured a stab of unease, it worked under my ribs, fixing itself into place. Maverick waved Francesca's phone, saying, "We don't know who he is. Not yet. You can't go anywhere until we've got this all tied up, Sammy."

The phrase "tied up" was hitting too close to how I already felt being here. "This is insane," I said. My eyes flashed to Kain. "Say something. Tell your dad it's fine." *I need to get out of here!* I wanted to ask Kain how my mother was—if he'd even gone there last night—but I really just wanted to see her myself.

She needed me.

Kain's face was placid, his eyes begging me to understand. "You're in danger," he said softly. "Until then, you're safer here than anywhere else."

I never suspected that his answer could cause me so much pain. Overnight, I'd gone from hating this man to relying on him. I knew what it was to *ache* for Kain. But I'd made the mistake of assuming he was on my side.

I knew better now.

Francesca cut the silence in two. "You guys are such assholes. Explain it to her better than that." Shaking her head, she came my way. "Sammy, look. There are people who hate this family—all of us. They're jealous, or cruel, or whatever. Doesn't matter." She tried to grab my wrist; I let her. "You got pulled into this because of me, no one else. So trust me when I say . . . let us protect you. We're the only ones who can."

Gently but firmly, I pulled my arm away. "You're probably right," I said slowly. Lifting my eyes, I watched her from under the loose pieces of my hair. "But since when is it okay to lock someone up just because you think you're doing them a favor?"

She actually looked wounded, and I felt kind of bad, but I knew what they were doing was wrong. The path to hell is paved with good intentions, and all that.

Marching past her, I ignored all of them.

"Sammy!" Kain's shout was a bullet that I sidestepped.

Let him call my name all he wants, I thought bitterly.

I may be on a leash.

But I'm not his damn dog.

- CHAPTER TWELVE -

KAIN

"Come on," Thorne said, opening his car door. "Let's go."

I was in a shit mood—this morning had *not* gone the way I'd wanted. Stepping out, I slammed the door as hard as I could.

He winced. "Fuck, man. This baby is new. Be gentle."

"Let's just get this over with."

"Fair enough." Climbing the steps to the front door, Hawthorne gave it a nudge. Sammy hadn't shut it when she'd burst out of her home last night. "Guess the guy who went after her didn't lock this up when he left."

"*If* he left," I mused. "There's a chance he's still in there. Be careful."

"Careful of what, shadows?" Chuckling, my brother led the way inside. "There's no way he stuck around."

In spite of his confidence, I put my hand under my jacket. I didn't usually carry a gun, but the warm handle felt comfortable in my grip. I wasn't going to chance getting shot for my assumptions.

Stepping quietly through the house, I noticed how sparse it all seemed. There were some boxes in a corner by the stairwell, and as I entered the kitchen, some more were stacked by the far wall.

I saw the shards on the floor seconds before I might have stepped on them. Under the edge of the sink's cupboards, there was half of a white coffee mug. Freezing, I glanced at my brother. "Guess this was where she fought him off."

Crouching, he nudged some of the pieces. "She's tough, I'll give her that. Not many people could take down someone that caught them off guard."

"Sammy's pretty surprising."

"Mm-hmm." Lifting a big piece of the mug, he turned it to show it to me. It was obviously part of a horse's face, the mane blowing in the breeze. "Surprising is a good word. Is this a fucking *pony*?"

"Huh. Maybe she likes riding them." She'd never mentioned anything about that.

Grinning, Hawthorne said, "I'll bet she likes riding something."

"If you're trying to insult me by comparing my cock to a horse, it isn't working."

"Tch." He stood smoothly, dusting off his jeans. "Let's scope out upstairs quick."

Together we ascended the stairs, the wood creaking as we went. "You come up with any reason this guy might be after her?" he asked me.

"Not a one." Gently, I nudged her bedroom door open. "If there's a connection between this guy, us, and her, I don't know what it could be." Bright light caught my attention. The window was flooding the room with sunbeams, they caused the bedspread to glow like a hellish white flare.

It blinded me, and apparently, it blinded Thorne, too—grunting, he dropped to the ground. Shielding my face, I grinned down at him where he'd ended up sprawled out. "You forget how walking works?" I asked.

Rolling his eyes, he reached up to grab my arm; I tugged him to his feet. Before he said anything else, he froze, staring down at the floor. We both saw the maid of honor dress that had tangled around his ankles, causing him to trip.

Carefully, he lifted it between us. "Here's a thought," he said, "And call me fucking crazy. But do you think this guy went after her because she seemed close to Frannie?"

Gripping the dress, I took it from him. My nostrils flared with the scent of Sammy. The room was already an echo chamber of her existence, this just rammed it home. "You might be onto something."

Looking around slowly, Hawthorne approached the window. "Fuck, the sun comes straight in here. Who could even sleep like this?"

Curling the dress in my fist, I didn't answer. My mind was roaming around, busy collecting scraps so that I could create a full picture. *Is that it? Did this guy want to hurt us so badly that he thought he'd target Sammy, thinking she was Francesca's best friend?* Fuck, it made a terrifying amount of sense. But since when were the Deep Shots so vengeful? *Was* the attack caused by them?

Could my dad be wrong, for once?

"Huh," my brother mumbled. Shade suddenly fell over the room. Lifting my eyes in confusion, I saw how he was blocking the window with a giant piece of cardboard. "This used to be up here. There's still tape stuck on the sill." With one toe, he nudged the pile of broken blinds on the floor.

Setting the dress on the bed, I joined him. Carefully, I ran my fingers over the window latch. Air was still blowing in through the bottom, where it hadn't been fully shut. "She said he broke in through her window, yeah." Lifting the glass pane with a grunt, I leaned out. The fire exit stairs were rusted, but reachable from the Dumpster below.

Imagining the bastard skulking around Sammy's home, waiting for her to return . . . it had my knuckles whitening from how hard I choked the sill.

"Shit!"

Banging my head on the window, I spun around to see what had made my brother cry out. Even with colors flashing in my eyes, I was groping for my gun. If the attacker had come back, then this was about to get messy.

Hawthorne faced me, his hands stretching up a pair of silky red panties. "Well, well, well," he said, smirking sharply. "Your lady friend has some surprisingly nice taste. Was she wearing something like this when you two—hey!"

Ripping the underwear away, I shoved him backward. "What the fuck is wrong with you?"

"What's wrong with *you*?" he countered. Eyeing me doubtfully, my older brother nodded at the open clothing drawer behind him. "I was just investigating. Chill."

"Investigating her fucking panties?" I threw the underwear back in with the others, slamming the dresser shut.

Hawthorne hadn't stopped watching me. His voice came out low and cautious. "You're not just messing around with this girl, are you? Holy shit."

"You think it'd be okay to dig through her stuff if I was treating her like a fling?"

"I think you'd care a whole lot less, yeah." Shrugging, he leaned on the dresser. "I haven't seen you like this before."

"Sure you have."

"Nope." Shaking his head, he messed with his short hair. "I've known you your whole life, Kain. I don't ever see you talking to the same girl after she does her walk of shame. You can't fool me, Sammy is more than just a hookup to you."

"So what if she is?" I asked suspiciously.

"That right there," he laughed. "Defensive as hell. Here's some advice for you, Brother. You're massively see-through."

Standing taller, I said, "Thanks for the insight. Can I give you some advice, too?"

"Shoot."

I gripped his shoulder solemnly. "It's creepy to dig through a woman's lingerie."

Pushing me off, he laughed. "Let's get out of here. Costello is waiting for us down by the Hill."

The Hill was a part of the city known for crime. It wasn't that long ago that people would warn against the area, unless you wanted to get a bullet in your guts. My father had done a lot of good in cleaning the area up—even if his methods were often questionable.

But why argue with the results?

Still, even with our thumbs crushing so many of the local gangs, one had recently made it a point to start ruffling our feathers. The Deep Shots were our major suspects in causing the police raid, so they were also our likely suspects as far as attacking Sammy went.

That meant it was time to meet up with them for a chat.

If Thorne is right about them trying to use her because they thought she had a personal relationship with our family, Francesca is going to feel awful.

On the way downstairs, something familiar flickered in my vision. Sammy's purse was hanging on the back of a kitchen chair. *She'd like to have that back, I'll bet.* Snatching it up, I brought it with me outside.

Hawthorne opened his car door, eyeing the purse. "New accessory. Nice."

With a wink, I hooked it on my shoulder. "Thanks. I hope the Deep Shots like it."

"I'm sure they will," he said, starting the engine. "About as much as they'll like seeing our pretty faces."

It had been a sore spot for some time that every strip club in the city was either owned by my family or the owners were being paid by my father to follow his rules. It might sound scummy, but my dad had a good reason for being so controlling.

Rhode Island had a dirty little secret—one few knew about unless they were in the game or looking to be a part of it. You see, while everyone treated Nevada like it was some magical place that you could go to legally fuck a girl for cash . . .

It wasn't some special, unique snowflake like people expected.

My state had one hell of a law, one that allowed people to pay for play all they wanted—as long as it was behind closed doors. That meant the strip clubs could *indeed* have full-on sex in the champagne rooms. Or the bathrooms, if someone was really desperate.

But we didn't like that law. Not me, and not my family.

We didn't want any of the girls working the clubs to feel like they could be forced into sucking a dick for a few bucks. That lifestyle led to bad shit, and my father had worked very hard to keep the bad shit out of our city.

And so, the sore spot I mentioned.

Since we owned or controlled the clubs, it meant people couldn't get their dicks wet. Every big gang in the area wanted to run a piece of the flesh-for-cash game, and we were stopping them.

Guess who definitely didn't like us for this?

Right. Our friends, the Deep Shots.

All that was left for them was siphoning cash out of dive bars and illegal betting. My dad didn't care about any of that, though. He always said that you had to let the rebels feel like they were sticking it to you somehow.

Otherwise, they actually *would.*

Hawthorne parked his car in the alley of the shit hole they called a bar. It was the kind of building that was all old brick and graffiti, no windows—no signs. It was magical that the place didn't crumble in on itself.

The Deep Shots loved money—who didn't?—but they were notorious for taking a cut from the businesses they controlled, then never putting anything back in to help them thrive. I wasn't kidding when I'd told Sammy that I figured we'd been attacked out of jealousy.

We were the Badds.

And we owned this city.

Who wouldn't hate us for that?

"Hey," Costello said, pushing off of the filthy wall by the bar entrance. He was dressed in a leather jacket that had to be making him sweat in this heat. Like always, his face was so calm that you'd think it was October instead of humid, sticky June.

Nodding at him, I eyed the crusty stairwell that led down to the door. Barnie's was a refurbished cellar that had been used in the glory days of Prohibition. The bar had a history, it was a place worth taking care of. The Deep Shots didn't give a shit.

Putting my hand on my holster out of instinct, I started past Costello. His hand gripped my elbow, freezing me. "You don't pull your gun," he said into my ear. The heat of his breath reminded me of a wolf snarling at my throat. "Not unless I do first."

"I'm not going to whip it out like it's a cock-measuring contest," I said. Staring him in the eye, I cracked a half grin. "Though, if it was, we all know it wouldn't be fair for me to get involved."

Costello didn't smile. "Keep it in your pants."

Shrugging away from him, I reached for the door. "You and Thorne just watch for anyone with a happier trigger finger than mine." Considering that I was expecting to face the people responsible for trying to hurt Sammy . . . they'd be hard-pressed to find someone edgier than me.

Barnie's was dark—not like a shadow, but the way the underside of your dirty fridge is dark. In spite of the smoking laws, gray clouds swam through the air, searing my nose and ruining the taste in my mouth.

Shoved back by a well-worn pool table, our hosts waited for us.

The table was just big enough to fit three men on one side. In the middle, more nose than much else, was Frock Monroe. He was topped with a mop of curly, red hair that he often shoved beneath a pale brown cabby hat. His thick beard climbed up his jaw like jungle vines. It was the same hair that made him and his son Brick look so similar.

Both of them were lean; I'd heard that in his twenties Frock had been an underground boxer. While the Deep Shots' leader was bent forward into the light, his son was reclining into whatever shadows he could find.

But even that couldn't hide Brick's bare chin. I almost didn't recognize him.

"Shit," Hawthorne hissed near my shoulder. "He lose a bet?"

Ignoring my brother, I scanned the last member of the trio in front of us. The guy on the left, I'd never seen him before. He was wearing a thin, green tank top, his white jacket spread open to show off his hard body. I was sure it was an intentional move.

The stranger was decked out in corded muscles that matched mine. Sitting like he was—one arm thrown over the back of his chair—he had a casual air to him. Either he was relaxed because he wasn't scared, or he was too stupid to think about who he was facing.

He gazed at me without a hint of emotion. As intense as his physique was, the guy had eyes that reminded me of a deer's. Soft, gentle—aware. It didn't matter if he was sweet or not, he hadn't stopped watching my brothers and me since we'd opened the door.

Guys like that are *always* deadly.

Frock spread his hands on the table. "Get them some chairs."

From the back wall, two heavily armed men approached with seats for us. *Reinforcements.* It made sense that the Deep Shots wouldn't let their guard down, but I was surprised to see so many bodyguards blending into the smoky corners.

"I'll stand," I said, "if it's all the same to you."

Hawthorne shrugged, dropping onto one of the cushions. "I'll park my ass, thanks."

All eyes turned to Costello. He just folded his arms. "We won't be here long enough for me to settle in. Standing is fine."

Brick rocked his chair forward, the feet clacking down. "Oh, shit. Big man on campus over here."

His father gave him a warning look. Linking his fingers, he stared not at me, but at Costello. "You said you wanted to talk about a little police action the other day."

"Some prick working for you cased our joint," I said. Brick grunted, drawing my eyes back to him. Squinting, I looked him over with a slow burn of suspicion. "Actually, the guy kind of looked like you, Brick. I didn't even think about it before because of that giant-ass beard you normally sport."

"Yeah," Hawthorne said, stretching over the table. "Kain's right. Where's your beard at, hm? Did you seriously fucking shave it just to pretend to be a waiter at our little party?"

"I don't have to answer you," Brick said, "but no. I wasn't there."

Clenching my fingers, I stared the man down. "I think you're a liar."

"You're calling me a *liar*?"

"He literally just fucking said you were." Thorne laughed. "Hey, Frock." My brother jerked a thumb at the leader's scowling son. "Your kid here caused a lot of trouble for us."

"He says he didn't. Besides, from what I heard, you guys didn't suffer much in that police raid. You were back on the street in a few hours, and you didn't lose any hardware."

"Bet that makes you *real* sad—"

Cutting off Hawthorne, I said, "We almost lost a friend."

Everyone went quiet. Next to me, Costello breathed through his tightened jaw. I knew I was about to say too much, but the longer

I stared at Brick—the more I realized it *was* him in the photo—the angrier I got.

This is the guy that attacked Sammy.

Frock lifted his hands, his voice eerily calm. "What are you talking about?"

"This asshole son of yours went after a girl the other night," I growled.

Frock shot a look at Brick. "What's he talking about?"

"I don't have a damn clue."

That was it; the denial was my breaking point. Bursting forward, I reached for Brick over the table. My hands coiled in the front of his shirt. The air rattled with surprised shouts and metallic clicks; every gun in the place was trained on me.

Wrenching him closer, I sent glasses tumbling to the floor. Someone had left an ashtray out; it spilled gray dust everywhere, making people cough as it rolled away. I didn't care that the ashes burned my nose. I was too focused on Brick.

This close, there was no doubting the fragile, red stubble growing over his face. If I stuck a suit on him, he'd be a ringer for the photo in Fran's phone.

Movement wobbled on either side of my view; I still didn't look away from Brick. His fingers dug into the backs of my arms, his sneer as vicious as mine.

I jerked him closer to me. "Tell them what you did."

"Nothing." His calmness just infuriated me further. "I didn't touch any damn girl."

Hawthorne groaned. "Fucking hell, Kain. This isn't the way to do this."

"Listen to your brother," Brick said, grinning so wide I saw his fillings.

My forearms tensed. "It's the only way to get him to admit what he did."

Frock barely moved, but he managed to lean into my view. "He says he didn't touch her."

"He's a fucking *liar*," I hissed.

"Yeah?" Brick asked, his lips pulling back. "Where's your proof? It's your word against mine."

"It's *her* word against yours, and I'd believe her over you any day."

Costello said, "This game is ridiculous. We know you were at the party, Brick. We have a photo of you there."

"You make a really cute waiter." Thorne chuckled.

Brick went deathly pale. He licked his lips, but his father spoke first. "You win. Fine. I sent my son to gather some intel on your family. Looking for illegal goods, you know the drill." He shrugged like we were chatting about the weather and not criminal activity. "It's obvious we're not happy with the current arrangement."

One of the Deep Shots, a guy with a big, red Mohawk, shouted, "Yeah! Fuck you guys! You're trying to keep us from making any damn cash out here! So what if you got raided?"

Brick was still staring at me. I think my silence made him the most nervous. He said, "That's the facts. You guys are screwing us while we're trying to make a dime. Everyone else is suffering, why shouldn't you?"

"I'm about to suffer from some busted knuckles when I slam them into your face," I growled. I'd heard enough—did no one get how furious I was? A cold, hard piece of metal dug into my temple. The man at the table—the one I didn't know by name—had stood up, his pistol pressing to my head.

"Slow and steady," he said, leaving no room for argument. "Let him go and stand down."

Instead, I shifted my hold so that I could wrap Brick's shirt around his neck. My veins popped; his did, too, as I started strangling him. From the corner of my eye, I saw that Costello was staring at me in disbelief. Hawthorne was copying him. They didn't fucking get it: this piece of shit in my hands was the man who'd gone after Sammy.

He tried to hurt her. If she hadn't fought back, who knows what could have happened to her?

"Brother, let him go," Costello said coolly. "Getting a bullet in your skull won't help her."

Brick was struggling, cutting into my skin, his face going a pretty shade of purple. The gun dug harder into my temple, and I knew . . . if I kept going, more than one gun would fire on me.

Shoving Brick back into his chair, I watched him topple over in it backward. He was gasping for air, sweat making his red face shiny. People hurried to help him up; he shoved them away, scrambling to his feet.

The ashtray was stuck to his cheek—he slapped it away, leaving black smudges all over his skin. Hawthorne snorted, covering his smirk with the back of one hand.

Frock waved his hand. "Put your gun away, Rush."

Flipping his pistol into his holster, the new guy faced me down. Rush—as he'd been called—gave me the barest hint of a smile. "Attacking the son of our gang's leader, right in front of everyone? Now that's ballsy."

"People tell me mine are pretty big." Flexing my fingers, I looked back at Frock. "Your son is bullshitting all of us, even you, but I guess it doesn't matter. I'll just say this: if he fucks around with the girl again—and he knows who I mean—he won't just get a coffee cup to the head as a result." I flicked my glare toward Brick. "Next time, I'll kill you myself."

Brick's mouth twitched, his chest flaring with rapid breathing.

His father shrugged, acting as if seeing his son getting threatened was normal. It probably was. "Your family and mine, we don't get along so well. Spilling blood will break whatever semblance of a truce that we have. My son says he's innocent, and we all know you aren't about to try and get the cops involved to investigate. So . . . my advice? Walk the fuck out of here, and forget about whatever your lady friend told you."

Twisting on a heel, I stormed for the exit. Only then did I notice the bar patrons were all standing, their hands resting on their weapons. It was a cold reminder that I was in Deep Shots' territory; as notorious as we were, any one of them would happily pull their triggers in respect for Frock and his gang.

Keeping my hand by my gun, I walked the slow march out, then up to the street. The sun felt refreshing on my skin after being soaked in the ash below.

I'll tear his fucking throat out.

"Kain!" Hawthorne's hand clasped my shoulder from behind. Spinning, I broke his contact and backed up. Costello was beside him, they both watched me as if I was some rabid animal. "Calm down, Kain."

"How can I calm down? That asshole down there is lying! He went after her!"

Thorne started to move forward, but Costello beat him. Rounding on me, my scarred brother ignored whatever fury was boiling in my eyes. One strong shove and he had me backed against Hawthorne's car. "Listen to me," he whispered. "Don't you *dare* do anything rash. Understand?"

Faced with the jagged cut that marred his face, I hesitated. Costello would always be a cold reminder of what could happen if you tried to take a serious situation into your own hands.

Ever so slightly, I relaxed. His pale irises warmed. Deliberately, he let me go and backed up. "It's obvious that Brick is lying. His father is right, though. We can't do anything about what happened. Unless you want to go to war?"

My chuckle was sour. "Might be fun."

Hawthorne sighed, his keys tossing up and down in his fingers. "Kain, don't be stupider than usual. Let's just go tell Dad what we learned. He might have a solution."

"He'll just tell us to keep everyone on lockdown until he's sure they won't try anything again."

"Then let that happen." Costello climbed into his own car, the door wide open as he talked to us. "You want her to be safe. Let her be safe with us."

As I settled into the car, I ran the situation through my head. I was positive that Brick had been posing as a waiter at our party. But why he'd targeted Sammy after the raid, I had no damn clue.

After all of this, I didn't feel an inch closer to an answer.

- CHAPTER THIRTEEN -

Sammy

The rosebushes blocked out most of the sky. Lifting my arm, I spread my fingers, pretending to grab one of the pink flowers. The world around me cascaded with birdsong, and the air smelled divine.

No one would have guessed how miserable I was.

I have to get out of this place. I'd already tried once; right after the morning meeting about my mystery attacker, I'd kicked the front door open and looked for an escape.

It was very dramatic, and I like to think I looked like a badass. But then I'd ended up wandering around like a lost puppy. The cars parked on the large, round driveway were all locked. Everything in the garage was no better.

Flustered, I'd stomped back into the front yard, ignoring how everyone was watching me through the windows. Their stares burned on my neck, reminding me that of course I was being watched.

Kain had come to the front doors, standing on the landing. "Sammy," he'd called to me. "Come inside, let me talk to you."

Holding my head high, I'd walked on stiff legs around the side of the house. My ears rang with my name on his tongue. There were a million things I wanted to say to him, many of them not meant for children to hear.

Let him simmer, I told myself. If I couldn't control my escape, then I'd control what I could. I didn't have to speak to any of them. Especially not Kain.

I'd thought he was on my side. That had been my mistake.

Afterward, I'd heard three of the cars rev up. Even lying in the backyard, I could tell they were driving east off the property. The metallic clang of the front gate slamming shut made my heart skip.

Since then, I'd been lying in my shaded part of the garden for a couple of hours. How was I going to get out of here? I needed to see my mother, and what was going to happen to my business? My appointments? Everything was turning to shit.

The scent of hay broke through the fragrance of roses. A shadow blocked out the sun, making me blink and look up. With a giant smile on her round face, Matilda looked down on me. "Hey, stranger, what are you doing back here?" she asked.

Sitting up, I dusted grass off of my back. "Didn't you hear? I'm . . ." I stopped myself. Matilda was watching me curiously. *Does she not know I'm supposed to be kept on the property?* The first seed of an idea grew. "You work with the horses, right?"

"Yup." Gripping the dirty sides of her torn jeans, Matilda beamed. "Have for around five years now."

The pride in her face made my heart swell. Standing, I ducked out from under the rosebush I'd been hiding beneath. "So if I wanted to ride one, you're the girl I need to see."

"Oh. Um." Her eyes darted back toward the stables. "Pretty much. Why, you wanna take one out?"

The pounding in my chest reached a crescendo. "Very, very much." It wasn't a lie. I'd wanted to touch those horses since I'd seen them. Their raw smell called back some of my fondest memories.

Matilda motioned to me, her steps light. "I don't see why not." Brightening her voice, she said, "I thought you might be a horse person from the minute I saw you."

"Oh, yeah?"

"Mm-hmm." She nudged the stables open, leading me inside. "The way you were looking at Rosel the other day gave it away."

My ears turned red. "I rode a bit when I was little."

She led me over to the same chestnut mare as before. Clicking her tongue, she reached out, her palm gliding over the animal's smooth flank. "You want help?"

"It's like riding a bike," I said, suddenly unsure. It had been thirteen years since I'd last sat on a horse. My determination gave me the courage to move forward with my plan.

Matilda set about saddling the horse. As she did, I walked closer, moving to Rosel's right flank. She set one big, round eye on me. Her massive nostrils flared. Swallowing, I extended my fingertips slowly toward her. "Hey, girl, relax. I'm not going to eat you. Though I once heard horse was a delicacy in some places. Ha-ha. Hah."

Matilda gave me a look.

With my smile twitching, I ran my hand over Rosel's muzzle. She was even softer than I expected, my head swimming with memories. The mare pushed forward, demanding more of my petting. For a minute, I forgot about what I was going to do. I was lost in the wonderment of this giant animal, how she could be so gentle—so sweet—when she was capable of crushing my skull.

"She likes you," Matilda said.

"I like her, too," I said softly.

Tightening the last strap, she gave the animal a quick tap. "I'll lead her out, then it's your turn." Taking the bridle, she guided Rosel out of the stable with me close behind.

Under the bright sun, the horse glistened like freshly poured caramel. I noticed the tip of her nose was pink and white, and there was a single sock of dark color on her rear left leg. Flicking her tail, she kept her eyes on me.

Matilda stepped back, so I took that as my cue. Gripping the saddle, I stuck my foot in the stirrup and prayed I wasn't about to fall on my ass. Maybe it wasn't like riding a bike, but then again, I'd never ridden a bike as a kid. My body remembered what to do, though. Grunting, I lifted myself onto the horse, straddling her.

The shift in position changed my worldview. I could see over the estate, the roses dotting the green in bright pops of color. There were a few trees in the distance, then beyond, I saw the hills of grass and hedges.

Beyond that is the road.

"Okay," Matilda said. "Let me just show you around, we'll take it slow."

"Listen. I'm really sorry," I said earnestly.

Laughing, she looked up at me with her brow in a knot. "For what?"

I didn't speak, I just dug my heels into Rosel. In a burst of muscle she flew forward, nearly knocking me from the saddle. It took several desperate, minor adjustments of my body's tension to make sure I was leaning over her in a way that would keep me afloat.

Behind me, Matilda shouted something. I didn't hear the words; I didn't need to.

I'm sorry, I thought for the fifth time. *I really am.* I'd make sure that Rosel would get back to her. I wished I could have explained that I just needed to do this, that it was the only way out.

The wind tore at me as we raced over the yard. The flat ground was broken up by the gardens. I spotted a gazebo to one side, a large storage facility on the other. As I passed, two men stumbled backward, watching me in abject shock.

They didn't stop me, but I expected them—or Matilda—to alert the rest of the Badds. People would come after me soon. I had to get to the road as fast as possible.

"Come on," I hissed into Rosel's ear. Over the rushing air that pushed her mane into my eyes, I wasn't sure she'd hear. My plan was to get to the street and follow it back to a rest stop. I could call for a taxi from there. I had no money on me, but if we went back to my house, I could pay them. As far as I knew, my purse was still hanging in the kitchen.

Unless that guy Jameson robbed me. Gritting my teeth, I decided to worry about that when it came up.

Rosel jumped some short bushes, my teeth rattling on the landing. Beyond the wall of green hedges surrounding us, I looked for a hint of pavement. Ahead of me, miles and miles of fields waved. *Keep going*, I told myself firmly. *It'll become a road eventually!*

The wind whipped, lightening my spirit. Years since I'd ridden . . . and it still made me feel so free. I was lightning, a leaf, the sun and the sky. I felt and tasted everything, Mother Nature calling my name.

It was kind of serene, when you thought about it.

"Sammy!"

That wasn't fucking Mother Nature at all. Twisting, I gawked back in disbelief at the figure in the distance. Like a knight out on patrol, Kain burst across the field upon a glossy, black stallion. I'd expected to be pursued, but I thought it would happen much later—and by someone else.

How was he already on my tail?

Something broke through the evergreen of the land. Flushing with excitement, I guided Rosel toward the mark on the horizon. Seconds before I couldn't turn away, I saw it was a fence. A large, black iron fence that stretched for miles.

No, there has to be a way around it!

Kain yelled again; he was much closer. Wildly I forced the mare to run, leading her along the fence without slowing down. The longer that my body shook with the force of Rosel's stride, the deeper my realization of my mistake sank in.

This family . . . they weren't stupid. They didn't care if I tried to run away on a damn horse. Their property was fenced in, it kept them . . . me . . . *safe*.

Dirt spat up, Kain's horse pulling up near mine. I shot him a look, wondering if my eyes were rolling as madly as my steed's. I was pushing Rosel too hard.

"Sammy!" he yelled again, his hair dancing over his cheekbones. "Stop this! Stop running from me!"

His words tangled in my chest. Running from *him*? Is that what he thought? Frantically, I scanned the fields, wishing something would appear—some escape, some rescue. I was part of some insane high-speed horse chase, and there was no way out.

Rosel reared, bucking so suddenly I wasn't ready for it. My body remembered how to ride, but as a kid, I'd never dealt with a panicked horse. The world spun, all clouds and grass and crisp blue.

The sky? I wondered from far away. *No. A different blue.*

Kain's terrified eyes.

Tumbling from the saddle, I rolled hard in the grass. I'd have to thank my mother for her blessed genetics; my thickly padded ass took the brunt of the impact. Gasping, I spun in the dust, landing on my back with my eyes still shaking in my skull.

So this is how I die. Thrown from a horse while wearing another woman's underwear.

No psychic would have ever guessed that.

"Sammy! Fuck, Sammy." He dropped down beside me, fingers hovering uncertainly—then catching me by my shoulders. Fear turned his healthy tan a sickly yellow, kissable lips pulled back over a grimace.

Looking at him, I said slowly, "You're making the ugly cry face, and you still look amazing. That seriously sucks."

Tension melted from his face. Grabbing me, he pulled me into his lap, his chin rubbing the top of my head. "Idiot," he growled. "What the hell were you thinking?"

Closing my eyes, I didn't speak. It was a miracle I had no broken bones, let alone that I wasn't dead. I'd done something so rash that I didn't doubt there'd be consequences. If pain wasn't one of them, it'd be something even worse.

But here . . . just for a little bit . . .

I wanted to forget about all of that.

Kain Badd—and I was starting to question if his last name even fit him—was holding me as if he'd been truly worried he'd almost lost me. Again and again, no matter how frustrated I was with my situation, this man came to the rescue.

He'd helped me at the jail, he'd driven me from my house when I'd been attacked, he'd bandaged my cut-up foot. Why had I been so angry with him this morning? It was hard to remember. So for a little bit, I didn't try. In ignorance, I could enjoy a moment with the man who kept breaking into my world like he belonged.

He breathed in deeply. "You're insane for running away."

The moment broke like a daisy in a storm.

Sitting up, I pulled out of his arms. I saw the horses milling nearby, neither of them seeming to be worse for wear. Gripping the grass by my thighs, I looked at him and smiled sadly. "How did you come after me so fast?"

"The second we pulled in, Matilda ran up and yanked me toward the stables, telling me what had happened."

My heart sank. "Is she going to get in trouble? It wasn't her fault, I just—"

"You didn't need to go this *far*, Sammy!"

"What else was I supposed to do? Let your father keep me trapped here? Let *you* keep me trapped here?"

"It's only temporary until we figure everything out!"

Studying his face—the hard lines that crossed his cheeks, the hollow indents beneath his eyes—I paused. "And did you figure everything out?"

Scraping fingers through his wind-tossed hair, Kain shut his eyes. "I know who did it, yes."

Prickling with surprise, I leaned toward him. "Please tell me he'll be taken care of so I can get out of here." Kain kept his head down, and my spirit joined him. "You're about to give me bad news."

"Sammy . . ." Filling his chest, he breathed out, meeting my wary stare. "The people who organized the raid? They're a gang that goes by the name of the Deep Shots. They're . . . not as powerful as my family, but they still have pull."

"What does that even mean?"

"It means we confronted them, and they denied everything."

"So *what*?" I dug my nails into the dirt. "I saw his face, I know who did it!"

"That's not enough!"

"Why?" Throwing up my arms, I shouted, "Bring me to them, let me call him out! That's what they do on TV, right? A lineup, a—"

"It doesn't work like that!" he snapped, two fingers massaging his temples. "Listen. Please. I want to get this fucker out of the way, to make sure he'll leave you alone, but it's your word against his . . . and to them, you're no one."

Barking out a sour laugh, I shook my head. "I'm not no one. Dammit, this is stupid. Maybe the cops really do need to take care of this if you guys can't."

"I am taking care of it," he hissed. His intensity made me sit back; he saw me move, and his next words came out so very, very tired. "Sammy, I don't want anything to happen to you. Not just you, but anyone you care about. I promise that I won't even sleep until I'm sure everything is under control."

Baffled, I tuned in to his promise.

Kain said, "The man who attacked you is the son of the Deep Shots' leader, a guy named Brick. I wanted to bust his face in when I recognized him from the photo, but . . ."

Brick? Not Jameson? Of course he'd use a fake name.

His fist was so tight I heard his tendons creak. That wasn't what I was focused on. Kain's exhaustion had felt out of place to me this morning. All day, I'd wondered about what he'd done that had made him so tired.

When he'd said he wouldn't sleep, it had clicked.

"Last night," I whispered, "I asked you to check in on my mother. I never got to ask you if you had." My fingertips swayed forward, gently brushing the bruises under his eyes. "You watched her all night, just to make sure she'd be safe. Didn't you?"

Kain's shoulders hunched. "Yes."

The snow that had started to crust on my heart melted away. I didn't move my palm from his cheek. "Why didn't you tell me you were a prince?"

There—that made his eyes flash to me. His surprise shifted, a smirk growing as he chuckled. "Who told you?" Before I answered, he said, "I don't know. It didn't come up."

Hesitating, I said, "I'd heard that you use that line to get girls in bed. You were trying so hard to get me to sleep with you, so why not try that if it worked before?"

His fingers circled my wrist, forcing my hand to remain on his jaw. The core of his voice was hot and smoky. "Because I didn't want you to care about it. I didn't want my blood to be what made you want me. Is that what you want to hear?"

Licking my lips, I said, "Yes."

His smirk vanished. "Fuck, you keep throwing me for such loops. Who would answer that question like that?"

"Someone who wants to be honest . . . because she wants the other person to tell the same truths." I tugged at my hand on his cheek; he held it firmly where it was. "Your family is royalty. It makes no sense. How are there even royal families anymore?" Laughing without humor, I looked away. "I know so little about you, Kain. So why do I feel like I already *get* you?"

My knees burned with the cuts from my fall. My stomach was a pile of snakes that wanted to escape. I probably needed to get checked out for a concussion.

And then he kissed me . . . and none of that mattered.

- CHAPTER FOURTEEN -

Kain

She'd asked me a question, but I didn't want to answer with words.

How could I even try?

I wasn't a poet—I didn't know how to phrase the colliding emotions inside of me that rose to the surface when Sammy was near. Besides, the way she'd been touching me had made me acutely aware of how soft she was.

How *warm*.

Could I be blamed for wanting to taste that sweet mouth of hers? Especially when her lips were glowing in the sun, her hair tossed by the wind and her fall?

There was a grass stain on her cheek; I kissed that next. Sammy threw her arms around my neck, holding me close as her whole body shivered. We came together, my weight pushing her down into the field.

I'd barely had a taste when she gripped my ears, forcing me back so roughly that I winced. Her pupils sucked me up like black holes. "Wait. Before we do this, I need to know more."

"More?" I asked, nuzzling her throat. "That's a nice word. Say that again." Her knee dug into my side; I gave up, leaning away. "We're rolling around in a field with no one to stop us, and you want to talk?"

Lying there with her hair swirling around her, she'd never been more beautiful. It made her demand slice even sharper. "I *want* to mess around with you—"

"Okay, then let's do that."

"But I'm not going to do anything with someone who's keeping secrets."

Groaning, I sat on my heels. The position exaggerated the shape of my hard-on. "This isn't exactly a secret, babe."

"Stop," she said, her eyes fixated on me.

"I don't think I can." Palming my erection, I hissed, "This is all you. It's not in my control."

Propping herself on her elbows, she threw a handful of grass at me. "Back at the jail, the detective warned me away from you and your family. Why? And don't say jealousy."

It was clear she wasn't going to give up. "Probably because we're known to dabble in gray areas of the law."

"Like?"

"Blackmail. Gambling. Weapons." I looked her in the eye. "Strip clubs."

It was amazing that she didn't flinch. "Do you hurt people?"

"Define 'people.'"

"*Innocent* people."

My head was starting to pound. "No one is innocent, but the folks we deal with definitely aren't." Sizing her up, I weighed the outcome of telling her what she wanted to hear versus what she needed to hear. With a great shrug, I went for the latter. "I'm not going to try and spin you some tale about how my family and I are heroes. We aren't. Never were, never will be."

"Then what are you?"

"Greedy." I bit the word off. "Determined. Power crazy." Sweat had collected under my throat; it fell down my collarbone when I leaned toward her. "We control this whole damn state, and it's better than it's ever been. Are we always kind? No. We couldn't be. But we aren't peddling drugs, and we aren't letting girls get pulled into the clubs when they don't wanna be there."

"So some girls get a choice about being trapped?" she asked bitterly.

My eyebrows lowered as much as my voice did. "Let it go."

"How? I don't want to be here!"

"But you do want to be alive!" I snapped back. A frailty cracked my words; I recovered, hoping she hadn't noticed. I was just . . . so damn tired. Tired of fighting, tired of having to prove I didn't want her to end up as a cold corpse. "The guy who attacked you knows we know about it. That makes him more deadly than ever."

Pushing up, she drew her knees to her chest and hugged them. I was spoiling for an argument, but Sammy was done. Nothing came out of her but gentle breaths that stirred the loose hairs that fell over her chin.

With the horses grazing behind her, she could have been a watercolor painting. No matter how fiercely she resisted me . . . or how she called me out on what I was doing wrong . . .

I couldn't stop wanting her.

"Your turn." I nodded at Rosel. "Where did you learn to ride?"

She followed my eyes. "When I was little, my dad used to take me riding. I loved it so much. My best memories are back then . . . with him." Sammy was far away in the past. I felt awful pulling her back to the present.

"How did he die?"

Her eyes flew wide. "What?"

Gently, I said, "You asked me to go watch your mother because you couldn't, and that meant no one else could, either. You talk about your father the way people talk about those they've lost. It was just a hunch."

I saw the moment when she debated not telling me anything. Then it passed, her voice steady when she began again. "I'm not entirely sure how he died. They never found his body." I couldn't stop my jaw from dropping—she saw. "That came out kind of cryptic, sorry. His car was found at the bottom of the Newport Bay. The police decided he must have drowned—suicide, they called it." Sammy shook her head, not softening her anger. "He wouldn't have. I know it. They did their investigation, then they told my mother and me it had to be suicide, body or not. Lots of corpses go missing in the ocean, they said."

Sammy was knotting up in front of my eyes; the last thing I wanted to do was push her on what was obviously a sensitive issue. I struggled to change the subject. "Where did he take you horseback riding?"

Shaking herself, she looked up at me. "White Rose Farms."

I did a double take. "You're kidding. I went there as a kid, too." Looking at the black stallion—Knight—I said, "It's just funny to think we might have seen each other years ago and not even realized it."

"I think I'd remember you." She chuckled. "Unless you were different as a kid."

"Weren't we all?"

"I was pretty much the same."

My eyebrows went up higher. "You must have been a handful, sugar."

That got her smiling, the shroud of sadness lifting into the sky. Sammy stuck her foot out, letting it rub almost accidentally on my thigh.

I squinted at her, trailing my fingers to her ankle and digging in. "Guess you really are a local."

"Did you *still* doubt that?"

Leaning forward, I brushed my lips on hers. When I pulled back, her eyes were shut, her face expectant for more. Whispering against her mouth, I said, "You still don't kiss like a local."

Sighing gently, she put her hands on the back of my head. "You're right. I kiss better."

And she did. She really fucking did.

With a wicked smile, I leaned on her until she buckled onto the grass. My knees straddled her, a hand creeping under her spine to encourage her to arch against me. Skating down her torso, I let the smooth cloth of her shirt caress my face.

Grass tickled my elbows as I settled between her thighs. In a great show of patience, I unbuttoned the black pants she had on. Looking up, I could see the high-speed curve of her hips as they led to her navel, the mounds of her breasts where they rose and fell.

Violently, I ripped the trousers down her legs; they caught on her flats, then they took the shoes with them. In front of me was my prize, the perfect triangle of her pussy hidden behind a pair of blue panties.

Kissing her hip, I said, "I've been wanting to eat your pussy since I first saw you naked. You smell so fucking *good*, Sammy. Did you ever think you'd get eaten out by actual royalty?"

"I'm pretty sure every girl writes about that in their diary, Your *Majesty*," she said, drawing the word out sarcastically.

Cupping her ass, I breathed along her stomach. "You're teasing, but I love that."

"It doesn't make you uncomfortable?"

I snorted loudly; she jumped as she felt it against her inner thigh. "In what world is it uncomfortable to have a hot woman treat you like the king you are?"

"Prince. You're not a king," she said with a weak chuckle. Her composure was cracking, it made it hard for her to joke around.

Flattening my tongue, I slid it along the front of her underwear. Her groan made my cock flood with lust. "And you're the expert?" Not letting her answer, I started to tug at her panties, pulling them inside of her so that her plump lower lips peeked out the sides.

Sammy grabbed my hands abruptly. "Let me get these off."

"Someone's in a hurry," I said, raising an eyebrow.

Biting her lip, she wriggled out of her underwear in a clumsy shift of her weight. Even that—seeing her flopping and grinding without any grace—was intoxicating. "Let's just say that letting you play with these particular panties would be . . . weird for me." I frowned with uncertainty. "Don't ask," she mumbled.

So I didn't. My lips had other ways to spend their energy.

I left indents in her soft flesh from gripping her ass so roughly. Sammy squeaked, acting as if my uncontrollable lust for her was out of the blue. There was no way she didn't realize how fucking *horny* she made me.

Her scent clouded my thoughts. It was clean and thick and everything in between, I wanted to smell her excitement till the end of my days. Growling, I pushed her knees to the dirt, spreading her out as fully as she could manage.

"Kain! Easy!" Her smile was nervous, the last remnant of her self-control locked inside of it.

Meeting her stare evenly, I lowered my nose to the triangle of hair above her swollen clit and had my first taste of Sammy Sage. She shut her eyes; I spoke into the wet heat of her folds. "Don't. You're going to watch me make you come. You're going to look me in the face as you cream all over my mouth. Got it?"

She trembled, a spasm that rolled through her until her knees twitched in my grip. It caught me off guard, her thighs clamping around my cheeks. "Yeah," she whispered. "I've got it."

Lapping around the edge of her clit, I pulled her pink lips apart. Every bit of her was slippery, engorged with her arousal. Knowing I'd done this to her was infusing me with a wild sort of power. Sammy was strong, she didn't give in easily—but she had with me.

Fuck, what a *rush* to know what I was doing to her.

In my jeans, my cock dug into the fabric. Every time I licked around her hard nub, my dick swelled more. The tension was unbelievable, I was coiled and ready to explode. Her heat was maddening; I could see her clit flex from my breath.

Lifting two of my fingers, I licked them patiently. Sammy stared, unblinking, at my display. I didn't need lube, I just wanted her to know what I was about to do. I wanted her to think about my fingers inside of her before they even began pushing in.

"Ready?" I asked.

"Of course I am," she said.

"I know." My fingertips ran along her entrance, then in a firm shove, I pumped them deep into her pussy. "I like making you say it," I said, her groan of delight muting my words. My fingers rubbing the inner roof of her wet walls, my thumb joined the fray, grinding on her clit. Sammy bucked against me, my cock thrumming instantly. She was squeezing my fingers, desperate for an orgasm to relieve the pressure I knew she was suffering—I was suffering it as well.

Bending low, I pushed my lips firmly against my thumb, licking around it as it made circles on her twitching clit. Her panting was all I heard, her soaked warmth was all I felt. Ripples moved down my fingers: the only warning I had before she crushed my head with her knees.

"I'm coming!" she shouted. The words echoed through the sky and grass, they filled my ears, and I felt them low in my belly.

"Don't you dare stop watching me," I hissed.

Sammy's lashes had been closing; she snapped them wide, her cheeks pink as she shook with her orgasm. I watched her the whole time, my breathing flaring my ribs so hard that I was rising from the ground in great waves.

Her juice soaked my face; my cock had never been so painfully rock-hard. "That felt like a good one. Fuck, I can't wait any longer." Kneeling on the grass, I pulled my shirt over my head. When I could see again, I caught how she'd been transfixed by the sight of my body in the sun.

Purposely I flexed my arms and my stomach muscles. She tried to laugh to hide how she'd been ogling me like a piece of meat, but she couldn't trick me—especially not with how her tits started rising faster with her excited breathing.

"Take off my jeans," I said.

"Yes, Your Majesty." She lacked the sarcasm that time. Rising up to sit, she fumbled with my belt. It fell away, her eagerness obvious when she didn't even savor pulling my zipper down.

The metal teeth parted, my erection shoving through the gap. The front of my tight briefs was wet with my precome. "That's beautiful," I whispered.

Her eyes flicked up to me. "What is?"

"Looking down on you as you stare hungrily at my cock."

Flushing, she reached out to pull my briefs away from my skin. The tip of my dick peeked out, stretching in a thick curve away from my belly with the underwear gone.

Taking her by the middle, I dropped onto my back, pulling her on top of me. Her naked thighs rested on mine, my length sliding along the outside of her pussy lips.

"If I keep this up, I'll come before I even get in you," I chuckled, but it was raw—strained.

"Let's fix that." Sitting back, Sammy rocked her clit across my road map of veins. Fisting the base of my dick, she lifted herself high, giving me a great view of her soaked inner thighs.

I groaned so long and low my throat went dry. "Wait. Hold on." Reluctantly, I grabbed her waist to stop her from sinking onto my cock head. Sweat slid down my forehead from the effort. "I don't have any condoms with me." Fuck, why hadn't I?

She looked me in the eye. "I'm a grown-ass woman. I take birth control."

My relief morphed into puzzlement. "What? Then why did you make me use one the first time we hooked up?"

"Because I'm also not an idiot. Do *you* bang strangers without protection?"

Without waiting for me to respond, she sank herself down on my fat shaft. I threw back my head, groaning with the sensation of her throttling me.

Inch by inch, she fed my length into her. The lips of her beautiful pussy glided down, dragging along my shaft until she was—with a final whimper—settled onto me completely. I was in her to my root, her thighs quivering where they tensed on either side of my body.

I was naked, but she still had on her shirt. It drifted down to her hips as she gyrated on top of me. In a way, it was sexier to see her half-hidden like that. It made the naked parts of her even *more* naked somehow.

She choked my cock with her desperation, her sudden cry of delight making the horses trot farther away nervously. The beat of her heart swam through to her pussy; I felt it on me, inside of me.

My climax hovered on the edge of my wavering vision. Was I going to come before she got a second orgasm? *No, focus!* This was like any other game between us. I'd win; I already had, she'd finished while I ate her out.

But the reality was that she was driving me to my edge, making *me* lose *myself.* I couldn't handle this fucking woman. I was supposed to be the one who broke people. I was the one who had them chasing me down, begging me for another go.

I created desperate people.

How could someone exist who could turn me into that?

"Kain! Ah—that's it, I'm . . . !" Her voice broke away, becoming a series of moans and whimpers. She shuddered through to her knees; they vised me harder. I was relieved that she was coming, my ego could lie a little longer to itself about how she was ruling my desires.

Seconds after she shivered, I lost the last of my strength. Tension built and built, finally exploding through my muscles and seeking the part of me that was deeper than anywhere else.

"Sammy . . . fuck, I'm going to fill you up. I'm coming, I'm coming and coming, and I'm not going to ever stop!" Warm, thick seed flooded into her pussy. Everything was wet and slippery, my cock twitching with electric fire every single time more of my thick, pearly liquid left me for better pastures.

The sensation was majestic. In spite of my claim, I eventually stopped coming deep inside of her clenching walls. I watched as she shuddered again, biting her lip and tilting her face to the fading sun. She'd turned parts of the white shirt see-through with her perspiration.

Her weight held me down, but it was her—her very being—that kept me locked in place. Sammy's presence glued me to the present. I would have let her sit on me for hours . . . forever . . . if we wouldn't have starved.

Or the horses starved.

Or . . .

It wasn't feasible.

But I still wanted it.

Wincing, she stepped off of me. I thought her legs gave out, because she sat so quickly onto the grass on her bare ass, it didn't feel intentional.

Grabbing my clothes, I redressed with speed. Her panties were a few feet away; I threw them to her, waiting for her to hide her perfect ass away from the world. She remained where she was, wriggling into the garments and tucking her toes into her flats.

I hopped up, reaching down to help her stand. "Can you walk?"

"Of course." She laughed, scrutinizing me like I'd said something insulting. "I'm fine, the fall off the horse wasn't that bad."

"I meant, can you walk after being fucked so hard?"

Her grin was sly. Gripping my hand, she let me tug her onto her feet. "You're really full of yourself."

Pulling her close to me, I scraped my nose just across the outer edge of her ear. "The same could be said about you five minutes ago."

Her waver of pleasure came and went. She pushed her lips together, disengaging and putting a foot between us. "Every counter I have, you'll just turn it into something dirtier."

"Is that so bad?" Reaching for Knight, I said, "Let's get out of here."

Poised where she was, just inches from the flattened grass we'd lost ourselves in, Sammy scanned the black horse as if he was a loaded rifle. "You're taking me back to the mansion?" She didn't try to hide her disappointment.

I motioned Rosel closer. The horse trotted my way, her agitation vanishing with a few nose rubs. "Yes. But only so we can get my bike. I'd rather take you out of here on something other than horseback. It'll be easier on your bruised ass."

Her shocked delight was almost as good as making her writhe with pleasure.

Almost.

Helping her onto Rosel, I slid my palm down the outside of her thigh. The way she jerked was a reminder of the contagious heat between us. "You're really going to help me?" she asked.

"Is it that shocking?"

Sammy looked over my head and toward the mansion in the distance. "I assumed your father had a hold over you. He wants me to stay on lockdown here."

Her observation made me flinch. I loathed the idea of anyone thinking I was under someone's thumb, especially my father's. "Let him get pissed. It's only a little ride."

I'd always look back on that moment—the way her green eyes bloomed with the first flicker of her appreciation for me. Sammy never looked more beautiful than when she was seeing the good inside of people . . .

The good inside of a rash idiot like me.

It was a powerful, wonderful memory.

One of my favorites.

I couldn't have guessed that I'd need it to survive the guilt brought on by the consequences of my arrogant actions.

- CHAPTER FIFTEEN -

KAIN

It wasn't hard to leave the estate.

But it was hard not to be seen.

As we pulled out of the driveway, I was sure someone would notice us. It didn't matter now, though; that was a problem for Future Kain. Present Kain was happily flying down the road with a cute girl clinging to his body, enjoying the afterglow of the rough sex he'd gotten to indulge in.

Hurrah for Present Kain.

Sammy had been delighted by my offer. I was dumb for making it, but I couldn't take it back, not now. Seeing her so depressed and knowing I could relieve even *some* of that pain . . . I couldn't have done anything else but help.

When I squeezed my motorcycle's handlebars, I imagined the glittery heels that had recently been dangling there. When I'd arrived home after visiting the Dirty Dolls yesterday, I'd taken them inside with the clear plan of handing them back to Fran. What use did I have for pre-worn wedding shoes?

Instead, I'd passed by her room and tucked the glittery heels away in mine.

Somehow, I couldn't give them up.

Maybe I need to see a therapist, I mused to myself. *Isn't this how freaky shrines with locks of hair get built?* I'd figure out what to do with the damn things later. After all, I'd found my Cinderella; she was clinging onto my muscled torso with all her might.

The apartment complex was an easy drive. Last night, I'd parked out of view so no one would report a suspicious man hanging around, peeping on the elderly. With Sammy here, I drove into a wide-open spot and cut the engine.

She climbed down quickly, straight-up running over the asphalt and jumping the steps to one of the doors on the motel-like building. I caught up to her just in time to hear her knocking rapidly. "Mom?" Sammy asked, testing the knob—she had no keys, but the door swung inward with ease. "Hey! Mom! Are you okay? Mom!"

I'd only peeked into the windows last night—just to make sure the woman was in bed and alive. Seeing the place in the full light of a few tea-leaf-brown lamps, I wondered where I was supposed to sit. Everything was cramped and covered with papers or books.

An older woman with hair far longer than Sammy's leaned into the main room. Small glasses were balanced on her nose. "You're the one who's late, give me a moment, I was just going through my planner—oh!" she squeaked, looking me up and down. "And who's this sexy beast!"

Sammy went from relieved to uncomfortable, all in a single second. "Mom, no—Mom."

Grinning madly, I made an exaggerated point of taking the older woman's hand and kissing the back of it with a deep bow. "Kain Badd, at your service."

When I stood back up, she was staring at me like she'd seen a ghost. I barely had a chance to process what I'd done wrong before that look was gone, replaced by a sweet and firm smile. "Nice to meet you. I'm Jean, but you can call me Mom."

"Jean is more fitting," I said politely. "You don't look like any moms I know." Inside, I was consumed with wonder over what had turned her skin so pale—well, paler, anyway. The woman didn't look exactly healthy.

Wincing, she eased onto the couch. "This is why I didn't see you this morning, hm? New boyfriend? The one you said wasn't going to work out?"

Sammy's jaw kept going lower. "Mom—"

"It's fine, it's fine!" She waved her hand by her cheek. "The guy is living man candy. I know you always had a sweet tooth."

Okay. I adored this woman.

"No reason to lie," I said, scooping an arm around Sammy's waist. "Jean is right. Sorry for stealing your daughter away."

Sammy was the brightest shade of crimson. Glancing at me, she said through her teeth, "I'll try not to make a habit of being late again. Maybe Kain can help me with that."

Her meaning was obvious. *She wants me to break her out of the estate again.* Right then, I might have promised to do it for her. I was sure my father would be upset, but Sammy and her mother . . . I could *feel* the love between them.

How could I choose to step between that?

Jean sat there with her head in her hands. "This is nice. So nice." She eyeballed me, saying sweetly, "So you met the other day, hm? How long until I get some of those grandbabies I've been wishing for?"

"Mom!"

The rest of the visit went like that; Sammy enduring her mother's jokes and me encouraging them with all my energy. As much as she blustered, Sammy was obviously having a great time.

I gave the older woman a hug good night—noting how she blatantly squeezed my ass. "So that's where your daughter gets it," I mumbled.

She just winked and cackled, shutting the door after a quick cheek kiss for Sammy.

Following Sammy down to the parking lot, I chuckled softly. "She's nice." When I looked up the stairs at the complex, I said, "I guess your dad wasn't the only one to teach you good manners."

"She's nicer now. Before she got sick, and before Dad passed, she was a little harder to deal with. She *hated* me going off to New York—she'd never say it to my face, but it was obvious when she never came to visit."

"People change." *Though not always for the better.* Thinking about Costello and Francesca brought a stab of sadness.

Climbing onto the motorcycle, Sammy lifted her helmet but hesitated before putting it on. "You know, it'd be a shame to go straight back."

Blinking, I made a face. "Oh, yeah?"

The edges of her mouth curled up. "Definitely. There's this ice cream place right around the corner. Really delicious, but they're only open on Thursdays, and . . . well, who knows when we'll be back here."

Starting the bike, I climbed on. "If you want ice cream, just ask nicely."

Her arms came around, linking on my belt and hugging me against her. Tenderness flowed through the heat of her body. Over the rumble of the engine, she whispered into my ear. Each breath made my heart thump quicker. "Can we *please* get ice cream?"

The urge to bend her over the seat and take her right here was overwhelming. My mind was whirling with the image of those whispering lips curling around the tip of my rock-hard cock.

Did she *know* how sexy she was?

Reaching down, I grabbed her right hand. Sammy squeezed back, a romantic gesture. That was nice. You know what was nicer? When I slid her palm down, making her feel my dick as it strained to escape my jeans.

"Holy shit," she gasped into my ear.

A sharp tingle rolled up my spine. Her honest exclamation was plain erotic. It also wasn't doing much for making me want to take her to get ice cream. *We'll have time for more fun later.* She'd be living with me for who knew how long.

I had a hunch we'd be taking advantage of that.

Fighting down my animal urge to rail her with my cock, I revved my motorcycle. "Put your helmet on," I said, the headlights setting the lot on fire. "There's only one cure for a massive hard-on."

"What's that?" she asked, teasing at my zipper like a damn succubus.

When I slammed the gas, propelling us forward, I clamped my hand on her arm to make sure she didn't fly off the bike. "Driving like a madman!" I shouted, the mechanical roar starting to blur my voice. "Fear of death is pretty good at making you focus on something beyond sex!"

"Ice cream isn't worth splattering on the road!" she laugh-screamed.

"Sorry," I shouted back. "I can't hear you when I ride like this!"

"What?" she cried.

Grinning, I raced into the encroaching night. I wasn't entirely lying to Sammy, but she seemed to believe me, because she stopped talking and instead just pointed to guide me to the ice cream shop.

It was quaint and small, mostly empty as well. Parking the bike, I pulled my helmet off. Next, I twisted and watched as she tugged hers away. Sammy stared at me with pink cheeks and glittering eyes, yet the centers were the sort of stillness you found on a lake just before a fish jumped to break the serenity.

"What's wrong?" I asked urgently.

She shook her head in a slow rhythm. "Nothing. I just haven't been here in a . . . really long time."

Her meaning was too grim for my liking. Lifting her off of the bike, I ignored her startled shout. It took some manhandling, but I managed to get her onto me, piggyback-style. "What are you doing? Kain!" she blurted, laughing in embarrassment at the attention we were drawing.

Stepping up to the outside window, I coughed politely. I didn't need to, of course; the attendant was giving us both all of her attention. "Hi there," I said, wincing as Sammy tugged at my hair and groaned. "I'll take a rocky road cone and—what do you want, princess?"

Covering her face, Sammy groaned some more.

"Come on," I said, smirking so all my teeth showed. "Tell the nice lady."

Sammy mumbled, "Abaniwacphone."

"Say again?" I chuckled.

"A vanilla cone!"

"There," I said, nodding at the wide-eyed woman taking our order. "That's all."

The attendant darted her eyes between us. "Um. Okay. That'll be ten fifty."

Wordlessly, I juggled my wallet out. It was an impressive feat. My card flicked onto the tiny counter, the solid black shape telling the world how much money I had at my disposal.

The woman eyeballed it, two fingers sliding it under her window. With a final stare between it, me, then Sammy, she hurried to make our ice cream.

"I hate you," Sammy whispered above me.

Squeezing her thighs, I turned my jaw enough to nip playfully at her knee. "I think you mean you adore me, sugar."

Our cold treats came quickly. I like to imagine they worked extra fast when they saw my fancy credit card. Patiently, I waited for Sammy to take the two cones. Then, I winked at the attendant, took my card in my teeth, and strode over to a free bench in front of the shop.

There was space inside, but I wanted to be alone.

Kneeling lower, I grunted as Sammy climbed over my head. It was mildly uncomfortable, but I *did* get nice and close to her delicious ass, so who was I to complain? She offered me my cone; I took it, quickly licking at some of the melting spots. "Huh, this is good."

"Told you," she said, sitting on the bench. Her eyes were low, focused on her snack as she kicked one foot like a giddy kid. She didn't say it out loud, but I was sure I'd cheered her up with my ridiculous actions.

"So," she said, wagging the ice cream side to side. "Is 'Badd' the normal surname for a rich, famous, and *oh-so-royal* family?"

Laughing in my throat, I said, "No. My father came here a long while ago. He didn't want to fight with his family back in his home country over who would rule there. Our actual last name is different." Going over-the-top with my enunciation, I said, "*Kain Fredrickson.* Less of a ring to it than Badd, if you ask me."

"Huh. How'd he get away with changing that?"

"He was always rich, but my mother . . . she's part of the Cassava family. They're wealthy as well, but she gave him a lot of connections in this state. Together, they've got power, and power can make hiding your identity very easy." On reflex, I touched my ribs where the crown tattoo was.

She watched me intently, her eyes glinting. "Francesca told me about that ink you all have."

Ice cream dripped onto my leg; I wiped it away quickly. "Did she really?" *Fucking hell, Sis.* What were secrets worth these days?

"I guess it's one way to make sure you remember your history, if you don't have your last name to track it back."

Shrugging, I threw the last bit of waffle cone at a nearby can. It bounced off the rim, falling inside. "It's a silly tradition, not one worth fighting."

Sammy looked like she wanted to say something. Instead, she licked the cold vanilla in her hands and went quiet.

We perched on that bench for some time. The quiet was comfortable—thoughtful. Both of us had a lot to weigh and measure when it came to what we were doing.

I looked down at her. The top of her head was at my shoulder, her eyelashes downcast and creating gentle shadows on her cheeks. "Are you okay?" I asked.

She smiled to herself. "Yeah. I mean—yeah. I think I'm just enjoying this more than I expected to." Hopping off the bench, she wiped sticky palms on her trousers.

"Don't be so shocked, I'm a super fun guy." Grinning, I followed her to the bike. Sammy gathered herself as if she was going to tease me in return. Instead she just climbed onto the motorcycle, hiding under the helmet wordlessly.

Settling in front of her, I had to wonder . . .

Was she hiding from me?

The drive back was faster somehow. Probably because I didn't want it to end. I had an awful sense that something was coming, and to avoid it, I just had to keep riding. It was getting dark, my headlights illuminating the way. Pulling through the gates, I kept going, pushing a button on my keys to make the garage open.

Inside, I guided my bike to a corner away from the other vehicles. Throwing down the kickstand, I turned to say . . . something. Sammy met me there, her mouth hungry and tasting like vanilla.

"Thanks," she said, breaking away. "For everything. Tonight was nice."

"Nice?" I teased. My hand slid up her knee. "I don't think that's the right word."

Pushing me away, she hopped down, but she didn't leave. Looking up at me so that the glaring white bulbs lit up her face, she said, "I'm serious. Thank you."

I readied another joke. "You're welcome." That wasn't what was supposed to come out.

She rocked on her heels, smiling as she backed up to the inner door. "I'll go upstairs. Real sneaky-like, so no one sees me."

My shrug was barely there. "They know we left. You can't trick them."

Sammy froze, her hand on the exit that connected the garage to the main house. "Wait, if you knew they'd find out, why did you take me?"

"I didn't want to see you sad." It was such a simple answer to a complicated situation.

Blushing, she ducked her head. "That's not your problem."

"It shouldn't be," I said somberly. "But it is."

On quick feet, she hurried my way again. Her movements were fast, but this time I wasn't caught off guard. Sammy stood on tiptoe, kissing me sweetly. It wasn't wet and raw, it wasn't meant to make my cock jump to attention, and it still did.

I'd never been kissed like that in all my life.

Scurrying away like she was worried she couldn't stop herself if she didn't abandon our kiss right then, she opened the door. Light slid in through the crack, turning her face into two halves; partly angelic, partly cool blue shadow. "Night." She vanished into the house and out of sight.

Touching my mouth, I shivered. *This girl is going to ruin me.*

Counting a full three minutes, I slid out of the garage. I'd figured I could avoid anyone this way. After all, it was pretty late. Everyone else should have been in bed or settling in. Whatever problems would arise from my decisions, they could come in the morning.

My father was waiting for me in the mudroom.

Ah, shit-tits.

The deep lines in his forehead gave away his fury. "What the hell were you thinking?"

I stuck my hands in my jacket. "You told me to get her anything she needed. She *needed* to go see her mother." I started to shove past him; his hand slammed into my chest, sending me back into the wall.

"You think it was smart to bring her out of the estate?" he asked. The anger burned low in his eyes. "If someone was following you, you led them right to her mother. How was that helping anyone?"

I swayed forward, our chests bumping. "No one would have to worry about that if you'd let us do something about Brick Monroe."

"Like what, kill him?"

My eye twitched. "Punish him. Make it clear he can't go after anyone he wants without consequences."

"Do you know why he attacked Sammy in the first place?"

My veins throbbed—I struggled for an answer.

He said, "Son, look at me." With reluctance I did. "I suspected the Deep Shots from the start. Ever since they changed leadership, they've become . . . reckless. What matters now is learning their motives. If they want to make a move to take us out, and she's somehow part of that . . ."

"You want to use her as *bait*?"

His nose became a row of grooves. I worried he might hit me—and that wasn't something he'd ever done. Lowering his hands to his sides, he breathed out like a dragon in its den. "Our family comes first. It's a shame you've forgotten that. I thought I could trust you to obey my rules. Apparently not."

"Rules," I said, rolling my eyes. "What are you going to do? Cut me off from our money? You can't hurt me, and I'm not some snot-nosed kid you can ground in his room anymore."

I was getting puffed up—cocky. I was positive he could do nothing to me.

Maverick was contemplating something. I watched him size me up, seeing how unimpressed I was with his threats. Half turning, he looked down the hall, toward the front stairs.

Toward Sammy.

"I can't trust you not to sneak her out again. I'll put someone else in charge."

My heart shriveled.

"And," he went on, "I don't trust *her* to listen to me, either. She's amazingly good at manipulating people."

"She didn't manipulate me! I—"

"You *what*?" he asked, fixing one cold eye on me. He dared me to say it. I didn't know what *it* even was. That I wanted her so bad that I'd risk getting in trouble with my own family?

That I cared for her?

That I . . .

My father was moving, his arms stone stiff beside him. Me and my brothers were gifted with his genetics, all of us tall and strong. But he was still larger, a man that would have looked more comfortable dragging a plow over a farm.

Or sitting on a gigantic throne.

"Stop," I hissed, following him up the stairs. "Where are you going?"

"I told you. I'm putting everyone's safety first."

"What the fuck does that mean?"

He knocked on Fran's door. Inside, I heard the chattering stop cold. Seconds later, my twin opened the door, blinking at us both. Behind her, Sammy sat on the floor in a pair of silky, two-piece, mint-green pajamas. "Uh, hi, Daddy. What's up?"

The girl I adored looked back at me with eyes that matched her outfit. Her smile was uncertain, failing the longer she realized that I wasn't even trying to look happy.

I'd been so fucking sure he could do *nothing* to me.

So sure . . .

That I'd forgotten he could do plenty to Sammy.

- CHAPTER SIXTEEN -

Sammy

"Where are you taking me?" My voice rose while I yanked frantically on the impossible vise that was Maverick's fist. He was pulling me easily through the mansion, both Fran and Kain close behind.

"Dad!" Francesca snapped, rushing toward my side. "Let her go! This is insane! *Daddy!*"

The tree of a man didn't even look at her.

My heels dug in; I skidded, close to falling, but Maverick righted me without even slowing a step. "Hey! Ha-ha, let's just talk about this like normal, non-dragging-girls-through-a-mansion kind of people!" In desperation, I twisted so violently my shoulder threatened to pop free. "Kain," I said, searching his face for some clue. "What's happening? Is this because you took me off the estate?"

Maverick ripped me around a corner. "Yes, you have my son to thank for what I'm being forced to do."

The scalding hate Kain aimed at the back of his father's head stunned me. "You don't have to do anything! You're overreacting!"

His father grunted, dismissing the accusation. "Sammy, I took you in to make sure nothing happened to you . . . and also to make sure you couldn't be used against us. You and my son seem to think that I'm joking around."

Our tiny parade was heading into a part of the house where I'd never been. The long walkway was flush with windows, the night sky peeking inside. Being forced along by muscle and fury, I actually thought that this place with its glowing white marble and angelic-halo lights couldn't hold back the darkness that Maverick Badd was burning with.

At the end of the hall, there was a door. It was deceptively simple, nothing about it should have scared me. Somehow I knew that if we reached that place . . . everything would end.

I would end.

My heart's rhythm was breaking down, the pattern erratic. "Hey—uh, wait! Just wait! I thought you said you liked me? Remember?" I tugged and tugged. "If you quit now, we can forget this whole thing! I'd like that—anyone else like that idea? No? Just me?"

Maverick's hand closed on the doorknob. His son's palm came down like a whip, clamping shut on top. Their fingers were pretzeled, the two men staring each other down. Sandwiched between, I was suffocating in their raw intensity.

"Kain," his father said softly. "Back off."

"I won't let you do this to her," he growled.

Do *what* to me?

"What's all of this?" The voice was flat; Costello stood in the hall behind us. His loose sweatpants hung off his slim hips, the top of his black boxers creeping above the lazily tied strings.

A tight, white shirt strangled his biceps, and though he was standing still, I had the impression that he was ready to jump into battle.

Maverick eyeballed his son. "Costello, come get your brother off of me."

The lighter-haired brother considered Kain, then his eyes crossed to where I was trapped between them. "Maybe you should explain what's going on here first."

"Fucking hell," Maverick spat. "Are all of you rebelling? I said get him away. Do as you're told."

There was a second when I met Costello's stare. His irises were sheer ice, but they weren't cruel. Why would he be sad? It didn't matter; quicker than a hummingbird's wings, the lean man slid his arms around Kain's neck.

"Shit—Costello!" Kain cried out, releasing his father to tangle with his attacker. The brothers wrenched away, Fran covering her mouth as she gawked along with me. Costello wasn't much bigger than Kain—I'd have said he was thinner, less muscular, if pressed for details.

Kain twisted, his torso showing as his shirt peeled higher. I saw every fiber under his skin flex. The two men tumbled against a wall, their impact reverberating through my teeth. I started to rush at them, hoping to get them to stop.

Taking advantage of the situation, Maverick opened the door and pulled me through.

Francesca had started to intervene with her brothers, but she must have thought my situation was worse, because she came after me instead. "Daddy! This is fucked up! What's wrong with you?"

"There's nothing wrong with me." Violently, he thrust me forward. "I'm doing what I have to, to keep everyone safe."

"This is your idea of safe?" I asked, stumbling away from him. My cynical laugh flew free. "Dragging me through your house and making your kids fight like some testosterone-fueled junkies?" I was going to say more . . . but I'd finally noticed where I was.

Flowers grew along the walls, weaving through the tiny holes to create hanging gardens. The ceiling was one big window, a peephole to the galaxies stretching above. Under my sock-clad feet, I saw I was standing on a plush, white rug. There was a large, round bed set in a corner, the gold blanket shiny—opulent.

I saw it as a private sanctuary for an emperor . . . or a queen.

How was this a punishment?

Then Maverick showed me a key. "This," he said, making sure I was listening, "is where you'll live for the rest of your stay, however long that may be."

"What? This one room?" I asked.

The man raised his eyes to the hallway, mine followed. Costello had his brother in a headlock so tight it had turned him purple. I started toward him in a panic; Maverick snatched my wrist again. "You're worried about him, aren't you?" he asked into my ear.

Bending away, I grimaced. "Of course I am!" My next shout was aimed at Costello. "How can you do that to your own brother? Let him go!"

Amazingly, Costello did. Kain dropped to the ground, hacking as he cupped his throat. The sight was awful. I struggled to get to him, but his father was an immovable object. This was too much; I felt a part of me snapping.

"Look at him," Maverick hissed at me. "If you care so much, how could you risk his life by making him take you off our property?"

"I *needed* to leave!"

"And I need people to listen to me so no one gets killed!" he roared.

Stunned, I stopped yanking at his tight grip. From the corner of my eye, I saw how horrified Fran looked. But . . . she didn't look surprised. *She's seen her father like this before*, I realized.

The big man took my shoulders, making me face him. "I had every intention of trusting you and Kain to follow my request. You didn't. Neither of you seems to get what's going on, how much danger we're all in. I care about this family, even if you don't."

"I *do* care," I insisted.

He went quiet. In my ears, Kain's dry coughing echoed. That sound rocked me with shame. My head was buzzing, making it too hard to decide which of Maverick's words were threats and which were advice. *Did I mess up? Is this my fault?*

Was Kain suffering because of *me*?

Letting me go, he walked out into the hall. "Costello," he said, handing over the key. "Take turns with Hawthorne. You're to make sure she never leaves this room."

Lightning exploded in my veins. "You're actually serious."

Costello stared at me for too long. Then he slid his eyes to Francesca. Something passed between them, a look that seemed to say, *This again?* It was the closest I'd seen them ever come to connecting.

Francesca spun away, her scowl beyond severe.

Costello closed his fingers on the key. "All right." Bending down, he helped Kain to his feet.

The other brother shoved him off, stepping back to glare at everyone except for me. "You're going to literally lock her up, and you think I'll allow that?"

"What will you do?" his dad asked quietly. "Fight all of us and flee away into the night? You'd tear this family apart for a stranger?"

"She isn't—" Kain cut himself off. "Yes. I'd fight everyone in the whole fucking world to make sure she didn't have to suffer through your perverse ideas of safety like the rest of us have. You haven't learned a damn thing from the past."

I was so overwhelmed by the full-body throb that fought with my growing pit of ice that I didn't consider the implication that this had happened before. *He'd fight his own blood . . . for me?* The thrill of that admission was crushed by my morbid guilt.

I saw it in my mind's eye: the suffering, the tears—the pain.

I saw how they faced off now, already acting like enemies.

I saw their family photo, all the genuine, unguarded smiles.

And I saw my mother standing in front of the empty casket belonging to my father.

"No." One by one, they all looked at me. But I only looked at Kain. "Don't fight your own family. I don't want to see anyone getting hurt because of me."

He took a step my way. "Sammy."

Lifting a hand to ward him off, I turned toward Maverick. "If you want me to stay in here, I'll do it. Just don't punish Kain because of what he did for me."

Pain rippled through Kain's frown. Ignoring everyone, he stalked my way, grabbing me up in his arms. I was lost in his touch, blown away by his open display of affection. This man, he didn't care at all what anyone thought.

And he'd said *I* was the tough one?

His lips found mine, the kiss too brief. "I'll get you out of here," he promised to me, so quiet no one else could hear.

I smiled indulgently, but I had no response.

- CHAPTER SEVENTEEN -

Sammy

A white horse circled me, letting me pet its side. It was all I could see, but that was fine; it was all I wanted to see. Under my touch, it was silver and gold, and then it was nothing but black.

"Sammy!"

My father's voice rang in my ears. Every time I tried to turn to see him, the horse would get in the way again. Fur became darkness; I couldn't even see my feet. Where was I? What was this?

The voice in my ears called again. I knew it was him, and that hurt deeper than any cut, because the voice of the dead can bring nothing but pain. My father was gone; I'd lost him. I'd come to terms with that.

And there he was, waving at me from the other side of the field. Stables white as clean sand stood tall behind him. *White Rose Farms.* I was a kid again, smiling as I trotted on the horse between my knobby knees.

Faces blurred around me; it was too hard to focus on any of them. Bit by bit, I urged my horse forward. I wanted to get closer to my dad, but the animal didn't care. I was bobbing in place, going nowhere.

"Dad!" I shouted.

It was all too real. Was this a dream or a memory?

A figure much bigger than any man should ever be came into the frame. He nearly swallowed my father whole, all by doing nothing but standing near him. I didn't remember this part. I didn't know any of this.

My dad looked away from me . . . and his frown was lower than the dirt.

I'd never seen that, either. Or had I?

They were talking. Whatever was being said, it made my father clench his fists and look back at me. He caught me watching, the raw determination in his stare stunning me cold.

"Careful," a voice said beside me.

When I looked, it was a young boy on a stark-midnight stallion. His dimples showed when he grinned, his blue eyes so saturated they blew out all the other colors in the world.

He thumbed his nose. "That horse is real big, can you even ride it?"

"Sammy!"

Desperately I urged my horse toward my father. What was he so scared of? Nothing scared him; I'd never seen him afraid. Not once.

The next time someone called my name, it came from my right. "Sammy," Kain said, and it was him, fully him, sitting tall astride the same horse he'd chased me down with on his estate. His fear matched my father's, a perfect mirror. "Sammy," he shouted, though his lips hardly moved. "Wake up."

Gasping, I sat up in the grand, golden bed. Sweat made my nightshirt cling to me. It took a bit for me to calibrate where I was. *My own sweet, terrible, private, and oh, did I mention terrible room.*

Thumping back onto the pillow, I stared straight up at the burning orange sunrise through the circular ceiling window.

"Sure," I said out loud to myself. "I may be trapped in the bowels of a giant mansion while powerful people decide what's best for me and my business rots to shit and my mother risks falling in her tub until she starves to death . . . but at least I have a great view."

My attempt to make myself laugh didn't work. *Mom.* Surely she was fine. I'd seen her just last night. I already itched to hear her voice again.

I decided that would be the first thing I'd ask for. As soon as someone showed up—*Wait. Wait, wait.* My eyes shot to the door. *Someone is supposed to be guarding me.* No matter who it was, surely they'd have a phone.

Tossing the blanket aside, I pushed my toes onto the soft rug. I didn't need any lights to see where I was, but I still shuffled toward the switch, flicking it so that the round room was lit brightly by the recessed lighting.

It was a little cold; I detoured briefly, digging through the wardrobe in the tiny hallway that led to my private bathroom. Every article of clothing was brand-name, well-made. Why would they keep so many nice things in here? Who had used this room before me?

I grabbed a long, thick cardigan, wrapping it around myself.

Satisfied that I was less vulnerable—and much warmer—I tiptoed to the door. On this side, the handle was like something from another time, surrounded by scrawling metalwork.

Wriggling the knob, I could barely get it to tick from side to side; locked, of course.

I cleared my throat. "Hey."

No answer.

I need to be louder. Bracing myself, I knocked on the door. It felt ridiculous to do that while I was *inside*. "Hey! Hey, open up! Mayday! Help! Fire!" I was starting to shout increasingly drastic stuff, but I needed someone to open the damn door.

It slid inward, making me retreat a step. Costello stared back at me—had he even slept? "Are you okay?" he asked, peering over my shoulder.

"I need to make a phone call."

His piercing eyes focused on me. "Excuse me?"

"Phones. You use them to talk to people miles and miles away? No? You've never seen them? Crazy devices, they—"

"Stop. I get it." Digging into his sweatpants, he tugged out a fancy smartphone. Before he gave it up, he narrowed in on me so fiercely I *felt* it. Costello's stare was as good as a shot of espresso, I was all jittery now, my eyes aching in their sockets. "Who are you calling?"

"It's just my mom." At this point, my mother was no longer a secret from the Badds. My palm went flat, ready for the phone. "I'm assuming you're trying to make sure I won't call the cops. Out of curiosity, how would you even stop me?"

"I don't need to stop you. I can tell you won't do it."

My heart took an extra beat. "How?"

His shrug was light, a poor excuse for an explanation. "I can just tell. Do you want the phone or not?"

"I do." Plucking it from his grip, I ran my thumb along the edge. "And . . . thanks."

He studied me and studied me until I shifted side to side with unease. Costello had a way of looking at you that made you feel like you were naked. Not just your bare skin, I mean down to your bleached bones—to your hidden, inner emotions.

I relaxed a hair when he glanced at the room behind me. He tracked his eyes from one curved edge to the next. "It was always a little cold down here, even in summer. I'll make sure the heat is turned up."

"You say that like you've spent time here," I said carefully.

Costello didn't respond, he just ducked his head and shut the door.

Fuck, I thought to myself. *What does it take to get a guy like him to open up?* I was incredibly curious about him. For now, I had other things to work on.

Scurrying to my bed, I sat lotus-style on top of it. Costello's phone was warm—strange, considering how his blue eyes and pale skin made him the personification of frost. Quickly I tapped the screen, calling my mother like I'd said I would.

He's really so sure I won't call the cops? It was probably obvious that I wouldn't. I'd chosen to stay in here to keep Kain from doing anything rash, and involving the authorities would create the perfect environment for tension and nullify my decision.

Yeah, that's all—it's just logical I wouldn't bother. I liked that better than thinking Costello could read me like a damn book.

"Hello?" My mother's voice was chipper—she always woke up at the ass crack of dawn.

Pushing a smile onto my face to make sure I, too, sounded happy, I said, "Hey! Hi, hi! Morning!"

"Sammy! This is a surprise. You never call so early."

"Uh-huh. I figured I'd remember what the sun looks like, is all." Chuckling, I leaned back on my pillows. The sky above was starting to gain a pink-and-blue tint. "How are you?"

"Good, good. You saw me last night, not much has changed."

Oh, a lot has changed, I thought dryly. "Right. I know, I just thought I'd check in anyway."

"Honey, is everything okay?"

"Sure! It's great! Why wouldn't it be?" On impulse, I glanced at my locked door.

She made a tiny noise. "What are you not telling me?"

Moms didn't have telepathic powers that I didn't know about, did they? "Uh. Nothing." Sitting up quickly, I struggled to change the topic.

My mother was much faster. "That boy last night."

"'Boy?'" I had to giggle. "Kain Badd, you mean."

"What a name," she said, a little softer than I understood. "What do you think of him?"

My jaw fell open, I saw it in the reflective surface of the metal trellis to my left. "I don't know. He's . . . loud?"

That made her laugh, and that soothed some of my nerves. "Is he nice to you?"

Thinking about how he'd fought tooth and nail with his own brother and father last night, I leaned into the phone. "Nice enough. Why are we talking about him?"

"I was just curious. I didn't expect you to show up with someone last night. Especially not . . ." Whatever she was going to say, she stopped and recovered. "He rides a motorcycle. It's very loud."

I lowered my voice. "Now *you're* not telling me something."

"I'm not hiding anything, Sammy."

"That means you are!"

She scoffed, then I heard her shuffling around. Her couch was notoriously loud. "If you were in any trouble, you'd tell me, right?"

Tiny palpitations attacked my heart. "Yes. Always." It never, *ever* feels good to lie to your mother.

Whether or not she believed me, I could tell she was smiling when she spoke again. "I should go. It's time for my pills. Will you come by again soon?"

The heartbeats got bigger, longer. "I'll . . . try. Work is crazy, you know, and . . ."

"Right, right. Well, you just swing by when you want. Don't put things aside for me, I'm fine."

I didn't believe that at all. "You got it. I love you, Mom."

"Love you too—oh, the mail is here. Bye, honey!" The line clicked, the cell phone going black in my hand. I fingered the device, almost depressed at the idea of giving it up.

What was she about to tell me? It bugged me that she'd been dodging around something. *Maybe she just didn't like Kain.* That wasn't hard to believe. Though she'd acted very friendly with him.

There was noise outside my door; voices. Blinking, I stepped toward it, my fingers hovering by the handle. Who was Costello talking to?

The knob jiggled, Kain entering the threshold with a disgruntled expression. When he saw me, he pulled up short, his eyes flickering with too many emotions for him to snatch them all back.

Behind him, Costello stood tall. "You've got a visitor."

"I can see that," I said, working through the initial wave of delight. Seeing Kain was better than any sunrise.

He swept me into his arms, a tight weave of his biceps and seeking fingers. It was as if he couldn't stop touching me, his need to explore and make sure every part of me was still here after being locked away overnight.

"Are you okay?" he asked into my ear.

Inhaling his pine-tree smell, I sighed. "I'm pretty good now, yeah."

Kain cradled my face, looking into my eyes to make sure I wasn't lying. "Dammit. This is all a huge mess because of me."

"No. It's my fault. I was the one who wanted to break out of here. You didn't have to let me."

"Of course I did." Kissing my brow, he breathed me in.

"I shouldn't have asked you. I should've found my own way out."

That made him chuckle. "You're so confident that you could have."

"I'm pretty resourceful. Things tend to work out for me." Waving around the room, I let the bitterness swim through my words. "I mean, check it out. I managed to get a beautiful, private suite fit for a queen, and all to myself."

I regretted my joke when I saw how he grimaced. "If I hadn't challenged Maverick, maybe he wouldn't have gone this far," he said.

Costello spoke up from the doorway. "You're right. It's not like you couldn't guess what he'd do if you stood up to him."

"Are you still here?" Kain shot back.

"I need my phone," he said calmly.

Tapping Kain's shoulder, I slid away. He clung to me, not willing to lose contact for a second. Stretching out, I held the phone out to his brother. "Thanks again."

He took it, the device vanishing away. "I'll leave you two alone." Before he left, he stared pointedly at Kain. "Don't do anything stupid. Please."

"I'll consider the warning." He chuckled. Alone with me, he brushed his fingers through my bedhead. "You could have used my phone again."

"I know, but I didn't know when I'd see you."

Pain dashed the heat in his eyes into pieces. "You thought I wouldn't come here immediately?"

"I didn't even know if you *could*." No one had explained the details of my imprisonment. Not beyond that I'd be guarded and couldn't leave. "Your dad seemed really pissed. For all I knew, he'd want to keep us apart."

"He couldn't if he wanted to." His hands clasped mine. "But he doesn't want to. He's just wrapped up in what he thinks is best. Costello is right, I should have known he could do this if he was pushed too far. In hindsight, this isn't a surprise."

My forehead creased tightly. "This has happened before, hasn't it?" The threads of evidence were all around me, I just needed to find the needle to stitch it all together.

"I really, *really* don't want to talk about that." Forcefully, he guided me toward the bed. "Is it awful that I just want to hold you against me until we forget about this damn mess?"

I wanted to say I couldn't forget it. Instead, I let him pull me onto the blankets. "Is this how you handle your bad moods? You just cuddle a girl?"

"Nope." Tugging me against his warm body so that we were spooning, he said against the back of my neck, "It has to be a beautiful girl. That's the secret."

He stroked the outside of my arm, the cardigan sliding down until he removed it completely. I was waiting for him to try and work me up—this man had a libido like no other—but . . . he never did.

Kain wrapped us in his arms and the blankets, and as the sun rose above and the world woke around us, we curled together like puzzle pieces left behind in the box. Alone like this, the bigger picture didn't matter at all.

He really did want to just hold me. Every time I thought I understood Kain Badd . . .

I learned something new instead.

Time came and went. Not just that morning, but in general for me. I had the window to tell me when day ended, I also wasn't without consistent meals or company. The family was treating me like a guest who just happened to be locked away.

What was most terrible was how I kept justifying that this was okay.

But fuck, that repeating image of Kain being strangled, of his father's cryptic words, it had left me with so much doubt. I'd been very close with my parents. It hadn't always been easy, sure—is it ever?—but I relished our little unit.

My dad was gone often; he worked as an independent landscaper, so his jobs were all over. In spite of that, for most of my life, money was there, we were comfortably middle class. The only time money came up was when he pulled me from riding, explaining that it was just beyond what we could afford.

I'd been distraught . . .

But I'd forgiven him.

After he'd passed, my mother began to fall ill. They were like two lovebirds; she was lost without him, and I was so busy with my new job I couldn't return to keep her company. All the money he'd squirreled away—and there was a good chunk—ended up being spent on my mother's health. I often wondered if quitting sooner and moving back here would have prevented some of her fading strength.

I loved them both so much. My father had taught me that family takes care of family.

How could I sit by and watch Kain throw his family away just for me? How could I watch him shed blood with his family for *me*? I couldn't.

I wouldn't.

So time passed. I'd call my mother here and there, I'd claim work was just filling my time, and I'd often send Kain to check in to make sure she was all right. The nights he wasn't with her, he was here—sleeping in the bed I was forced to see every single day. We'd tangle our bodies together, we'd watch the stars and the sun as they crossed the sky.

It all blurred together, so much of it the same.

Until one night it changed.

In a small way, but it changed.

Lying on the pillows, I realized how Kain was looking at me. It was the same look I'd glimpsed on our first night together, that real brand of tenderness no hookup should ever create.

And as I faded away, I had the funniest thought.

That's what a man in love looks like.

- CHAPTER EIGHTEEN -

Sammy

A torrent of envelopes rained down onto the table, some of them sticking to the side of the pancakes I'd been about to eat.

"Look out below," Kain said, standing over me with a smile.

Lifting an envelope, I stared at him dubiously. "Usually you're supposed to say that before you drop things on someone. What is all this?"

"It's the mail from your shop."

Perking up, I stacked everything neatly. I'd been at the estate for over two weeks now. Most of it had been spent inside of this beautiful excuse for a prison. It had its upsides—my own bath, a nice fresh smell from the flowers, books to read, and all the stars at night I could count.

Oh . . . and I was lucky enough that no one stopped Kain from seeing me.

Getting kissed under the stars—even through a window—was pretty amazing.

Regardless, being stuck as I was, I couldn't see my mother or run my business. Kain had returned my purse and phone to me, which did help some; I could call her freely, but it was clear she doubted my reasons for not stopping by.

Blaming work was a shaky lie, it wasn't keeping me busy at all. It was a mixed blessing that Fran's wedding had ended so abruptly. No one was blogging or gabbing about the dress she'd worn—the one I'd made. That meant I didn't have the explosion of business I really needed . . . and it also meant I didn't have to field calls about dresses I couldn't make because I wasn't able to get to work.

Kain's father wasn't going to let me go anywhere.

In a last-ditch effort to not lose everything, I'd given Kain my bridal shop key, asking him to collect my mail.

And . . . he'd done it.

"There's a lot of stuff," he said.

Frowning, I started digging through the pile. Most of the stack consisted of bills. Kain saw too many for me to bother hiding them. "What?" I finally asked. "Is it that shocking?"

Dropping into a chair beside me, he pulled one of the envelopes closer. "When Fran and I went to your shop that first time, it looked like you were doing really well."

"Appearances." I shuffled another bill aside. "They say if you act rich, you'll become rich." *It almost worked, too. Maybe the police will still turn those checks over to me someday.*

"If it helps, after seeing what you did in such a short time for us, I think you're one hell of a wedding planner."

That had me smiling helplessly. I almost shoved a small, white envelope in with the rest, but at the last second, I saw the name on it. *This is* . . . Peeling it open, I pulled the photos into the light. They weren't even all the way out before I was shaking.

Hazel looked beautiful in her wedding dress. It fit her perfectly—of course it did, I'd made it—but it was her smile that really made her glow. She was standing in front of a man dressed as Elvis, her husband grinning in a mismatched blue-and-tan suit.

It was easily the trashiest wedding photo I'd ever seen.

I *loved* it.

"Whoa, hey, you okay?" Kain asked me.

I couldn't answer, I was so overwhelmed. *She looked so happy.*

There was a knock at the door. I heard someone outside talking—was Costello on guard duty or Hawthorne? When the chatting continued, I knew it had to be Fran and Hawthorne. She never talked to Costello beyond a few blunt sentences.

Heels clicked through the door, Francesca swaying into my prison. Mic followed her closely. She said, "I was going to ask if you wanted breakfast, but it looks like someone else brought it to you." She leaned over my shoulder. "Wow. That's got to be the *worst* wedding I've ever seen!"

Heat burned up to my ears.

"Are they seriously in Vegas! Ha-ha, wow, who does that? Gawd, that's . . . Sammy? Are you *crying*?"

Wiping tears from my eyes, I folded the envelope. "No, of course not."

Kain touched my knee under the table. It was comforting, I sent him a quick smile.

Next to me, Frannie folded her arms. "I didn't mean to make you sad."

"I'm not sad. I'm happy." Sliding my chair back, I took a deep breath. "It just feels good to know Hazel got the wedding she'd always hoped for." How could I explain how I was feeling? I'd spent hours on that dress, and I'd given it all up just to keep Hazel from missing out on her big dream.

Mic made a tiny whimper. Lifting my head, I realized Francesca was looking at her feet. Her hair had fallen over her forehead, hiding most of her expression. It dawned on me that her silence wasn't because she was being snotty.

"Fran," I said, starting toward her.

Shaking her head, she forced out a loud, fake laugh. "What? Stop looking at me like I'm some little orphan on the side of the road." Mic whined again; she bent down, scooping him up. "He's hungry, I've gotta feed him before he throws a fit."

Faster than normal, she hurried from the room.

"Huh," Kain said. "What was that all about?"

Twisting the corner of the envelope, I watched the doorway she'd vanished through. "I'm so dumb. I was talking about happy weddings, not even considering how she must feel with how hers ended. She didn't even get to kiss the groom."

Slumping forward, he put his elbows on the table. "With everything going on, I forgot, too. I feel like a shit brother right now."

Tilting my chin high, I looked back at him. "Let's fix it."

"Fix it how? You're not supposed to leave this room."

Chewing my thumbnail, I started to smile. "Then let's get me out of here."

He chuckled. "I'd love to. Even if I did, I don't know how we'd fix Fran's mood. She wants a wedding, I wouldn't know where to begin."

Lifting my eyebrows, I winked. "Then aren't you lucky that you happen to know one hell of a wedding planner?"

We were lucky Costello wasn't guarding my room. Where he seemed to respect his father's requests, Hawthorne . . .

Hawthorne was a bit different.

Leaning on the wall outside my door, he just eyed me and Kain. "You want to leave?" He looked at the floor. "Fine, I don't see you."

"I—what?" I asked, stumbling on the words.

His eyes darted up to me, then to Kain. "The story is Costello let her leave, not me. And you'll owe me for this."

Grinning, Kain punched his brother lightly in the shoulder. "Fine with me."

It was too easy. It felt like a trap.

With Hawthorne humming loudly, I followed Kain down the hall. I didn't stop looking over my shoulder for a long while. He cupped my elbow, saying, "Relax. Thorne can be a dick, but he'll keep his word. What do we do about this wedding you want to throw?"

Breathing easier, I scanned the windows. "I need music, flowers, and Midas. Can you handle some of that?"

"I'll call him, he can get here easily. Flowers . . . I'll talk to Matilda."

I was relieved to know she was still working here after my horse-escape attempt. "Good call, she has the whole garden at her disposal."

Nodding, he pointed to a staircase. "There's a music room up there, third room on the right. You can find whatever you need."

He started to leave. Before he could, I took his hand, standing tall to kiss his warm mouth. Sparks danced into my belly, all from one dumb, little kiss. "Man," I whispered, watching him through half-shut eyes. "That never gets old."

Breathing in so deep his chest rubbed mine, he cradled my cheek. "Sammy, about you getting locked into that room, I—"

"Shh. It's fine."

"It's not. I'll figure something out."

I wasn't sure what to say. Kain thought he needed to break me free, but he was missing the real problem. Getting out of the room and off the property wasn't hard; I'd just been let free without any fanfare, I was sure Hawthorne would let it happen again if we asked.

Escape was pointless if Kain was left to deal with the repercussions.

Ever since Maverick had made me watch Kain gasping for air . . . writhing in pain . . .

I'd realized *that* was what I needed to prevent.

I didn't want to do anything that could put him at risk again. My new problem was choosing between protecting my mother and protecting him. There was no easy answer.

Maybe no answer at all.

The music room was exactly where Kain had said it would be. Wandering the huge room, I gazed up at the domed ceiling. There was a small stage, a giant bay window, and huge instruments all along the walls: a piano, a cello, and some things I couldn't identify.

What I was after was the wall of CDs. Walking toward it, I ran my fingers down the spines until I found a suitable choice for tonight. *Perfect!* Grabbing one that contained instrumentals, I grinned in delight. The CD player sitting on the nearby desk was the last thing I needed to make sure we'd have music tonight.

"And where are you going with all of that?"

The voice cut through to my core. No one should have a sword for a tongue, especially not one that could also make your heart sizzle. It was barely a relief that the source wasn't Maverick.

Hawthorne was sitting at the piano. I hadn't noticed him—had he stalked inside while I was looking away, had he been following me and Kain since the start?

Hugging the CD player tightly, I searched for where my voice had buried itself. "You scared me," I finally managed to say. Fuck, it had come out like a ragged squeak. "Why aren't you standing guard outside my room?"

Narrowing his liquid-coal eyes, the man rose gracefully. He had on dark jeans and a braided belt and a long-sleeved red shirt rolled up to his elbows. His patterns of ink cut off in a perfect line at his wrist; for a second, I'd thought he'd had on a second shirt.

He moved as lightly as fingers playing over a flute, approaching until he stood before me with his arms linking at the small of his back. "I asked you a question."

Flicking my stare down to the equipment in my grip, I said, "I need it for something important."

"Oh, well, then you can tell me what that is."

Hesitating, I considered my position. I didn't know Hawthorne well, but he *was* Fran's brother. It didn't make sense to cut him out of my surprise . . . and at the same time, he made me realize how he could help.

Gesturing with the CD player, I smiled. "Okay. But don't tell her. Tonight I want to surprise Francesca by finishing her wedding ceremony."

His eyebrows crinkled deeply. "Excuse me?"

"It's not fair that she didn't get to finish out her wedding. I want to fix that."

He stared at the items I was hugging. It was a long moment, so I was disarmed when he stabbed that fierce set of eyes back at me. I couldn't break away from them—did all these damn brothers have such haunting stares? "Are you sure she'll like being surprised?"

"I've got a hunch." My smile struggled to grow. "Now, I need to ask you a favor."

He straight-up laughed. *"Me?"*

I leaned toward him. "Tell your mom and dad to come to the gazebo around eight. They should be there when this goes down."

"What, don't want to waltz up and ask them yourself?"

"You know I'm not supposed to leave that room. I'm trying to mend things, not make them worse."

He considered me with his head angling to one side. "Fair enough."

"So . . . you'll ask them?"

Breathing in deeply, the dark-haired man looked at the ceiling. "My father will be furious . . . and there's a chance he'll know I let you out." His palm rubbed down his face. "*Why* did I agree to let you out again?"

"Something about wanting a favor from Kain."

"Right. Maybe he'll agree to take the beating good ol' Dad will want to give me, instead."

I ignored his sarcasm. "Just tell them. She'd like it better if they were there. Let Costello know, too."

"That definitely won't happen."

I'd started to walk away. Now I turned back. "Do you just like being difficult?"

"Yes." His grin split his handsome face. For a second, it was easy to see that he and Kain were brothers. "But I'm not being a dick. Costello and Fran . . . they don't get along. Didn't you realize?"

"She *is* weird with him, but . . ."

"Fran didn't invite him to her *first* wedding. Why would she want him at this half-cocked version?"

Now that he mentioned it, I hadn't seen Costello at the wedding *or* the dinner I'd organized. "He must have burned her pretty bad to get so ostracized."

Hawthorne glanced away. "In a way."

"Can you tell me what happened?"

"Not my place. Sorry." I didn't think he was sorry, but I didn't argue. I had enough on my plate, I wasn't ready to dive into more family politics.

Deciding the conversation was over, I walked toward the door. Hawthorne clasped my wrist, halting me so abruptly I stumbled. "Hey," he said, an uncertainty in his dark eyes that I hadn't seen before. "Why are you doing this?"

Pulling away, I asked, "What, helping Fran?"

"Not just that—you're asking for my father to be there to watch. He's locked you in a room for almost two weeks. I'd want to kick his nuts in, if I were you."

My head moved side to side. "Even if I did want to hurt him, Fran isn't part of that. No matter what he's done, she loves him, she'd want him there . . . and she deserves a happily ever after."

"A happily ever after," he mused. His angled brows crawled higher. "If I see my parents, I'll tell them to come by the gazebo tonight. No promises they will."

It might have been something in his pose, but I believed him. With a real smile on my lips, I said, "Thanks."

Hawthorne shrugged into his ears, acting like he didn't give a shit one way or the other.

I suspected he definitely did.

◆ ◆ ◆

Night came on too slowly. I was eager to make things happen.

Kain was helping me decorate the gazebo in the backyard. Matilda was on lookout, her job to warn us if Fran came anywhere near us before we wanted her to.

"You know," he said, hooking a light up on one of the tall beams. He reached it without stretching. "I think we've got one small problem."

I'd stopped working, too busy eating up the sight of him in his tight, white dress shirt that he'd left undone at the collar. Damn, he always looked delicious when he cleaned up.

He caught me staring; I looked away quickly. "What's the problem?"

"Well . . . don't we need a priest to officiate this thing?"

A private grin broke out on my face. "Let me tell you a funny story."

"Ha, all right." Leaning against the structure, he tied off another light. In the growing evening, the balls blinked like tiny fairies.

Tossing some flowers I'd pilfered from the garden over the beams, I flicked a loose twig away. "Few years ago, I decided to go to New York—design school and all. Wanted to show the world what I could do." *That feels so long ago now.* It was a bubble where my father still lived and my mother was still healthy.

Walking down memory lane made my stomach flip, especially when I thought about going for ice cream with Kain. As we'd sat there eating, I'd looked into the store at all the happy families . . . and I'd actually thought that I'd seen my father.

It was impossible, and still, that moment had stayed with me.

But he was dead.

No one came back from dead.

Shaking off the trickle of black mood, I tied off another vine. "My friends wanted to take me out before I left town. We . . . went a little wild."

"You've got my attention."

Stringing up the last of the long ivy vines, I said, "The short of it is that things got a little crazy."

"Oh-ho," he chuckled. "This is getting even better. Tell me this is going to end with you kissing some chick." Kain inched closer to me, eager for more of my story.

Rolling my eyes, I picked a leaf off of his head. "It ends with me filling out a form online."

His blank stare said he wasn't impressed. "Your definition of crazy and mine are miles apart."

"Shh. The point is that we don't need a priest." Bowing dramatically, I flicked my hair so that it whacked him in the chin. "You're looking at a registered officiant. We don't need to bring someone else in to marry these two."

His lower lip stretched out. "Pretty impressive, sugar. I still like my version better, though."

"Do you think that's what happens when girls go out and drink? They just start making out?"

"It's only natural. Scientific, even."

Reaching out to give him a soft push, I instead found myself being yanked into his arms. Kain dug one palm into my lower back, gliding it down so he was cupping my ass. His other fingers caught my jaw, forcing me to look up at him. "Wha—"

His breath was warm. "You know what I like better than imagining you kissing other girls?" Kain squeezed my hip, nudging his stomach against mine. "Kissing you myself."

"Psst!" Matilda peeked into the gazebo, her hand tapping the wood like it was Morse code. "Someone's coming!" She froze, noticing how Kain had me shoved up against one of the wooden beams.

He winked at her, saying, "Delay them for another ten—maybe fifteen minutes."

"No!" Scoffing, I wriggled out from under him. I hadn't noticed that he'd unhooked my bra; with Matilda watching with wide eyes, I quickly reached back to snap it together.

Scanning the gardens, I saw a figure coming our way. When I recognized those hard eyes, I stood stone still.

Hawthorne was here.

He nodded at Kain, giving me a side eye. "Where should I stand?" he asked.

I hadn't honestly expected him to come. "What about—"

"Mom and Dad didn't seem keen." He said no more, as if the conversation was over. Biting my lip, I motioned for him to hide around back where Matilda was with Midas. I didn't know if it was better or worse to have only some of the family.

It was more than I'd expected, but . . . it made it feel emptier, somehow.

Hawthorne trailed behind the gazebo. Over his shoulder, I spotted Midas. He was torn between grinning and fidgeting, his skin slick in the tiny lights woven through the flowers above.

He was wearing—from what I could tell—the same suit he'd had on at the wedding. It was a shame that Francesca wouldn't have her dress, but surprising her would make it worth it.

Matilda squeaked. "Okay, now she's coming!"

Fran was making a beeline for the gazebo.

"Everyone, get into position!" I said excitedly.

Bending low, Kain said into my ear, "You *were* in position, I was just about to start teasing that perfect pussy of yours."

Fire poured into my veins. "I'm about to perform a wedding, give me some breathing room."

"I don't know, this feels a lot like how her wedding began before." He cupped my hip, chuckling against my ear.

My eyes fluttered, and if I hadn't heard Fran swishing along the grass toward us, I might have given in to Kain. Groaning, I stepped away. "Just stand over there, please."

In a long, red skirt and a floral, too-tight top, the would-be bride finished her trip across the grass toward us. "I got your text earlier. Why did you need me?" Fran asked, climbing the steps into the gazebo. It took her a second, but her eyes trained up, taking in the soft lighting and fresh flowers we'd arranged. "What the hell is all of this?"

On cue, Matilda pressed the CD player button from where she was ducked behind the gazebo. Gentle, sweet violins began to play. Still Fran blinked, turning from me to Kain, then back again.

Hawthorne wandered into view, standing back enough to watch everything. It wasn't until Midas cleared his throat, climbing the stairs behind her, that what we were doing registered with her. "Midas?" she gasped, spinning to gawk at me. "Sammy, did you . . . ?"

Folding my hands in front of me, I lifted my voice. "Ahem. Dearly beloved, we're gathered here tonight—"

"Oh! Em! Gee!" she squealed.

"To celebrate the uniting of Francesca Badd and Midas . . ." Shit. I didn't remember his last name!

"Tengelico," Kain whispered at me.

"Midas Tengelico," I said, giving the couple an apologetic look. Behind me in the darkness, I heard Matilda giggle. "Did you two write any vows?"

Midas nodded, facing Fran. "Frannie," he said, "I knew the day that I met you that we'd be perfect together. Everything I do, I want to do it with you. You're perfect . . . you're my light, my world. I love you so much."

Her eyes welled with tears. Inhaling deeply, she gathered herself. "Midas," she began, "I wrote a whole bunch of stuff down. I don't have that, so I'll just say this: I love you, too. I love your eyes, your smile, how you always let me try your food when we go out to eat." Beaming, she dabbed at her eyes. "Oh. And if you ever, *ever* sleep with one of my friends, I'll cut your balls off."

I covered my mouth hastily.

Kain didn't look surprised at all. I guessed he was used to his sister's relationship, and Midas must have been, too, because he hadn't even flinched.

Love could be fucking weird.

"Uh, please join hands," I said. They did, their fingers linking. "If no one objects, then by the power vested in me by the state, I now pronounce you husband and wife." I prepared to speak the final words—the whole you-may-kiss-the-bride-thing.

Francesca never let me.

She threw her arms around Midas, dragging him to the ground with a kiss too passionate to handle while standing.

I jumped back, my hands held up like I was being arrested. Wide-eyed, I looked at Kain; he was busy bending at the middle and laughing. It was contagious, that big grin of his. With the pair making out in the middle of the gazebo to the sound of violins, I couldn't hold myself together.

My dad had taught me that when things get hard or ugly, that was when you needed to laugh the most.

So I did.

Wiping my eyes, I looked out over the gardens. It was then that I saw them—three figures looking on like statues meant to stand forever. Fran's parents were hugging, Costello hovering by their elbows.

Each of them was smiling.

- CHAPTER NINETEEN -

KAIN

"I want to talk about Sammy," I said.

My father lifted his head from the tablet he'd been scrolling through. Wearing thin-framed glasses, he almost looked like a nice grandfather instead of a dangerous beast.

Putting it aside, he folded his hands. "Talk."

"I want her out of that room. I want Costello and Thorne to stop guarding her."

His forehead strained under his heavy eyebrows. "And why should I do that?"

I'd thought this over for a while. It had been over three weeks since Sammy had been locked away. Far too long, by any standard—but especially my own. I knew my father, he was stubborn and didn't like being challenged. But he also appreciated someone who could admit their mistakes. While I didn't agree one bit that taking Sammy to see her mother was a mistake . . .

He certainly did.

Lifting my jaw, I said, "Because this time, I'll watch her every move. She won't leave the estate until *you* think it's safe to do so. I promise that."

Tapping his chin, he puffed out some air. "Done."

My mouth fell open. I'd been prepping for a much harder fight. "You're really agreeing to this?"

"Did you want me to argue?"

"I expected you to," I said gravely.

Chuckling, he slid deeper into his chair. "I've got other things to worry about." Without prompting, he went on. "I'm starting to think that Brick wanted *Sammy* specifically. That he wasn't after our family at all."

My father's words turned my blood cold. "But why? She's got no history with him." He didn't blink, he just kept watching me thoughtfully. "Dad. She doesn't *know* him. She couldn't."

"Maybe. And maybe not."

"That's fucking cryptic as hell," I said. "If you learned something about her, tell me."

Pinching the bridge of his nose, he said, "Sammy might have a more solid relationship with the Deep Shots than I initially assumed. I've got people looking into it. We'll know soon."

What he was saying was impossible. The Deep Shots were a *gang*, they were all about guns and gambling. Sammy made wedding dresses and liked vanilla ice cream. Her deepest secret was her boring story about drunkenly registering online to marry people.

He was wrong about her. He'd learn that for certain soon enough.

I considered my words. "I guess it's a waiting game again."

"It always is." He sounded resigned, pushing himself out of his chair with a labored grunt. "Just keep that girl *here*." His finger stabbed into my collarbone. "Brick will slip up eventually, and if not, my informants will reveal the truth—whatever it is. Then we can decide what to do."

His informants. I had a suspicion he was putting every one of the Badd Maids to work overtime to figure this mystery out.

There IS no mystery, I reminded myself firmly. But what if I was wrong? This was ballooning in a way I hadn't expected.

I'd only just started to understand who Sammy was to me.

Who the hell was she to everyone else?

Swimming in a sea of disconnection, I struggled for the shore. Everything he said, it made no sense. Sammy Sage was *no one*. Well, to me she was someone, but to this gang, she had no connection.

I was sure of it.

He started to move past me. "I'm going to call around some more, see what I can dig up. We'll consult on this later." Pausing, Maverick gripped my upper arms. "You know I meant well when I put her down there, right?"

Sourness bubbled in my stomach. But the longer I looked into his hard face, the more I sensed the desperation behind his question. People often said we had the same eyes. I saw them imploring me, and fuck it, I thought about the way I'd implored Sammy to understand me.

I didn't agree with his decisions . . .

But I knew the need to be understood.

"Yes," I whispered.

He gripped me harder, then he released me with a gentle shoulder pat. "Good man. Go get her, bring her upstairs. It's time."

It was the first thing he'd said that I definitely agreed with.

Costello was blocking the door to her chambers. His eyes came up, focusing on me the closer I got. "At ease," I teased him. "I'm going in, and you can go upstairs and eat."

His lips stretched out in a thin line. "Is this a trick? I'm still amazed you talked Thorne into letting her out that one time."

In spite of his doubt, he unlocked the door and opened it for me. "It's not a trick," I said. Tapping the door hinges, I alerted Sammy that I was there. "Dad says she's free to leave this room now."

Costello's icy eyes froze over. "You're definitely lying."

"I'm not. Ask him yourself." We were close enough that I sensed my brother tensing up. My veins flickered; I didn't want another fight, the guy was a fucking animal when he had to be. But if I had to tear through him to get to Sammy . . .

"Hey!" she chirped, ruining the intensity. Waving, she crossed around the big, round bed and came to meet me. She was wearing a pair of long, white pants and a matching top that flowed with her movements.

Sweeping her into my arms, I kissed her throat and thrilled with her shock. Even like this, her body yielded to me; she breathed out sharply, her nails clinging to my shoulders.

Dipping her farther, I crept my hand to the small of her back, licking her lower lip. The heat in her eyes mirrored mine. "I've got good news," I mumbled.

Swallowing, she looked past me to where Costello was guarding the open door.

Following her eyes, I asked, "Are you going to stand there and watch us screw like some kind of perv?" Nipping Sammy's ear, I made her whimper. "Because I'll fuck her, regardless of if you're watching or not. Nothing is going to stop me."

Wordlessly he closed the door, leaving us alone.

Spinning her in a circle, I scooped her up just to drop her on the bed. She bounced once, shaking off some of her dizzying passion so she could talk. "The good news better not be that you're about to fuck me. And for the record, I wouldn't let you do it with an audience."

Climbing on top of her, I snatched her wrists and pushed them into the mattress. "No?" I asked, smirking. "I think you'd let me do anything if I got you hot enough."

Her glare wavered. "Let's not find out."

Laughing, I rubbed my nose on her collarbone, speaking into her chest. I heard my voice bounce inside of her ribs. "Maverick says you're free to leave this room."

"He's not joking?" she asked. "He really means it, no catch?"

"The catch is that I have to watch you." Taking her chin, I leaned into her with a grin. *"Closely."*

Her smile went ear to ear. "Gross. I'll stay locked up, thanks."

Laughing, I wrapped her hair in my fist. She copied me, tugging at my nape so that my senses burned from the mild pain and pressure. When we kissed like that, the world vanished so easily. I felt lighter knowing the weight of her situation was gone. I needed to channel this energy somewhere, and Sammy gave me the perfect solution.

In seconds I tugged my shirt away; her eyes flashed, then she hurried to mimic me. I would have gone slower, but I worried that if I waited, I wouldn't be able to control this fucking urge. I was along for the ride; one misstep and it'd take over and leave me blind with lust.

Our bare skin connected, our lips locking into their familiar seal. Her knees circled me, clutching to keep us pressed together. My hot, hard cock was sandwiched on her navel. Her lips whispered useless vowels by my ear, my brain thumping as I worked to keep up with my insane arousal.

Her hand came between us, perfectly accurate as she guided me inside of her. It was smooth; as thick as I was, she was slippery down to the crevice of her ass with how badly she ached for me.

I pushed her legs off of my back, shoving them under me in a straight line. "Point your toes," I demanded. "Squeeze them together hard as you fucking can."

She couldn't deny me. Sammy was too cloudy with lust to even wonder what I was thinking. She had the presence of mind to ask, "Why?"

When my hands cradled her lower back, forcing her to arch into me so that my pelvis ground on hers, rubbing her swollen clit with every subtle movement of my body, she understood.

Friction built between us. Desperately, Sammy thrust against my hard muscles, her nails buried in my shoulder blades. I guided her from above and below, creating a pace that was going to leave us both frantic.

"Kain," she whimpered in my ear.

"Call me your king," I growled. I wasn't a king, I might never be, but I loved the feeling of being worshiped. It went both ways. I was eager to lavish attention on her body, to make her shake with pleasure.

Someday . . . she could be mine. Sammy could be an actual princess.

My Cinderella, for real.

The idea sent a spark of raw energy into my core. My cock thrilled each time I buried it deep inside of her. Every thrust took more of me, stole more of her. I fucked her like I'd never touch her again.

Crying out, she was pinned under me—right on the edge of orgasm. "Don't stop," she begged me.

My insides flipped, lightning that forked and came around again. "I said to call me your king. I'll let you come when you do."

"Let me fucking *come*, King Asshole!" she groaned.

Nipping her earlobe, I slid out until just the ridge of my cock head was in her. She tried to reach me; my hands gripped her ass, keeping her trapped. She couldn't get more of me in her pussy, but she also couldn't escape the sensation of my swollen tip.

"Say it."

Kissing my throat, she gripped my ass and squeezed; it made my cock jump. "You're my king! Let me fucking *come!*"

I sensed the edge of her humor, but I was too far gone to care. Trusting that she wouldn't get pregnant, I pumped back into her. Panting, I braced my body on hers. My palms massaged her perfect ass, slamming her with my full length.

She strangled my shaft, thrumming through her tensed thigh muscles as she came. "You're my king," she whispered across my damp shoulder. Closing my eyes, I took two more strokes before I finished.

Sammy was still fluttering with aftershocks, the sensation glorious.

I wanted to lie in the sheets, I really did. This pocket was ours, even if it led to nowhere. *Outside is freedom. She's finally been granted it.* How insane to smile over being given back your basic rights.

Her stomach grumbled—her laugh following right after. "Come on," she said, sitting up. "Brunch sounds amazing right now."

Resisting my desire to yank her into the shower and take her again, I let her clean up in peace. When we were changed into our clothes, I walked to the door. Sammy's hand on my elbow froze me.

"Let me," she said. Her fingers clutched the handle, testing it like she doubted it would open. When it did, her lips jerked at the corners. "It's really not locked."

It would have been awful if Costello hadn't left it unlocked for us.

Together, we exited that room. I wondered what Sammy was thinking. Yes, we'd done this before, but that had been a temporary ruse.

This was . . . real.

Everyone was gathered in the bright, granite kitchen. My mother was shoveling eggs onto a plate for Hawthorne. She spotted me, not noticing Sammy with my body blocking the way. "Kain! Could you take any longer? There's hardly anything left."

Piles and piles of food on the counter disagreed.

Swinging her way, I gave my mother an emphatic kiss on her cheek. "You'd make more if I asked."

"Tch." She swatted me away, but her pretend offense didn't disguise her pleased smile. My mother was no pushover, but her heart was dedicated to her children. Even with enough servants on our estate to handle meals, she still loved helping with brunch.

The light in her eyes stilled; she'd spotted Sammy.

For a moment, the chatter and energy slowed to a halt. Everyone was either staring at the girl beside me or at my father where he was slumped comfortably at the kitchen table. Hawthorne twirled a biscuit between his fingers, eyeballing me with the unspoken question of, "What the fuck is she doing out of her cage?"

Ignoring all of them, I wrapped my arm around Sammy's waist and nudged her toward the food. "Go on, grab something."

Clearing her throat too loudly, she started stacking a plate high with bacon and tiny quiches. "Wow! This sure does look great! Doesn't it?" Her eyes snapped to Costello; he said nothing, her grin went tighter. "Ha-ha. So good you can't even speak, I get it."

Realizing that nothing was going to remove the discomfort besides an answer, I looked pointedly at Maverick. "He said it's fine. Everyone stop gawking already."

At once, the air shifted. My mother placed a new pitcher of orange juice on the table. Francesca was grinning, her hands clapping softly at her chest. No one wanted to call my father out for the insane move he'd pulled, but we were all thinking how good it was for it to be over with.

How could any of us sleep well knowing we had a prisoner in our home?

Sammy sat down next to Francesca, reaching for the carafe of coffee. Frannie gave her a small shove, then another, until finally Sammy laughed. "Okay, yes, I noticed you. Hi there."

"Gawd, I'm just happy to see you up here eating with us!" Grasping her in a quick hug, my twin bent in, whispering into Sammy's ear. They both laughed, and when Sammy looked my way, her green eyes lit up like jewels.

Passing Costello, I gave him a gentle shove. His half smile was as good as a toothy grin for the serious man. Dropping beside Sammy, I leaned close to kiss her on the cheek. Hawthorne pointed his fork. "None of that while I'm eating."

I ignored him, too busy enjoying how red Sammy was getting.

Let everyone roll their eyes at me, I thought, my cock still half-hard from fucking Sammy minutes ago. *I don't give a shit what anyone thinks.*

Everything was as close to perfect as it could possibly get.

Juice spilled over the table, soaking the patterned cloth.

"Frannie!" My mother gasped, mopping at it in a panic. "Be careful! This will stain and you *know* how hard it is to . . ." She trailed off, her eyes moving to where my sister's were.

Where everyone's were.

The woman in the archway was tall like my father, curvy like my mother. She was pale snow and midnight eyes, a smile that could go on for days, and—I knew from experience—a tongue that could cut you apart if you tried to mess with her.

She stood there as if she hadn't been gone for ten years.

Lulabelle.

My older sister.

- CHAPTER TWENTY -

SAMMY

"Lula!" Frannie squealed, jumping onto the other woman. Where the twin was tan, Lula was light. Her dark eyes were more like Hawthorne's, her long hair pulled into a loose tail that ran closer to caramel brown than the rich mahogany of her sister's hair.

I barely recognized her from the family photo, but I was smart enough to realize who she had to be.

Holding her tightly, Lula said something into Fran's ear. I couldn't hear it, but it made Fran pull back, her eyes suddenly narrowed. "I know," she said, "and I don't care. Gawd, it was just a wedding, you had your reasons for not making it."

It was plain as day that whatever Fran said, she was hurt by her sister not being here for her big day. Lula hesitated, then she just gave the girl another quick hug. Pulling free, she eyed the large kitchen. Her hand came up, waving casually at all of us. "Hey," she said. "Long time no see."

Maverick rushed forward, breaking the frozen moment. Crushing his daughter in his arms, he held her so long it should have been awkward. It wasn't.

Her mother hadn't moved, she—much like Costello—just stared from where she was.

Puffing out a bit of air, Kain said, "Don't hog her, Dad."

The large man deflated, patting the woman on the shoulders even as he disengaged. Standing aside, he let Kain and Hawthorne take turns embracing Lula.

Thorne motioned at her suitcase. "How long are you staying, Lulabelle?"

"I don't know yet." Her glance at Costello was so fast I almost missed it.

Dropping beside me again, Kain gripped one of my hands under the table. I clasped it in return, smiling at him. The tension was thick, and still, I understood so little of it.

I realized Lulabelle was staring at me. Leaning away from Kain, I waved a hand. "Hey. I'm Sammy." *I'm the girl who's trapped here.* I didn't say it, of course, but I kind of wanted to.

Mama Badd stood up, shoving her chair backward from the table. "Well. Tonight we should have a nice celebration. We can bring in a florist, some live music . . . the works."

"How?" Fran mumbled. "Daddy won't let us bring anyone onto the estate, he thinks everyone is out to murder us."

"Frannie!" her mother snapped.

I'd seen them all together once before. That photo where they were all smiling . . .

Where the future looked bright.

None of them looked happy now. Especially not Francesca.

Lulabelle shifted enough to face her father. "You know what, I don't even want to know what she's talking about. It was a long flight, I'll be happy just to get settled in."

He held out a wide arm, corralling her from the kitchen.

The rest of us were left to the silence. Mama Badd hovered by the sink, her lips trembling, moving from an uncertain smile to a much more solid frown. The appearance of Lulabelle had thrown their world for a loop.

Hawthorne ran his hands down the front of his shirt. "Come on, Mom." Heading to her, he scooped up her elbow. I wasn't used to seeing him acting so . . . kind. "Let's go look over some ideas. Lula might not want a celebration, but fuck her, we can still throw something together anyway. Dad isn't stopping me from going anywhere, I'll buy whatever you want."

Patting his arm, she let him lead her from the kitchen. "Buying me things? You always know how to cheer me up."

Costello had been as still as a suit of armor in a museum. Abruptly he pushed off the wall, his legs cutting a path from the room.

And then there were three.

Peering from Kain to Fran, I asked flatly, "What am I missing?"

"It's personal," Francesca said. Grabbing the pile of wet napkins from the juice spill, she slammed them into the trash. "Family stuff."

"Family stuff," I repeated. "All right."

Resting his forehead on his fist, Kain eyed his sister. "It doesn't have to be a big secret, Fran. What happened between Costello and Lula—"

"It didn't just happen to them," she said sharply.

Kain narrowed his eyes. "Funny, you always act like it's *you* everything happened to."

"Oh!" She scowled, flailing her hands like she was going to slap him. He gripped her wrists, stopping her before she could get far. Scooting my chair away, I stood quickly. I wasn't going to get a black eye from some crazy sibling fight.

Kain didn't stand, he remained where he was with her stuck firmly in front of him. "Frannie, listen. You've been taking this grudge too far."

Seething, she said, "Screw you, Kain. I'll be pissed as long as I want."

"And how long is that?"

"For as long as he's around!"

"Fran, he didn't make her leave!"

"He did!" That was her breaking point; she wrenched away, and I knew Kain let her go, because I'd felt his grip before. He could have held her there for hours.

Without another word, Francesca stomped from the kitchen. I heard her feet clomping down the hall, then up the stairs . . . and then nothing.

Ever so slowly, I looked back at Kain. He was sitting there with his hands on the table, shoulders knotted like he was still busy holding his sister in front of him.

I clapped my hands sharply; he jumped. "Kain, it's all right, you don't need to tell me what's going on. I get it."

He snagged my arm, pulling me into his lap. I started to argue, but his sudden, hungry embrace shut me up. Kain circled me fully, his warmth . . . his strain . . . full of so much more than I could understand.

Whatever had happened to this family, it had left a wound that was still raw.

The day vanished with everyone passing like ships in the night.

Hawthorne disappeared—presumably to shop for his mother.

I had no clue where Costello was.

Maverick dragged Kain off into the den to talk in heated secrecy.

And Fran . . . well, I caught her whispering with Lulabelle in the room I'd slept in accidentally that one night. The door was shut, but through the wood, their voices were buzzing. I caught no words, I only grasped that one of them was upset.

I was sure I heard crying.

When the sky finally turned purple and Hawthorne returned with bags, I decided I should get ready for whatever "celebration" they were going to concoct. Francesca wasn't in her room, so I helped myself to one of the outfits she'd set aside for me once it became clear I'd be here for a while.

It was a simple thing—well, simple for Fran. Just a long, white dress, the edges lacy and the top tying around my neck. Studying myself in the mirror, I gave a spin, watching how the cloth rippled.

It almost looks like a wedding dress. Not one I'd ever choose, no, but I could see someone wearing something similar. *My wedding dress would have lots of ribbons, probably a mermaid design, and . . .* Gripping the hem, I stopped short.

Why the fuck am I thinking about that?

Yeah, I'd fantasized about a wedding with Kain way back when, but that had been just silly fun. Nothing serious.

Get a grip. Standing tall, I breathed in—then out. *Date the guy once this mess is done, then maybe think about marriage, jeez.*

I was still chuckling to myself about my insanity when I entered the hall. Clicking Fran's door shut, I turned . . . and then I saw her.

Lulabelle.

What is she doing in Kain's room? She hadn't noticed me. Closing his door, she began to head my way. The shoes in her hands were, without a doubt, the ones I'd worn at the wedding. I'd know those hellish glitter monsters anywhere.

"Oh," she said loudly, as if I'd caught her doing something wrong. "I almost didn't see you there. Sammy, right?"

"Yeah, that's me." My attention dropped to the shoes, then back to her face.

Lulabelle followed my eyes. Smiling, she lifted the heels and gave them a little twirl. "Ugly, aren't they? Either Kain's been moonlighting as a stripper with bad taste, or I'm guessing these belong to my dear little sister."

My fingers twitched at my sides; why did I want to grab those shoes so badly? I'd hated the things. I'd been relieved to chuck them at Kain to get rid of them.

That was almost a month ago, I thought with budding wonder. *He kept them this whole time?* If I was still angry with the guy, learning that he'd kept my shoes in secret would have been terror inducing.

Instead . . .

I found it stupidly sweet.

"Actually," I said, reaching out. "Those belong to me."

Lulabelle scanned me from top to bottom, not hiding her confusion. I was sure she was thinking that I did *not* look like the sort who wore shoes like these. And she was right, I wasn't. They were the worst things I'd ever had to stumble around in.

I wanted them more than anything.

With some uncertainty, she handed them over to me. I squeezed them tight, hugging them to my chest. "Thanks," I said softly.

"No problem." Her mouth opened, as if she had more to say. In the end, Lula just pushed her long hair behind her ears and looked at Kain's door. I was relieved when she didn't ask why my shoes had been inside. I didn't have an answer, anyway.

How much did she know about what was going on?

She rubbed her ankle with her opposite foot. "Okay. Uh, good talk."

On impulse, I stepped toward her. "Wait. Why were you in his room?"

Rocking side to side, she peered at me thoughtfully. "I was hoping to talk to him alone. He's not in there, though."

Nodding almost absently, I said, “He’s probably with your dad still.”

“Mm. Probably.” Casting her eyes to one side, she spoke to herself. “Or he’s avoiding me.”

“Why would he do that?”

Her lips twisted up benevolently. “Do you have siblings?”

“No.”

“Then you can’t understand.” Studying me long and hard, Lulabelle walked down the curving staircase. “But you don’t have to. This is between family.”

Family family family. I was starting to think that word was becoming an excuse for their bad behavior. Left alone, I grazed my fingers over the high heels. I was marveling over how he’d hung on to the things.

Kain Badd was the fucking *opposite* of bad. He was kind, dedicated, and possibly—fingers crossed—hopelessly addicted to me.

Because I certainly was to him.

With a bounce in my step, I hid the shoes away under my old pajamas in the guest room Fran had helped me set up. I didn’t want anything to happen to those glittery shoes.

Strolling through the mansion, I walked headfirst into Kain just as he was rounding the corner. Stumbling backward, I was grateful that he helped keep me on my feet. I’d been eager to run into him—but I hadn’t meant it literally.

“Whoa there.” He chuckled, steadying me. “Someone is in a rush.”

“Well, you have to go-go-go . . . or something.” I floundered under his baffled stare, quickly rushing to change the subject. “Hey, your sister was looking for you.”

“Fran?”

“No, Lula.”

His hands curled into loose fists. “Ah.”

“What’s that mean, ‘Ah’?”

"Nothing." He saw my stare, and though he looked to the side, I just shifted to keep my face in his line of sight. "Damn, you're determined."

"I'm just trying to understand you guys. There's a lot happening that's going over my head."

"We're a complicated family."

"What family isn't?"

Palming the nape of his neck, he sighed loudly. "It's not the same. You're not just talking about petty squabbles, you're mixing old history, politics, hurt feelings, and a ton of tiny mistakes that no one as proud as these people will ever own up to."

"You're one of them," I reminded him.

He shot me a cynical smile. "I'm aware. I'm probably prouder than all of them combined."

"So what do we do? Just act like things are normal?"

"You," he said, clamping onto my shoulders, "need to hang on tight. I promise that this morning was just a baby crocodile tooth when compared to the massively jagged mouth that is the drama of this family. Let's go outside, they're setting dinner up."

He placed his hand possessively on my hip. Thrilling with the touch, I followed him through the home and out into the rose gardens. Night wasn't far away, a long table had been set up under a few heated lamps to keep the shadows from ruining the meal.

On top of the white cloth, there were bottles of wine in metal buckets—far too many for eight people. *Or maybe just enough, if things go as crazy as Kain suggested.* Eyeballing the seats, I tried to weigh my options. What was the most tactical place to sit?

Kain decided for me. Pulling out a chair, he dropped me on the far end, away from the head of the table, where Maverick would sit. Sitting across from me, Kain poured a glass of rich, red wine.

"Aren't we waiting for the others?" I asked.

His eyebrows went up as, on cue, voices began drifting into the garden. "Mom!" Fran groaned, allowing her mother to stop and fix the deep *V* of her dress. "It's fine. Come on."

"It's fine for a street whore, not my daughter."

"Please. You only care because Lula is here."

"Watch your fucking tone, missy!"

Kain passed me the glass; I took a grateful sip.

From there the others trickled in. Mama Badd sat on a corner by Maverick, Lulabelle sat on the other. Francesca plopped beside her, and I was pleased to see Midas join us. I'd barely seen the man since the surprise ceremony.

Hawthorne pulled out a chair beside Kain, leaving a space beside me for . . .

"Uh, hi," I said, looking up at Costello.

He pulled into place, his wolfish eyes darting to me for too long of a second. "Hey there." I was relieved when he grabbed a glass of wine, freeing me from his intense energy. Of all the people in this family, I still struggled with him the most.

I'd watched him fight with Kain at his father's orders. I'd watched him smile at a distance as Frannie got her wedding, all while knowing he'd originally been denied being a part of it. And that facial scar of his . . .

He was a mystery to me. I didn't like unknowns.

Polished shoes clicked over the paved stones that led to our table on the grass. Seeing the servers, I endured a brief blast of fear. *Great, did Jameson or Brick or whatever his name is give me PTSD over waiters?* Going out to a restaurant was going to suck, if so. I decided that, when this was all over, I was going to mail that bastard a bill for my therapy.

As plates of tiny beet salads and candied walnuts were placed in front of us, Mama Badd said, "I'm really sorry, Lulabelle. I wish we could have done more. If we'd known you were coming—"

"No. It's fine." Looking down at the food, she poked it with a half smile. "I, uh, didn't want you to make a big deal. Even this is a little much."

"Please," Francesca scoffed. "There isn't even any live music. It's a poor excuse for a celebration."

Hawthorne tilted back a big gulp of wine. "I did my best, okay? I'm the only one who even bothered making a shopping trip."

"The food is fine," Lulabelle insisted.

Fran rolled her eyes several times. "The food is whatever. I'm talking about entertainment."

"I said," Lulabelle whispered, "that it's *fine*."

"It's not!" Fran shouted, slamming her palms onto the table. The silverware shook with a miniquake.

"Frannie—"

"Don't *Frannie* me, Costello!" She stabbed her eyes at her brother viciously. Beside me, I felt him twitch. "This is your fault!"

Kain and I shared a look. He started to half stand. "Fran, no, it's no one's fucking fault that we're on lockdown. No one but the Deep Shots, anyway."

She said, "You know I'm not talking about that! I'm talking about how he drove Lula away!"

Large and heavy, Maverick's fist came down on his untouched plate. Beets splattered all over, a few sticking to Lula's cheek. "That's *enough!* Everyone needs to sit down and be quiet so we can have this damn celebration in peace!"

"Peace," Hawthorne mused.

Mama Badd put her hand by her lips, like she could block her voice. "Fran, shut up and listen to your father."

"I won't! This family is a stupid mess, and no one wants to talk about the tall fucking elephant in the room!" Her polished nail flashed, indicating Costello.

Still, he hadn't moved.

"Go ahead," Fran said. Her body shook with her fast breathing. "Apologize to her for what you did. For what you did to this whole family."

Costello lifted his eyes just enough to watch his younger sister. Slowly, subtly, I scooted my chair away from him. It was as if the air was crackling around him. Was he going to flip out? Attack Fran? What the hell was happening?

His voice was a mere ghost of his emotions. "I've apologized before, it didn't matter back then. Why would it now?"

In a flurry of orange sequins and too much boob, Francesca tried to leap over the whole damn table. Kain moved faster, knocking his chair upside down as he rushed to hook his arms around her middle. "Holy fuck, Fran! Relax!"

In a crescendo of voices, the table exploded. Everyone shouted at one another, hands waving or fingers jabbing in the air. Some of it was aimed at Costello, who, through it all, sat beside me in silence.

His hands were in his lap; I saw how bone-white his knuckles were. Who was his quiet fury aimed at?

Over all the mess, Lulabelle's voice rang the truest. "This is exactly what I didn't want. Maybe I shouldn't have come back, I've made it all worse." Wiping purple stains from her cheek, she jumped to her feet.

"Lula!" Maverick shouted.

She wiped her hands on a napkin, throwing it down. "Thanks for the food. I'm going to bed." Sidestepping the table, she walked toward the mansion with her head held high.

It amazed me to see Maverick put his face in his hands, hang his chin, and go still.

Thorne was shielding his mother from Fran's furiously flailing elbows. Kain was struggling to hold her back; she was intent on getting at Costello, who finally walked off in silence.

Across the table, Kain met my eyes. His lips parted, silently mouthing "Sorry" at me. I smiled partially, hoping he understood I didn't blame him. He wasn't responsible for this drama—I didn't think so, anyway.

I did wonder, though, as I sat there among a broken family that was busy knocking over wineglasses and screaming instead of talking, if I would ever learn about their old secrets.

And if I even wanted to.

- CHAPTER TWENTY-ONE -

Kain

My shoes brushed over the hallway rugs. Even with the mansion's lights turned down low, it was easy to see all around. Besides, I'd walked this way a thousand and more times. I knew where Lula's room was.

She just hadn't been inside of it for ten years.

Tapping the door, I whispered, "You in there?"

"Yeah." Her answer came fast; she must have been awake in spite of claiming she was going to bed a few hours ago. "Come in."

Cracking the door, I leaned inside. Lula was sitting on the edge of her bed, half facing me. Her hand twirled; she wanted me to shut the door. I did it softly. "Hey," I said, approaching slowly. "Are you okay?"

"Why are you here?" The haughtiness in her voice sent me reeling. Lula made me feel like I was a kid all over again, hanging around her room for advice on how to solve one of the many stupid problems I'd come up with.

Shrugging, I said, "I wanted to make sure everything was good. You left pretty quick earlier."

"Can you blame me?" Leaning back on the bed, she looked as stiff as a board. None of her muscles seemed capable of relaxing. "Some family dinner. I thought it might get messy, but still . . . maybe I shouldn't have come back."

Taking a step forward, I almost sat on the bed—her energy warned me away, but it didn't stop the question that had been burning in me. "Why *did* you?"

Her dark eyes floated to me like moths ready to dive into a fire. "Oh, little brother. Because I'm a sappy idiot who missed her family."

She motioned for me to sit. My chuckle mixed with the squeak of the springs. "Even fuckups like me?"

"Please. You're not the fuckup." Lula managed a tiny smile. That gave me even worse nostalgia. "I'm the one who caused this family to fall apart."

"We haven't fallen apart."

"I'm pretty sure your little friend out there would disagree."

"Sammy?" I asked, thinking about her sitting in her room—her new room, one that wasn't a prison. Had anyone told Lula about what was going on?

My sister eyed me closely, like she'd read my mind. "Fran told me what Father did to her. How could you let it happen?"

I went red at her implication. I'd never *let* anything happen. "I tried to stop it. Sammy insisted she stay in there. I don't have a damn clue why."

Covering her mouth couldn't hide her smile. "You're seriously that oblivious. Kain, she was doing it because she was worried about you."

Knitting my eyebrows, I said, "You just got back home. How would you know anything that's going on?" My words weren't meant to hurt; I saw her flinch slightly and realized they had. "Lula—"

"It's fine. You're right." Stretching back on her pillows, she stared around at the blue walls. I followed her eyes curiously, wondering what she was seeing. "But that girl . . . she's still a person. I like to think I understand *people*, Kain. You broke her out to host Fran's wedding recently, right?"

Unsure where she was going, I nodded. "Yeah. That was her idea."

Lula brushed some of her hair from her cheek. Her eyes cut through me, like I could hide nothing from her. And maybe I couldn't. "Escaping after that would have been easy, especially if she asked you for help. She didn't, right?" She didn't let me get a word in. "I don't know Sammy, but she obviously cares about you. So she sat in that damn room like a good little pet, and she sits in another room now, doing as she's told."

She spit that last word out; a cold knife stabbed into my guts. "You came back because you missed us. Why did you run in the first place? Was it really because Dad tried to lock you in that room?"

She threw an arm over her face. "Of course not. You know it was more than that."

Keeping my tone even, I said, "No. I don't."

Her arm fell away, showing me how wide her eyes were. "What? Of course you do. How would you . . ." She trailed off, and then she grinned, but it was a broken excuse for one. "No one ever told you why it happened. Amazing."

I didn't know how she could look so smug. Was it because she'd just realized that, once again, our family had done something fucked up? "I know some of it," I said. "Clearly not enough to understand why you left for ten years."

Sitting up on her elbows, she asked, "What *do* you remember about that night?"

Hunching on the bed, I folded my arms over my chest. That time was so long ago . . . it came to me in fragments. "I remember being in my room, hearing Costello shouting for help. I came downstairs to find out what the hell was going on." The first thing I'd noticed was our normally shiny and clean floors had a trail of blood from the front door to the foyer. "He was half dragging you. Screaming. Your clothes were all red, the both of you."

It had stuck out to me so starkly at the time because Lula was always so serene—so put-together. But there she'd been, sprawled on the floorboards with her shirt half torn apart, and Costello was no better.

I whispered, "At the time, I'd thought the blood was his. He was saturated in it." Unable to blink, I stared right at her. "I didn't know most of it was yours."

She shivered, reliving the memory with me. I didn't need to see her scars, the memories of the fresh wounds were enough. "I don't remember much after I was attacked. I was so dizzy. I'd lost so much blood, it's a blessing Costello got us out of there."

"You almost died," I said seriously.

Lula chuckled dryly. "It turned out fine."

"No, it didn't." Frowning, I shook my chin side to side. "You still haven't said why you two were attacked in the first place."

Like she had too much energy, she hopped off the bed and started pacing. "Right, Father's dirty little part in this. A group of nobodies had learned who we were—who our family was—and decided to use it against us."

That confused me enough that I stood up as well. "Use it against us how? That's not even a secret."

"Our royal heritage is more of a weakness than you think, Brother." She was so pale I could see the veins beneath her skin, like she was made of plastic wrap. "Being royalty is about more than using it as a pickup line to get girls."

There—the biting side of Lula I knew so well.

She went quiet. I almost said something, but Lula began again. "And here we come to the real issue. My actions that split this family apart. After I healed from the attack, I told Father I was leaving. I didn't want to be so close to him and the danger that being related to him brought. That was why he panicked and tried to lock me away."

That was a night I *did* remember. I'd stood in that hallway, looking on as Maverick shoved Lula into the room, explaining it was for her own good. Costello had assured me it would be fine when I'd tried—in my teenage rage—to intervene.

I'd been pissed at him for stopping me.

We sat in uneasy silence. I wanted to comfort Lula. I thought there had to be some way to make everything better.

She turned to face the wall, touching a shelf of books absently. "I used to imagine being a real princess, or even a queen. Did you know that?"

I smiled sadly. "I remember when you made me pretend to be your steed as you ran around, giving orders to all of us."

She laughed suddenly. "Then Thorne threw water on me and told me to melt because I was secretly a witch. That's right. I was so furious."

Her joy was contagious. But my mind was elsewhere. Not in the fond memories of childhood, but in the heavy future waiting for my family. I'd never taken my heritage seriously. Lula was right, it had been all fun and games for me.

Had our father hidden the truth of this attack so we'd never think poorly of who we were?

Studying my sister, I pressed my fingertips to my right ribs. "That's why you never got the tattoo."

"The tattoos," she snorted, brushing her own ribs thoughtfully. "I love this family, Kain. And I hate it at the same time."

My hand fell to my side. "I guess that's fair."

Her lips twisted when she stared at me, one eyebrow riding high. "You want to talk about fairness, do you? Then let's talk about how *fair* it is to keep that poor girl here. Why haven't you run away together yet?"

Inch by inch, blood filled my veins. "What?"

Lulabelle whispered, "No one deserves to be locked up. No one."

"She isn't locked up anymore, Lula."

"Please." Her hands reached for mine, folding tight and calling back to all the times she'd chided me when I'd done something she didn't find "princely" as a kid. "A cage without bars is still a cage. What's keeping you here? Don't you like her?"

A spasm went through my fingertips. "Of course I do," I said quickly.

"Kain," Lulabelle said. "What do you want to do?"

What DO I want to do?

I'd never considered running away. Perhaps part of me associated it with pain; I'd seen how Fran had handled Lula's escape. Could I really do the same thing? Was it so bad to sit here . . . sit in this safe place . . . and wait until—*Until what?* I asked myself. *Until Dad decides we can do as we please?*

Lula was right.

A cage without bars was still a damn cage.

Pulling my sister in, I hugged her as tightly as I could. This was a real hug—nothing like the one this morning in the kitchen.

"Treat her right, Brother." She held me at a distance. "Everyone deserves that much."

After all this time, she still gave the best advice.

- CHAPTER TWENTY-TWO -

SAMMY

I wasn't quite asleep when the knock came.

Sitting up, I hurried to the bedroom door. My intuition said this was Kain, it had to be, but I still peeked through the slim opening to make sure. His eyes were warm when they saw me—I couldn't have kept him out if I'd wanted to.

"It's late," I whispered, letting him in. "I was wondering if you would come and see me. Check out my fancy bed. It's not as good as the garden-prison one, but still."

Kain was blurry in the shadows, it took me a minute to realize he wasn't dressed in pajamas, like me, but rather the same clothes as earlier . . . shoes and all.

Nervously, I asked, "What's going on?"

Scooping me into his embrace, he played his lips across mine. It was sweet and soft; my center started to melt. "I just had a very long talk that opened my mind."

Who did he talk with? I wondered. Tracing his cheek, I tried to read his smile; why did he seem like he was ready to start sprinting around the room? "All right, Mr. Open Mind. What are you here to share with me?"

"How about a wish?"

Blinking, I stared up into his perfectly blue eyes. "Are you offering to grant one?"

"If you tell me what it is, I might."

Flushing, I started to back away; he crushed me against him, preventing my retreat. This no longer felt like a lighthearted game. Wishes were silly things, but under Kain's intensity, they became so real they could cut me open. If I dared to speak my mind, this little world I was pretending was good and fine would crumble. I'd see the edges and know it was fake.

"I can't," I said. "It's too much to ask."

His face went hard, all the humor between us fading into the night. "Ask me," he whispered. "I'll do it if you just ask. I came here because I share your wish, too. I'm ready for it."

"I couldn't. Last time we left, your father—"

"I'll go with you."

"Of course you will, how else would I—"

"No. I'll *go with you.*" Fire swirled in his pupils. "I'll take you to your mother, we'll leave, and none of us will come back. You, me, and her. I've got the money. If my father tries to cut me off, I'll make sure I take out enough to get us settled first. We can go anywhere. We'd be safe."

Safe with Kain. I adored that concept. But this was happening too fast, I'd missed something major. "The person that opened your mind," I said quietly. "Who was it?"

"Lulabelle." His fingernails slid down my bare arms; I was wearing too little to be having such serious talks with Kain at this hour. His full attire gave him armor that I didn't have. "She helped me realize how crazy I was to keep you here. You deserve more than a cage, Sammy."

He wasn't lying before; he knew what I wanted, he'd thought it over . . . and he'd come here to offer it. But I needed to make sure he wouldn't regret this.

I couldn't be the one who ruined his connection to his family.

"Fran will want to kill us if we vanish. Your father might try to hunt us down. If we do this—Kain, you have to tell me you're okay with the aftermath. I need to know. Be certain, be really, *really* certain."

Like the slow crawl of winter turning into spring, Kain looped his fingers around my forearms and erased every chill. His lips could have met mine, we could have kissed again and again, but he chose to spill his heart instead. "If you asked me to, I'd slash and burn every connection to this place . . . just to plant myself somewhere else with you. Forever."

He was offering me everything on a silver platter.

All I had to do was ask.

Standing on tiptoe, I teased my mouth over his. My teeth caught his tongue, my nose grinding along his cheek. I kissed him until I saw spots of light behind my eyelids, and then, I kissed him some more.

My voice was broken and hushed when I pulled back. "Take us away from here, Your Majesty."

Kain cupped my cheeks, his breath tickling my eyelashes.

"Your wish is my command."

- CHAPTER TWENTY-THREE -

KAIN

A month had passed since I'd first kissed Sammy.

Yes, that was how I was measuring my time.

My father had talked again and again about the danger she was in—that we could all be in, though he clearly suspected this was all about her somehow.

And still . . . no one could come up with a reason why.

Each time I looked at Sammy, I tried to make sense of her. I'd see her clever green eyes, and I'd ask myself, "Who is she?" I'd watch her smoothing her wild hair, how she'd laugh so easily, and I'd tell myself it was all a mistake.

Brick Monroe was just a dangerous idiot.

That was all it was.

So why did I suddenly feel so uneasy?

I didn't know. But I found comfort in slipping my gun under my jacket. I had no clue what we would face after tonight, I wanted to be prepared.

Sammy met me in the driveway, a backpack strapped over her white lace dress. I figured it was whatever small items she'd gathered since her time here. Her steps were light as she bounced toward me. Her ever-present smile told me she didn't sense what I did.

Because nothing is wrong.

"I'll have to mail this dress back to Fran," she said, climbing up behind me. "I hope she isn't too mad. It's nice, though—nice and light with this warm weather. I was starting to think summer would come and go without any of those sweaty, nostalgic evenings."

Under her casual chatter, I let my guard down. "Sweetheart, I'm pretty sure I've given you a few sweaty summer nights to get nostalgic over."

Hiding behind the helmet, she just flashed me a thumbs-up.

Riding down the highway and out of Newport, we entered a stretch of road that was free of light pollution. Along my right side floated a field of black grass, the sky above glowing as if it were nuclear.

Sammy tapped me—then she did it again, insistent.

Turning, I saw what she wanted me to see. Breathing in, I gazed at the twinkling lights that bobbed over the field. It had been a long time since I'd noticed fireflies. In the serenity of a summer night that was often reserved for carefree kids, we rode along with our bodies pressing close, the engine vibrating our bones while our joy shook our hearts.

In my ear, she whispered a sentence. It shouldn't have been loud enough to climb above the white noise of the bike, but sometimes words have a way of ignoring the rules.

"I know you can't hear me, but I'm not mad at you anymore."

I'd warned her before that the engine's roar had a way of cutting up conversation and making it useless. But my ears were sharp, and she was so very close.

I smiled to myself, enjoying what she thought was a private confession.

"Actually, I think . . . that I might even love you."

The front tire of my bike kicked up grass; I nearly spun us off the road. Every firefly for miles fled in our wake, the world rocking with the weight of her admission.

Yanking my helmet off, I twisted to face her. She'd pulled hers aside as well, fresh fear from our near spill creating apples in her cheeks. Or maybe it was fear from what she'd let slip from her lips.

"Kain." My name was the single breath she'd had in her lungs. "I—I didn't think you could hear me!"

I couldn't break our stare, I was locked on and trying so hard to understand what she'd said—what I would say in return.

Suddenly, she sat up straighter. The doubt marring her lovely face changed into something that dared me to tell her she was wrong for admitting her inner secret. Again and again, this woman and I, we faced off to see who would win.

But looking deep into the starbursts of her eyes . . .

I realized I'd lost long ago.

Cupping her cheeks with a fury, I brought her to me. She was sweet and salty and more than my taste buds could make sense of. Love didn't change who she was, it only made her more grounded. I was touching a woman who couldn't be knocked down.

Sammy's love for me was solid as steel.

Together we suffocated; oxygen was for the weak. But love doesn't make you immortal, funny as that is.

She ripped away, gasping, with tears on the edges of her eyes. Was it from needing to breathe or from her emotions?

"Well?" she asked, her palms finding my jaw. She forced me to look at her. "Talk to me, because I'm about to feel really stupid if you don't just say something."

Say something? What the hell could I say?

The truth. Tell her.

But I didn't know what the truth was—*No. It's not that.* I did know, I'd known for some time. If I tried to tell her, what would happen?

And then my lips parted, and everything ran out of me before I could stop it. My voice was a syrup so thick that I couldn't clean it up, a stain that would last an eternity.

"I love you, too." I didn't whisper it. It wasn't a shout. Yet my admission rang between us, a song that would become so addicting we'd never forget the lyrics. "Fuck. I *love you.*" I said it again. It felt fucking amazing to feel it on my tongue.

I didn't want to stop, but her two fingers on my lips shut me up. "Okay," she said softly, a smile breaking over her glossy lips. "I heard you the first time."

"I don't give a damn if you heard me once." Sinking my lips onto hers, I pulled her to me. My mouth demanded more of her—more than anyone should be able to give. Sammy rose to the challenge, her eyes shutting behind her rows of thick lashes. "I won't ever stop saying it. I'm going to repeat it a million times, until my tongue dries out and my heart stops beating, and even then . . . I might never quit."

The wetness in her eyes finally tipped over the edges. Sammy had always hidden away when she cried. This time, she watched me dead-on and didn't try to stop it.

I kissed the corner of her cheekbone, wiping away the wetness there. Her nose brushed my ear, her tone the sensation of silk over bare skin. "I also love you for not driving us into a ditch and killing us in an empty field."

Hunching over with a laugh, I held her tighter. We lingered for a long while. The fireflies returned, the two of us trying to count them as we cuddled on my motorcycle.

Eventually, she looked at her phone. "We should go, I don't want Mom to fall asleep. Explaining to her that we need to pack up and leave is going to be messy as is."

The reminder that I'd offered to sweep them both away and off into the sunset should have been sobering. I was too busy relishing the blockade being gone from my heart. I'd never told a woman I loved her. I'd never *felt* like I'd loved someone before. Sammy had opened me up without my say, she'd gotten inside of me before I'd realized.

But maybe I couldn't have stopped her even if I'd seen this coming.

Maybe I wouldn't have tried to.

Pulling into the parking lot, I turned the engine off. Sliding down, I helped Sammy to the ground. My hands glided down her arms, one of them finally linking with hers. She tightened up in surprise, not trying to get away from my touch.

Hand in hand, we climbed the stairs.

I got to watch Sammy's joy as it became her state of mind.

And when she opened the unit, finding only darkness and not her mother . . .

I got to watch it melt away.

- CHAPTER TWENTY-FOUR -

Kain

"It happened. It finally happened." She was pacing, holding her head and talking to herself rapidly.

"Sammy, calm down."

Spinning on me, she let the last bit of her composure fall to pieces. "He took her! Oh fuck, oh no—what if he hurt her? What if he—"

Grabbing her roughly, I forced her around to face me. "Stop it!" I growled. The light came back into her eyes—she was listening. "Call the hospital first. Maybe she was taken there."

Her shaking chin made it obvious that possibility wasn't much better. I looked on as she dialed, her voice frantic as she spoke to someone on the line. Sammy's fist went white on the phone—when her arm dropped, my heart went with it.

Hanging up, she challenged me with her wild glare. "She's not there. I'm telling you, this Brick guy took her. It has to be that, she'd never leave without telling me."

With purpose, I started toward the door. "I believe you. I know where Brick is, we can leave right now."

"If he's done anything to her . . . I'll kill him." She said it so strongly that I didn't doubt it. Sammy wasn't violent, but when faced with losing the last person in her family, she was willing to take off her gloves.

I'd have done the same.

"Come on." Forcing the heavy helmet back into her hands, I lifted her onto the bike. Her focus was solid, she followed my lead. Sammy became a faceless eight ball behind the helmet.

Is this the right thing to do? I asked myself. Our plan had gone from escape to rescue. That is, if Jean could even *be* rescued—*No. Don't.* I tightened my jaw, my molars grinding. *We can save her. Everything will be fine.*

Robbed of her expressive eyes, I didn't linger in asking her thoughts. Sammy was as good as a one-direction robot. She cared about nothing but finding her mother. And I felt . . . no, I knew . . . that if it was a bleak outcome, she was ready to destroy the people who were responsible.

My front lights guided us down the road, rubber squealing. Sammy melded against my back, leaning into me for strength. Twisting the handlebars, I pushed my motorcycle to the limit. We cut corners, flying back the way we'd come.

The highway exit I wanted was just beyond the firefly field. It was late, and the road was usually barren anyway, so I didn't bother slowing down. As we cut over the bend of asphalt, revealing the straight shot in the distance, I spotted headlights.

My eyes cast slightly down; it allowed me to still see and not be blinded. *Just beyond here, we'll get to the highway, then the Hill, and then I'll kick Barnie's door down and strangle Brick Monroe for real.*

No one would stop me from getting to him. Not this time.

I wasn't afraid of guns.

I was afraid of seeing Sammy's heart torn to shreds.

Up ahead, the car drew near. In a sudden flash of high beams, it swung into our lane. It was an unexpected obstacle—and I was going too damn fast.

It rammed toward us on that stretch of quiet road.

The same place where so recently Sammy had told me she loved me.

Wrenching my bike to one side, I threw us into the grass. We skidded—we bounced. Every bone in my body took a turn punching into my skull, and when it was all said and done, I was lying face-up so I could see the stars.

Groaning, I rolled onto my elbow. *Move, go!* This was all wrong, the car had come at us on purpose. I knew what an ambush was, I wasn't a fucking idiot.

But I *was* hurt.

Grimacing, I clutched my ribs and stumbled toward Sammy. We'd both had on our helmets, the field cushioning us miraculously. Kneeling beside her, I helped her sit up; she yanked the helmet free, spitting into the dirt.

Breathing rapidly so her chest rose and fell, she looked up at me. Then she stared over my shoulder. "Don't!" she shouted.

Spinning, I looked into the barrel of a handgun. Brick spoke with a sneer I could *taste*. "Hey, asshole, remember me?"

My eyes darted up to his twisting features. *I have to get to my gun.* It was in my holster under my jacket, but he was too close for me to chance it.

The muzzle jammed into my temple; I grunted. "I asked a question," Brick said.

"Yeah, I fucking remember you. How could I forget a dick bag like you?"

His sudden kick to my ribs made me think twice about the next insult I'd readied. "You," he said, motioning at Sammy. "Get up."

She watched me nervously. On unsteady legs, she rose up, her backpack hanging limply in one hand. I realized she was slightly taller than Brick; that made me grin, because he noticed, too. Jerking the gun, he said, "Get back by the car."

"What are you going to do?"

"Just move, honey."

Licking her lower lip, she eyeballed the distance between her and the car. It was only a few feet away, we hadn't rolled far. "You're the guy who attacked me in my house."

"Good memory."

"What did you do with my mother?"

"Shut up and get over there," he growled, motioning with the gun.

Stiff-legged, she did as he said, passing him with a wary look at me. I tried to console her with my eyes. I wanted her to know everything was fine—because it had to be.

Somehow, it had to be.

Brick slid his stare to where I was sitting in the grass. "Thanks for making this easy. You'd think someone would have warned you to stay off the roads, but taking the same route over and over every week . . ." Snorting, he wagged the pistol lazily. "I figured you were smart when you pinned me for breaking into Sammy's place, but damn. Guess not."

Nothing stirred the air but crickets. Would anyone hear us out here? I couldn't see any headlights on the mile-long stretch. *I need to stall.* "So you attacked her, and now what, you'll kill her? What's the point? She's a nobody. There are better ways to hurt my family."

Though no better way to hurt me.

He steered his weapon, keeping it trained on me lazily. "Your asshole family thinks everything is about them. It isn't. And if you got your head out of your ass, you might have seen this coming."

Perking up, I looked to Sammy. She was shaking her head in blank confusion. "I don't even know who you are," she said.

He wrinkled his brow. "Maybe not my face, but you know who I am. I'm a Deep Shot, baby. Just like your daddy was."

My brain short-circuited, unable to comprehend what he'd said. Sammy threw up her hands—so fast that Brick pointed the gun at her nervously. "You've got me confused with someone else. My dad was Bastian Sage—a landscaper! He wasn't a member of some gang!"

"A *landscaper*?" he laughed. "Nice try. You know he was our fucking leader. Until he stepped down, anyway." Scratching at his cheek with the gun's muzzle, he chuckled. "Stop acting stupid. When I saw you rubbing elbows with the Badds, I got it. It clicked. You'd figured out I'd ordered that hit on him and it wasn't some suicide."

Her eyes were wild. "Holy shit, you're nuts!"

"I'm not nuts, I'm a damn go-getter!" His laugh was deep, the edges cracking like cheap pottery. He was unhinged; I wished I'd realized sooner. I'd thought he was violent and stupid, but was he really saying what I thought he was?

I whispered, "You had him murdered?" *Didn't Sammy say his car was found in Newport Bay?*

"Yeah, I'll take the credit for that." Fuck, did he look proud. "Had a guy do a drive-by shooting, but the dude went all-out and shoved the car off the road and right into the ocean. Points for the extra effort, there."

Sammy had gone white, her whole body shaking as she stood there. I saw her knuckles crunching, skin straining as she gripped the backpack.

Brick flipped the gun like he was a movie star. "I just needed time. My dad was going to let me lead the Deep Shots, and I had ideas, you know? Wanted to get you fucking Badds out of the picture . . . get you fucked by the police a few more times until your lawyer couldn't rescue you. Didn't expect to discover you working with this bitch. Jackpot! Revenge plot spotted!"

He was busy sneering at me. This man wasn't afraid of spraying his plans at us, because soon, he'd be spraying our brains all over as well.

I just needed a chance to get at my gun.

And that beautiful girl . . . she gave it to me.

Bursting into motion, Sammy chucked something at his head from inside of her backpack. Glittery and surreal, the high heel clicked off his scalp, sending him falling as he groped at the back of his skull.

Any other time, and I would have stared blankly at the fact that not only did Sammy *have* the shoes I'd thought I'd hidden away in my room . . .

She's just used one as a fucking weapon.

I didn't have the luxury of being shocked. My gun was hot in my palm; I yanked it free, aiming it at Brick. I was fast, but he wasn't scared of hitting someone he cared about like I was.

The muzzle flashed, his first shot worming through my shoulder. He was spinning in the dirt, firing blindly. Bullets pierced the sky, vanishing off into the stars.

With a scream, Sammy dropped to the pavement.

"No!" I roared, pointing my gun blindly. Each and every shot went astray. Brick grunted, half turning as I landed one slug in his upper thigh.

I had one bullet left, but I didn't waste it. All I could see was Sammy. I stretched over the ground, struggling toward her. I could hardly move, I was leaking life all over the place. How many bullets had he buried in me? My legs weren't working right, everything was on fire.

Sammy doubled over, leaning on the car's front tire. Hair stuck to her forehead; she lifted her hand, the crimson staining through her snowy-white dress.

Brick coughed, wiping at his scalp. He didn't even check the hole in his damn leg. Studying the redness on his fingers, he looked from me . . . to Sammy. Purposefully, he cocked his handgun. "Enough of this."

No no no no!

His other shots had been on reflex; he'd hit me and her entirely by accident. I didn't know how bad her wound was; she was cradling her stomach and looking at the ground. I couldn't even see her face.

If Brick shot her intentionally this time, I knew she'd be done.

My soul was capsizing. I wouldn't let Sammy die—I couldn't. Let me die instead; I'd rise from my damn grave, cursing the heavens and guaranteeing that anyone who touched a freckle on her cheek would get dragged back into the cold ground with me.

Fear is the perfect divider for separating you from your fucked-up thoughts.

The last time I'd thought about that, I'd been plowing down the highway with Sammy hanging on to my back. I wouldn't have guessed that this was where we'd end up someday.

I want to ride with her again.

I want to hold her.

Kiss her.

I wanted to have our damn fairy tale.

As I lifted my pistol, aiming it with the hope that after every fucking thing I'd been through—that *she* had been through—some karma would give me some luck, I realized . . .

This was it.

One shot was all I'd been offered.

So I took it.

My last bullet slammed into Brick's knee. He went down in a fury of arms, swearing and shouting through the burst of pain. I knew it hurt, I had lead burning away at me, too.

"You motherfucking piece of shit! I should've killed you first!" he bellowed.

Digging into my pocket with blood soaking my everything, I opened my phone. Smudges stained my screen, my message sending on its way to my father. It was a bare little text, it only read: HLP.

I didn't have time to hit the *E*, but he'd understand.

Pushing himself to his feet, Brick braced one arm on his uninjured leg. The other was dragging uselessly as he limped toward me.

His gun shook as he raised it—red veins popped in the boiled eggs that were a poor excuse for his eyes. "You're dead," he breathed heavily. "Fucking dead."

I knew I was smiling, I couldn't control it. "Shoot me, go on! I won't die. I'm too damn tough to die." If I kept talking, I could give my family time to get here. I just had to drag this out . . . I just . . .

The black hole in the muzzle of his gun became the only thing I could focus on. Some feet away, Sammy groaned weakly.

Brick pressed the warm, metal tip between my eyes. "Guess we'll find out," he said, squeezing the trigger.

Blood splattered.

It wasn't mine.

Brick rocked forward, coughing as liquid filled his throat. He toppled to the ground, leaving me more lost than ever as he rolled around in pain. Where had that shot come from?

On the empty road, I saw a new car. Its lights were off, none of us had heard it approaching. My savior was a big man with an even bigger gun. For a second I thought it was my father, but he was thinner—paler. I didn't know him, but I did know that he'd saved my life.

Her life.

"Sammy!" I shouted, dragging myself over the pavement toward her. She was propped against the car's tire, her stare fixed straight ahead on the stranger. In the distance, the first howls of police sirens began over the hill.

Someone had finally heard the gunshots and reported them.

She swayed, sliding sideways and to the street. Closing the distance, ignoring my pain, I scooped her into my lap. "Sammy! Sammy, look at me!"

She wouldn't, she was too busy fixating on the stranger. "It's him," she said in disbelief.

Was this new man dangerous? Was he going to aim at us next?

"Who is he?" I asked urgently.

Finally, she looked up at me. "That's my father."

- CHAPTER TWENTY-FIVE -

Sammy

"Sammy?"

This is nice. This is warm.

"Sammy! Sammy, please . . ."

Leave me alone. I can finally sleep. I haven't felt so relaxed in forever.

"I love you . . . so please, just . . . wake up."

Kain?

My eyes snapped open. Wincing at the bright lights overhead, I tried to shield my eyes; something tugged my arm, keeping it locked in place. In a panic I started to thrash, too confused to make sense of what was going on.

I'd been dreaming . . .

But before that, hadn't I died?

Strong, solid fingers captured my shoulders. "Sammy, you're awake, I thought you might never . . ." Kain never finished. His pupils were tiny, they were lost in the white expanse of the rest of his face.

The ringing in my ears faded so fast I barely realized it had been there. Turning my cheek to the pillow, I saw the machines beside me, the IV in my arm. "I'm in a hospital," I said stupidly.

Kain cupped my chin, trying to get my attention. "You're fine, you're alive."

Keeping my voice calm, I said, "Someone else better be paying these medical bills."

His lips cracked into a surprised pucker. The grin that grew after that lifted some of the weight from my soul. *That* was what I needed.

"If you want," he said slowly, "I can take care of them for you. But you know it'll cost you, right?"

"How could I *not* know that by now?" I meant it as a joke. His wince reminded me of why we were here—the favor he'd done when he'd taken me to see my mother.

Sitting up, I looked him over with rising fear. "Oh, fuck, you were shot! I was shot. I—my mother, oh, no." Covering my mouth, I let my tears rise and fall. I didn't have the energy to stop them.

"Shh," he soothed me. "I'm fine, and you're fine."

"But how?" Brick had us locked down. I remembered sitting there, *knowing* that we were both about to die. And then . . . my attention swam up, I stared Kain down in wonder. "I must have been fading away, because before I blacked out, I swear I saw my father."

Kain's eyes darted to the door.

"Stop," I said quickly. "Don't fuck with me. My dad's dead, I know that. I was hallucinating."

Gently, he disengaged from me. That was when I realized he was limping. Ice sank in my gut; how injured was he? Each step toward the door thudded like a drum in my heart. Twisting the knob, he leaned into the hallway. "I think you should come inside," he said to someone.

Without waiting for me to ready myself, *he* entered the room. He was wearing a long-sleeved, tan shirt, and I instantly thought it looked too big on him. Too big on a man that had always been a giant to me.

It had been over a year since I'd last seen him alive, and in that time, my father had thinned out. It didn't look right, his gaunt cheeks, knobby fingers, fading hair.

But there was no doubt it was him.

I'd know that smile half a world away.

"Sammy," he said softly.

Yanking the IV stand along the floor, ignoring how every machine began to beep, I threw myself into my father's arms and *bawled*.

He was alive.

Impossibly . . .

My father had come back to me.

We sat for hours. We talked continuously.

I still had trouble wrapping my brain around everything.

"Mom is seriously okay?" I asked, knowing I was repeating myself. I just didn't know how to handle being so lucky.

Nodding, my dad said, "I got her out of there the night before. I'd seen Brick on the road once nearby, that was enough for me."

My head wagged side to side in gentle disbelief. "How did she handle seeing you? Her poor heart."

"She slapped me a bit."

Chuckling at the image, I said, "She probably had no clue what to think. I don't even know what to think. Is everything Brick said true? You led the Deep Shots?"

He frowned severely; it made me miss his comfortable smile. "It's true. I was their leader until about a year and change ago. The rising trouble within the ranks of the Deep Shots, the number of times my life seemed to be in danger, I'd decided it wasn't worth it anymore. When I told them I was stepping down and backing off, I assumed that was that. Frock was a good enough guy. I never pictured one of his own putting a hit out on me."

"Brick." I spit his name out like it was dirty dishwater. "What happened to him?"

Kain cleared his throat. "Dead."

It was such a blunt, ugly word. As much as I hated the man for trying to kill me and so many people that I loved, I didn't want him—or anyone—dead. Shifting uneasily, I looked back at my father. "Then, when that car was found in the water, you weren't ever in it."

His laugh was gritty. "Oh, I was. The hit man Brick hired was a cheap one, some upstart punk desperate for money, I'd guess. He came out of nowhere on the road, shot at me through the window—and he missed. But the shattered glass got me." Tilting his head, he combed back his hair to show off the reddish scarring. "It was the last straw. I realized then that as long as I was around, whoever was after me would keep trying. It put you and your mother in danger. So when my car went off that edge and I managed to swim to shore without anyone seeing . . . I let everyone think I was gone."

The reminder made me shiver.

Reaching out, he took my fingers and squeezed. "I'm so, so sorry you had to go on so long suffering like this, Sammy. I thought I was doing what was right."

"I'm kind of tired of everyone trying to do what they think is 'right' for me," I mumbled. Kain's eyes went downcast at that. "Listen, I'm still struggling here. How did you run the Deep Shots for so long without me ever knowing?"

"How could you even guess? I went by a different name, I made sure to keep my private life and my family life apart. Until Brick decided to make sure I never tried to come back and take control from his father . . . it was working."

Turning, he said to Kain, "I never expected your family to get involved with Sammy. I always kept the Deep Shots away from the Badds, didn't want to start a gang war we couldn't win, but I did meet your dad once—only once."

Kain blinked. "When?"

"It was years and years ago. I used to take Sammy riding at this farm—"

"White Rose," he whispered.

My dad smiled kindly. "That's it. Anyway, usually your parents sent you there with a nanny. But one time, you were completing this course. Your father showed up to watch. I knew who he was, of course. He didn't speak to me, but my wife, Jean, she went right up to him and scolded him for letting you pick on Sammy."

That memory was so fuzzy. I gripped my forehead, trying to recall it. "Huh," I said. "I guess you *were* a jerk as a kid."

Kain wasn't listening, he was busy staring at my dad. "Jean said that?" Something crossed his face. "That's why she acted so strange when I introduced myself. She knew who I was."

"Speaking of Jean, I should call her and tell her everyone is fine." My father stood with a brief wince. At my nervous glance, he waved me away. "I'm just sore. I hadn't fired a gun in a long while."

I suspected, from how he looked, that it was more than that. A man who'd been hiding out for so long, watching his family from afar . . . of course he'd suffered from it. The bags under his eyes gave his stress away.

The door clicked shut as he left; I turned toward Kain. "That did just happen, right? I'm not still dreaming?"

"It happened. That, or I shook the hand of a very firm ghost."

"You shook his hand?" I asked, stunned as I tried to picture that. "Why?"

"Well, he *did* save my life, for one. But you don't remember, do you? Back at the jail, I joked about your looks and manners and . . . never mind." Sitting beside me on the bed, he grunted. I noticed how he favored one leg. Before he could stop me, I sat up, pulling at his belt.

"Whoa!" he laughed, eyeing me closely. "Down, girl, I don't think you're ready for this ride just yet."

Ignoring him, I yanked his pants down so that I could see the top of his thigh. The bandages were thick, the sight of them made me freeze.

"Sammy," he said insistently.

Reaching out, I snatched the hem of his shirt and ripped it over his head. His hair stuck up in places; it would have been funny, but the padding on his left shoulder sobered me. We were inches away, I snapped my eyes to his. "Your dad was right. You got hurt because of me."

"Yeah. I did get hurt." He said it so crisply that I did a double take. "Before you came into my life, things were much easier. I didn't struggle as much, I *definitely* didn't make as many risky decisions."

His honesty wasn't making me feel better.

"But you know what else?" Kain asked, leaning into me. "I also didn't smile as much . . . or feel as much. I didn't try to make sure someone else—someone besides me—was having the time of their life." His eyes twinkled, silver flecks set deep in crystal. "My world is a *much* better place since you came along."

The center of my heart stretched and strained. It couldn't fit inside of me, this sensation of expanding was too much for anyone. A small sound fled my lips; a hiccup, then a sniffle.

"Sammy, are you all right?"

Pushing my hands into his chest, I laughed and smiled and welled with tears, all at the same time. It was the only way to keep from shattering into pieces—my love for this man pushed my body to its limits.

Sobbing, I said, "Stop making me cry!"

Kain bent over me, kissing the corner of each of my eyes. "Is this that ugly cry you were telling me about?" Grabbing his shirt, I flapped it into my face. He chuckled, snatching my wrists, forcing my arms down. "Don't hide."

"You literally just called me ugly!"

"No, not at all. I was going to say if *this* is your ugly cry, then it's not so bad. I don't know why you acted like mine was so impressive." He smirked sharply. "Or do I need to make you cry more to see the real thing?"

"Please, no." I laughed softly, dabbing at my eyes. "You'll get more snot, that's all."

Snuggling me against his bare chest, he slid us more comfortably onto the hospital bed. Well, as comfortably as one could ever get on one of these hard things. But truthfully, in Kain's arms, I could have sat on jagged rock and felt wonderful.

My eyes tracked over his naked torso. His tattoos glimmered in the hospital lights, the red-and-black crown a heavy reminder of who Kain was.

But it wasn't his history that had caused our conflict. It was mine. *A past I knew nothing about.* What would happen from here? Was my father going to return, would things get easier . . . or would they get worse?

How could things get worse? I asked myself, studying the old scar on his stomach. *We've already been nearly killed.* "We match now," I said suddenly.

He blinked. "What?"

Lifting my pale green gown, I touched the gauze and padding that was strapped over my belly. "We've both got bullet wounds on our stomachs. It's kind of neat."

At first he was silent. The initial shakes of his laughter startled me, but his full-on bellow turned me to stone. Calming himself, he took my hand, placing it on his old scar. "It's from having my appendix removed."

My eyes ached from how wide they were, they were drying out as I considered this revelation. "You mean . . . that for weeks, I've been thinking that you had this old wound from some wicked gunfight . . . and it was just . . ."

"Yup. Though I did get to stay out of school for a bit. That's pretty wicked, right?"

I lost the ability to talk. In the quietness, the knock on the door made me jump.

Not knowing who to expect, I was beyond lost at seeing the familiar face of Detective Stapler. He was peering into the room, one hand holding a white envelope tied to a gigantic, teddy-bear balloon. The instant he saw Kain and me—him shirtless—tangled on the bed, his whole head flushed.

"Oh—I—I'll come back," he stuttered.

Ignoring Kain's giant grin, I flapped a hand. "Wait! It's fine." Was it fine? "What are you doing here?"

His eyes tracked all over the room, but not at us directly. "Mmff. I just wanted to make sure you were all right. Heard what had happened." He glanced at Kain, then away, like seeing a member of the Badd family wasn't what he was hoping for.

I wondered if he'd come to chide me, pointing out that he'd been right about the Badds being dangerous. He'd walked into something else entirely, of course.

Kain's grin became a cheeky smirk. "Hey there, boss."

The detective inched my way, handing over the balloon with the card attached. "Thanks," I said earnestly, taking it. The colorful bear was smiling for all eternity. In the mirrored back of the balloon, I saw how pale I was. "Were you with the cops that arrived at the scene?"

"I was," he said grimly. "I wasn't shocked to hear about a fight between the Badds and the Deep Shots, but when word came down that there was a young woman seriously injured at the scene . . ." He shook his head, seeming to relive last night. "Actually, I had a question that one of you can hopefully answer." Finally he looked at me, his warm, brown eyes shifting with curiosity.

"Shoot," I said, instantly regretting my choice of phrasing.

The detective didn't get the joke, or he knew enough to ignore it. "We found something at the scene that I couldn't make sense of."

I glanced at Kain—did he have any idea what this was about? "What was it?"

"A very pink high heel."

"Pffftt." It was the only sound I could make. My lips fluttered as I tried not to crack up. I'd forgotten all about that fucking shoe.

Kain tapped his fingers on my headboard. "That *is* weird."

"I could swear I'd seen those heels before," Stapler said.

Tears broke through the corners of my eyes. Not from sadness, but from the sheer pressure of trying not to explode at the absurdity of all of this. The detective froze, noticing the wetness as I rubbed at it and entirely misunderstanding. "Forgive me, you're still recovering, and everything is so fresh. I didn't mean to bring up memories of the attack. I'll go, I'll—right. Farewell."

"Hold on!" Tapping the card he'd given me against my palm, I offered him a genuine smile. "Thanks for checking in on me. And . . . thanks for being one of the good guys."

He flushed all over. "Yeah, well, I just hope I never have to see you again, Miss Sage." Tipping his head at us both, he backtracked to the door. "Enjoy the card."

Alone with Kain again, I met his stare with my own. "Wow," I mumbled.

"I think you have a fan."

"Is that good or bad?"

"I don't usually like cops following me around like puppies, but in this case . . . it might not be the worst. He did have a keen eye and a good question. Why *were* those shoes with you? I thought that I'd—"

"Hidden them away in your bedroom to worship in private?"

His grin cut sideways. "What's creepier, me keeping them or you sneaking into my room to take them back?"

"I didn't sneak in at all. Lula gave them to me."

Kain's eyes widened while his smile crumbled to dust. "Okay. Now I'm really fucking lost."

"It doesn't matter. Why *did* you keep those ridiculous shoes?"

His arm slid around me possessively. "Saying it out loud will sound insane."

"Then let it," I said earnestly.

Kain looked down at me, judging how serious I was being. I passed the test, I suppose, because he began to talk. "The day of the wedding, when I took you to the impound lot, I was spending so much time just thinking of a way to keep you from avoiding me. I wanted to prove I was better than . . . well, I guess better than someone who'd gotten you thrown into jail."

The contours of his warm voice slid through my ears and into my heart. Which was good, because the memory of being handcuffed was a cold one.

He said, "But then you climbed into your car, and you didn't even give me a damn moment to say good-bye. There was nothing, no opening—you were done."

My hand clutched at my lungs. He sounded so damn *sad*. Had he really felt like that? "Kain . . ."

Blue skies free of clouds—that was what his eyes reminded me of. This man, he stared at me without a hint of doubt, speaking from a soul I would have once called tarnished and sinful. "Then you handed me those shoes. They were sparkly and pink and everything you weren't. I'd helped you walk in them, they were all I had to represent the tangled-up way I felt about you."

Abruptly he laughed, his hair falling across his eyebrows with how his head swung low. He whispered, "I actually thought—well, if I'm a prince, and these were the shoes you'd cast off, I'd keep them . . . I'd use them to find you . . . because you were my own personal Cinderella."

My heart opened up, tingles spreading up my throat and to my brain. They made my nose tickle, a sneeze that never came because the pressure in my skull was from something sweeter entirely.

"What about you?" he asked, pulling me in for a kiss. "Why did you keep them?"

Flushing wildly, I let myself smile. "I'd never wear them again, but the fact you'd hid them away made me understand how much every minute we'd spent together had *meant* to you. I guess I couldn't let them go."

"But you did. Into Brick's head."

"Right. The mystery weapon." *The shoe that saved our lives.* I remembered the envelope Detective Stapler had given me. Peeling it open, I slid out the big and bright get-well card. It had a pair of dancing mice on it. "Why pick mice, of all the . . ." I didn't finish.

Inside the envelope, the detective had left me two very familiar slips of paper.

The ink on the bottom right of one was a messy scrawl: Kain's signature.

Mama Badd's was much neater.

I hadn't expected to see that thirty grand ever again.

- EPILOGUE -

SAMMY

Kain had tried to warn me that the meeting would be intimidating.

I'd been sure I was ready.

Then I'd entered the den.

Every chair had a person, every corner . . . every wall . . . they were covered. Each of them belonged to either the Deep Shots or to the Badds. The ocean of faces was useless to me; I only knew a few.

Kain stood with his brothers. I also noted that while his sisters weren't present, his mother was. She stood right behind Maverick in his recliner. My father was seated beside him, and right smack on the other side of the blue-eyed patriarch was someone I'd never met.

"Sammy," my father said. "This is Frock Monroe, leader of the Deep Shots."

Snap snap went my thoughts. *Brick's dad.*

His attention hadn't left me since I'd entered the room. This setting was supposed to be neutral ground. The Deep Shots wanted a white flag, to make it clear they'd had no part in the violent scene out on the road.

My dad motioned for me to come closer. Hesitantly I did, staring at Frock with mixed emotions. The red-bearded man leaned forward.

His elbows rested on his knees, hands folded between them like he was praying. "You're so much bigger than when I last saw you."

Hairs lifted on my neck. "I've never met you before."

Frock side eyed my dad. "You really did keep your family out of it."

"Not entirely. My wife knew what I was involved in."

Maverick shook his head in wonder. "I'm almost ashamed I didn't realize it before. I know a thing or two about hiding an identity, and still, I never suspected that Sammy Sage was the daughter of The Bear—or that you were still alive, Bastian."

The Bear? So that had been his alias. This was still too weird for me. Turning, I faced the leader of the gang my dad had apparently once run. "Your son tried to murder me. That's all I know."

Frock stretched toward me from his chair. "I want you to understand that I explicitly told Brick not to get involved with you."

"You *knew* he wanted me dead?" I gasped.

"No. No." His hands came up defensively. "I didn't know his plans. I didn't even know you were the girl he'd attacked. But I believed Kain when he came to our bar. His rage was real. So I told Brick, right after everyone was gone, to stop whatever the hell he was doing." Shade crept into his pause. His tone was weaker now. "He didn't listen."

Confronted by a man that had lost his son, I struggled with a wave of sadness. "As awful as what he did was, I'm still sorry for your loss."

Frock's smile never touched his eyes. "Thank you."

It was fleeting, but my father reached over to pat Frock on the knee. The other man gripped that hand, held it, and then they parted like seeds from a shedding dandelion.

Kain crossed the room, capturing my hand firmly in his. "Let's get out of here."

"That was all you needed me for?" I asked the room, resisting Kain.

Maverick breathed in deep, the buttons on his shirt straining. "No. Bastian," he said to my father. "I wanted you here with Frock to discuss the future of the Deep Shots. The dissent in the ranks needs to be crushed right away."

My dad said, "If you're asking me to take over, I won't. I'm done with that life."

I was relieved to hear that. I wanted to hear more, but Kain was pushing me carefully toward the exit. He wasn't interested in what this group would decide. Kain had been almost a hundred percent interested in one thing only these days.

Me.

"You know," Kain said as we walked the bustling halls of his home. The place was full of all kinds of people now that Maverick wasn't worried about some plot to harm anyone here. "Technically, you can step in if you want."

My knees turned into cement, then quickly, so did the rest of me. Kain crushed my fingers. "Me? Why?"

"Your father was the leader," he explained patiently. "He put Frock in charge when he left, but he was always viewed as the real leader—until his death. That was probably what began Brick's madness, the fear he'd never get to control the Deep Shots if Bastian ever returned . . . or you did. But your father is here, he's alive. And as his daughter, it's your right."

This revelation was almost laugh-worthy. Me? Lead a *gang*? I couldn't stop it; I started giggling. "You're joking. Do I look like I want to take over a group of crazy killers?"

"I'll say this," he replied, "I don't want you to do it . . . but I don't doubt at all that you could."

I couldn't blink. "What?"

"You're a leader at heart. You're tough, you don't back down, and more than that, you take on the burden of everyone you want to help. You're concerned about the people close to you. Combining that and your new ties to my family, and I think . . . in a way, you'd be perfect."

Is he right? Compliments aside, there was more to controlling a group like this. People would be jealous of my power, I'd deal with threats and danger and a million other problems.

Kain brushed my fingertips.

But would it be much different than the danger of staying near Kain?

Gingerly, I clutched the bandages on my stomach. It had only been five days since my injury. The pain was a harsh reminder of this world I was dabbling in. *Dabbling*, I mused. *I've been in with both feet first for a while.*

I considered what I would say. "Gang Leader Sammy has a nice ring to it, in a twisted way." With clear intention, I grasped Kain's hand and held it. "I'm still adjusting to being near one group of crazy assholes. I think I'll hold off from taking control of a second one."

Kain didn't laugh like I expected. Instead, he pushed me against a section of wallpaper. A maid who'd been rounding the corner saw us entwined; her face went red as she shuffled off.

She reminded me about what Fran had told me forever ago, the thing about their Badd Maids company. Maybe it was real after all. I wondered if that meant the girl was a real maid, a spy, or something else. Then Kain started nibbling my throat, and I stopped wondering anything at all.

There was still so much I wanted to learn about the Badds. The number of old secrets and bad blood ran deep. At least with an uneasy truce settling in, the Deep Shots would take a break from exacerbating those issues.

That meant I'd get some peaceful times with all of them.

With Kain.

Or at least . . .

That was what I hoped for.

"You know," Francesca said, pointing a forkful of bank-breaking levels of salmon, "I was thinking."

Thorne's eyebrows rolled upward. "That's surprising."

She tossed the fork at him, and I lamented the waste of food. There'd been caviar wrapped up in the fish as well. "Shut up and listen," she insisted, eyeing me closely. "It's supposed to be very *in* for winter weddings, isn't it?"

A flutter of paranoia moved through me. "Uh. Well, sure. I was actually thinking about my lineup for the season." That thirty grand had gone a long way toward paying off my debt and giving me the breathing room for new dress designs.

The photos from Fran's wedding had finally started leaking into the public. I was pretty sure she was the one to thank for that. My business had been booming wildly since then.

"If you ever need help fitting your customers into their dresses, by the way," Hawthorne said, "I might be able to swing some time."

I pursed my lips. "You realize they're engaged?"

Popping a cracker into his mouth, he shrugged. "Just helping them get into their dresses. You're the one with the dirty mind."

"Gawd, let me finish!" Fran snapped. Her scowl became a toothy smile fixed right on me. "So I'm saying, I figure red is a great color for a maid of honor dress. And I look fuckin' *great* in red."

"Fran," Mama Badd scolded.

I looked less good in red, especially when it was my skin turning into the color. Shooting a glance at Kain beside me, I said, "Frannie, give me a break. You're acting like I'm getting married or something."

"Well, duh," she scoffed.

Laughing nervously, I gave Kain a light shove. "Tell her she's being crazy."

Under the table, he grabbed my thigh. "You're being crazy, Fran." His words were rolling off of a smile, but something in his eyes made me knot up.

Our "little" table was set up on a high deck overlooking Martha's Vineyard. It was a gorgeous area. Maverick had taken us all for a weekend trip—including my parents. I suspected it was his own disconnected way of apologizing for everything he'd put me through.

I hadn't entirely forgiven him for the missteps, but I was working on it. I understood his heart was in the right place. He'd also been right—a fact that shamed me—about Brick tracking Kain to my mother's place, using that route to catch him and me off guard.

It was a private relief that the huge man hadn't driven that point home.

Now, he watched me from his chair, sipping idly at a mimosa. It should have made him cartoony and less scary.

It didn't.

My mother was grinning at me, hell—everyone was. When Kain knelt at my side, I startled so much that I tipped my coffee over. No one paid any attention to it as it dribbled onto the patio.

"Kain," I said through my teeth. My head swam with my old visions of the pretend fantasy wedding I'd had with him back when the possibility wasn't . . . well, possible. Now that it was, the reality was smothering me.

His hand went into his pocket; Francesca started to squeal. Lula's midnight eyes were shiny, was she about to cry? Wasn't that my job? "Sammy," he started.

My hand clamped over his mouth. "Don't."

Kain's eyebrows knotted. "Ffwhy?" he muffled.

Parting my lips, I found . . . no answer. I had nothing inside of me but the ever-increasing speed of my own heart. Colors whirled through my brain, a poor excuse for words. I didn't know why I was stopping him.

Deep down, when he pulled my hand away, I was grateful.

"Sammy." The fierce glint in his stare said he wasn't backing down. Why had I even tried? "I thought, at one point, that I'd never ask this of someone. And then I thought, even if I wanted to ask you, how could I? I love you, but you deserve to have the world looking on when I finally declare that I'll protect you . . . adore you . . . obsess and love and every other damn thing humans can do for the rest of my too-short life."

Shit, I was trembling. I mouthed his name; no sound came out.

He looked across the table at my parents, then at his own. "It's not the whole world, but this is everyone we have sitting in front of us. There'll never be a better time than now." His fingers linked with mine, a gesture he'd made a number of times.

He'd held me like that when we'd first twirled in stunned attraction in his driveway.

He'd clutched me when I ran to him in terror as my home was broken into.

And he did it now as he slid a small ring onto my finger. The silver was twisted in a loop: two horses running together. It was topped by a diamond bigger than the marble-size caviar everyone had been eating moments ago.

I'd never seen anything so beautiful.

"Sammy Sage," he said, making me thrill with how his tongue rolled my full name. "Will you marry me?"

Francesca slammed her hands onto the table. "Yes! She says yes! Sammy, say yes!"

At some point I'd started smiling. It became a grin, touching my eyes and making my muscles ache as happy tears rolled free. "See this?" I asked him, flapping my fingers by my cheeks. "Ugly cry. This is an actual ugly cry *and* a yes, okay?"

Sweeping me into his arms, he kissed me in front of all of them. I think they were clapping, cheering, but my ears were ringing with the sweet insanity of a moment I'd dared to hope for and had actually been granted.

I made wedding dresses for a living. I talked to brides that were in love and many that were painfully not. I helped along the ones that had found their counterparts, and for the others, I struggled to bite my tongue to keep from talking sense into them. I wasn't always successful.

I didn't know why some people chose an ending that didn't make them dizzy with joy.

But I did know this:

Everyone should get their happily ever after.

Just like me.

AN EXCERPT FROM *ROYALLY RUINED* (BAD BOY ROYALS BOOK 2)

Editor's Note: This is an early excerpt and may not reflect the finished book.

Once upon a time, I would have been a king.

Firstborn.

Royal blood.

A family full of money and power and everything you could possibly dream of. I would have ruled fairly, justly, taken care of my loved ones and done my best for my country. The key words in all of this are "would have."

Modern-day princes like me? Guys with mafia roots that stay in control thanks to threats instead of our lineage? We're often the bad guys.

I sure am.

It's why I was checking my handgun under my coat—I didn't need to look to know that it was loaded. And it's why I was staring down the young woman who wanted *nothing* to do with me.

"Hold up," she said, her voice tangling high in her throat, the sign of someone struggling to remain calm. "You don't need to do this. Thorne knows me, ask him!"

Thorne was my brother. He'd made a point of stepping out of the dressing room when I'd demanded we check every girl here—dancer or otherwise—to make sure they weren't wearing a wire. Weapons were a problem, too, sure. But for me . . . it was all about the cops.

I *hated* cops.

I'd already searched the five strippers on shift. It was this waitress's poor luck that she was working tonight, too. No one had warned her why her boss had told her to go to the dressing room. She certainly hadn't expected to see me down here.

When I said nothing else, the woman lifted her arms. Was she going to fight me or was she surrendering? Her tongue darted over her lower lip. "I work *here*, not for the damn cops! Seriously, ask Hawthorne, he knows me!"

"But I don't know you," I said softly, feeling for my gun like it was a nervous tic—it wasn't, I don't get nervous that easily. "I'm not asking much. I only want you to take off your clothes so I can search you."

Her face flushed pink, the color bringing out her freckles. The tiny piercing in the corner of her nose glinted when she scowled. "Oh? That's all? Well then, gee, I—no! Get Thorne. I've been here for three years, I've seen plenty of bad shit and never said a word before. I deserve better than this!"

With clean precision I slid the tip of my pistol between us. There wasn't much space as it was; I'd set up my little "check station" in the corner of the dressing room farthest from the door. The beaten-up and vandalized lockers the girls stored their everyday clothes in were keeping the waitress from bolting one direction.

My body prevented the other.

"Hey," she said, flicking her brown eyes to the weapon, then back to me. I was surprised she held my stare so evenly. Few people could. "Can't we be nice about this?"

"Do I seem nice?" I asked.

"No." The edge of her mouth went up in an out-of-place smile. "And I thought your brother was the asshole of your family."

When I was younger, that would have hurt. But I'd been called far worse things for over ten years. "I'm not playing around. Clothes off. Now."

She stood taller. It brought her chin close to mine, I could smell the sweetness of her skin. I'd expected typical stripper smell, but this wasn't cotton candy and baby powder. This was something . . . richer. Like the inside of a treasure chest: metal and leather. I didn't know any women who smelled like that. It was familiar in a way that nagged me.

Her voice was low and anything but soft. "If you're going to see me naked, you should know my name."

"You don't need to be naked, your bra and panties are—"

She spoke over me. "Scotch. My name is Scotch." Again, her piercing shone from how hard she scrunched her nose. "And you? You're Costello, right?"

I expected her to know my name. After all, my family owned every single strip club in this city, including the one we were standing in. "If you don't take your clothes off, I'm going to take them off for you."

Scotch peered at me. I wondered if she doubted my promise. If she was smart, she wouldn't. To keep me, my brother, and our new relationship with the Deep Shots safe, I'd do whatever it took. If that included stripping a waitress who refused to prove her allegiance, so be it.

She turned away and faced the lockers and curled her nails under her shirt, peeling it up so it exposed her back to me. "Get this over with. I have drinks to serve upstairs."

Tucking the gun into my jacket, I said, "Smart girl." I bent close, and that damn scent hit me again, confusing me and making me dizzy.

Fighting through it, I brushed my hands over her skin, reaching around to feel for anything hidden on her stomach.

Scotch trembled, her heart kicking at my chest through her spine. She was warm as a perfect cup of tea, smooth as ivory. I was supposed to be feeling for a wire but I couldn't stop thinking about how *good* she felt. How solid and strong and fucking soft, all at once.

When I trailed my fingertips over her hips toward her skirt, she inhaled through her nose. It wasn't a scared sound—it was too thick. Static passed between us and together we stiffened.

She asked me, "Why are you going so slow?"

Sweat crept over my brow. "I'm not. I'm being precise."

"Oh?" and it came out like a *purr*. "How's this for precise?" I pride myself on my speed, but this woman rammed her ass right against the front of my slacks before I could dodge. I'm not sure I would have dodged.

My blood raced, battling with the excitement that was curling in my lower belly. How had this simple task become such a game of wills? How was this damn stranger getting under my skin so quick? *Get your shit together!* I reprimanded myself. Scotch was grinning, I could see it even with her face turned away.

She wanted to play.

I didn't. Or I did, but . . . no. I didn't. I had a job to do.

Snatching her wrists, I pressed her hands above her head on the lockers so hard that the green metal rattled. Over it all, I heard her surprised gasp and endured a thrill from it. "Not the wisest move you could have made," I whispered in her ear.

"Wait," she said quickly, struggling to face me. I didn't let her. "Hold on. What are you doing?"

Binding her hands in one of mine, I hooked the top of her skirt with my other. "What I promised I'd do from the start." I pulled it lower, a mere inch, showing me the fishtail of her black thong. My cock swelled painfully. "Taking your clothes off for you."

She was breathing heavily, her heart ramming audibly against her ribs. My mouth was a tingling mess, and my senses were getting fried. But no matter how this girl was turning me on—and fuck, she really was—I was done playing games.

It didn't matter if Scotch was terrified.

What she wanted paled when it came to keeping my family safe.

Once upon a time, I would have been a king.

Now?

I'm just a monster.

ABOUT THE AUTHOR

Photo © 2016 Kristen Carter

A *USA Today* bestselling author, Nora Flite lives in Southern California, where the weather is warm and she doesn't have to shovel snow—something she never grew to love in her tiny home state of Rhode Island. All her romances involve passionate, filthy, and slightly obsessive heroes—because those are clearly the best kind! She's always been a writer, and you'll probably have to pry her keyboard/pen/magical future writing device out of her cold, dead fingers before she'll stop. Visit her at www.NoraFlite.com, or drop her a line at noraflite@gmail.com.